S.K. SHARP

I KNOW WHAT I SAW

arrow books

1 3 5 7 9 10 8 6 4 2

Arrow Books
20 Vauxhall Bridge Road
London SW1V 2SA

Arrow Books is part of the Penguin Random House group of companies
whose addresses can be found at global.penguinrandomhouse.com.

Penguin
Random House
UK

First published in ebook by Arrow Books in 2020
This paperback edition first published in the UK by Arrow Books in 2021

www.penguin.co.uk

A CIP catalogue record for this book is available from the British Library.

ISBN 9781787465312

Typeset in 11.5/16.25 pt Times New Roman by Jouve (UK), Milton Keynes
Printed and bound in Great Britain by Clays Ltd, Elcograf S.p.A.

The authorised representative in the EEA is Penguin Random House Ireland,
Morrison Chambers, 32 Nassau Street, Dublin D02 YH68

MIX
Paper from
responsible sources
FSC® C018179

Penguin Random House is committed to a
sustainable future for our business, our readers
and our planet. This book is made from Forest
Stewardship Council® certified paper.

For all the people we can't forget

Imagine a heart ready to burst with joy. Christmas mornings as a child, passing your final exams, the thrill of a first kiss – all that and more. Imagine being able to reach and find those glorious moments whenever you want, the feelings fresh and intense, undiminished by time. Imagine sinking into them when the world grows heavy, always there whenever you call. If I describe my perfect memory to you like this, does it sound like a gift? Something precious, even something to envy?

I've been this way for as long as I can remember. As a child, blissfully ignorant that I was different from anyone else, steadily more aware through my teens of how it made me special. It *did* feel like a gift back then, the way I could summon any moment of my life and live it again, fresh and bright and with nothing faded. Tests and exams were easy. I could remember – *can* remember, even now – everything my teachers said in the classroom.

And then boys. The day I first saw Declan. The look in his eye, the first words he ever spoke to me, the first time we kissed; that first summer when we discovered each other, the sense of a love that went far beyond anything I'll find again. Even now, after a bad day, I can lie awake and relive those memories and it's all as vivid as ever: the colour and the joy, the anticipation, the love that brings tears to my eyes. My mind is wired differently from yours. The doctors have a name for it and there are only a handful of people in the world who live their lives as I do.

But a blessing?

Imagine the moments that broke your heart and crushed you flat. A loss, a humiliation, a betrayal. Imagine every slight, every rejection, every disappointment, all kept polished for safe keeping in a little chest inside you. Imagine the things you did and wish you hadn't; every word spoken or received in anger; every regret as fresh as the moment it was made. Imagine every mistake and all the words never said that might have changed your life. Imagine them forever lurking, never knowing when they might steal out and take you.

A gift?

They say that time heals, but for me it festers. Where

your scars fade, mine stay raw. On good days, my memory will take me to places that others can only dream of finding. On bad days, it rips the soul from my chest and shreds it in front of me.

Right now . . . ?

Right now, the phone is ringing. My hand hovers over the receiver. Whatever happens next, I will remember its every detail for the rest of my life.

I close my eyes and force myself to breathe.

It's been a long, long day and I have a sense that something terrible is coming.

1

Saturday 1st February 2020

I suppose it's a cliché for someone with a perfect memory that I work in the British Library archives, but there's a truth in that, too: most archivists *do* have good memories. I've worked here for ten years, ever since I came back from America. I like it because it's a quiet place where everyone does their own thing and keeps to themselves. Today being a Saturday, I have the office to myself and so I have the radio on, tuned to Absolute 80s, the music of my youth.

It's 3.17 in the afternoon and I'm humming to 'Eye of the Tiger' when the phone rings. I pick it up, expecting to hear Joy from reception asking if I want to go out for a drink after work; but the voice on the other end is deep and male.

'Mrs Nicola Robbins?'

5

Robbins? I roll the name around my tongue, wondering what to do with it. No one's called me *Robbins* for two decades.

'Walker,' I say at last. 'Nicola Walker. Mr Robbins and I separated twenty-five years ago.' This is probably some telemarketing nonsense, so why do I feel the need to explain myself? Yet I do.

'Mrs . . . sorry, Walker. I'm Detective Sergeant Jason Scott. I'm with the London Metropolitan Police, Wordsworth Park.'

Another jolt from the past. Wordsworth Park is where I grew up. Where Mum still lives with that arsehole Dave Crane who used to be Dad's best friend. It's just another suburb of London now, stuck at the end of the Metropolitan Line between Harrow and Pinner, but when I was young it was the sort of place where everyone still knew their neighbours.

My thoughts race ahead: *Has something happened? Is Mum in hospital?*

The question catches in my throat. All that comes out is silence.

Dave? The next thought is gleeful. *Could it be Dave?*

'I'm sorry to have to ask this, Mrs Walker, but . . . is it correct that you were previously married to a Mr Declan Robbins?'

'Declan? Yes. And it's *Ms* Walker.'

'Sorry. *Ms* Walker.'

'What was your name again?' I don't need to ask, not really. It's right there in my head, every word of the conversation between us. I'm just stalling.

'Detective Sergeant Jason Scott, Ms Walker.'

I knew a Jason at primary school. He was nice enough, kept himself to himself and didn't bother people; had a handful of friends but not a crowd. He was quiet and gentle. Jason Scott? I worked with a David Scott a few years ago. Brisk, business-like, kept things going, always moving but with a warmth to him. Someone you could talk to.

'What's this about?'

'I'm sorry to trouble you at work, but Mr Robbins has asked to speak with you. Is that OK?'

Twenty-five years apart and Declan's name still sends a chill through me. A surge of longing and regret and a dull stab of bitterness. That's the thing: all it takes is a name or a sound and I'm spiralling back to some stupid moment that anybody else would have forgotten decades ago.

'Yes . . .' The truth is: I don't know. I haven't talked to Declan for—

'Nix?' And there he is: Declan, sounding exactly as I remember him. 'Nix? Are you there?'

Nix? How long since anyone called me *Nix*? Declan went back to calling me *Nicola* after the divorce, always with an edge of ice that tried, and failed, to hide the hurt.

Anger bristles. As if it was *my* fault that he was seeing another woman . . .

'Hello, Declan. What do you want?' The last time we spoke was a decade ago and now here he is, stirring everything up, rattling the bones of memories kept closeted for twenty-five years.

'Bloody hell, Nix. How long has it been?'

I could tell him it's been nine years, three months and seventeen days since we last spoke. I was drunk and morose. I'd just come back from America. I was wearing my charcoal cardigan, the one with the crocheted belt. It was three days after I'd had my hair cut, an inch too short, and the hairdresser had given me a discount after I insisted on speaking to her manager, a lady named Grace. All these details are as vivid as yesterday. That night, I called Declan and tried to tell him I was sorry. I'm not entirely sure exactly what I said – as I found out when I was seventeen, drinking too much affects my memory like it does anyone else – but I *do* remember his reply, cold and bitter. *Go to hell, Nicola. Don't call me again.*

'A long time,' I say.

'I . . . I need your help.' He doesn't sound bitter or cold today, only scared.

'*My* help?' I'm an archivist. The only people who ever need my help are academics and journalists writing local-history pieces.

'I've been arrested.'

All I can think is that he's been caught speeding or something like that. The idea of Declan doing anything serious makes me want to laugh.

'Nix, it's . . .' There's a long pause, then: 'Did you see the news?'

'What news?'

'Wordsworth Park. Nix, they found my dad.'

For the second time in as many minutes, I don't know what to say. Arthur Robbins vanished on Sunday 9th June 1985, on the night of his fiftieth birthday party in the Mary Shelley. The police search went on for weeks. You don't need a special memory to remember *that*, not if you grew up there. It was the talk of the neighbourhood for months.

'What are you talking about?'

'You remember? The night we—'

'Declan, what's going on?' I remember the police were at my house when I got home that night, already looking for Arthur. *Good riddance to bad rubbish* was Dad's judgement, which I would have thought odd right up until that night, because everybody loved Arty Robbins, pillar of the community.

Not me, though. *I* was glad when he disappeared.

'Nix, they think I did it.'

Declan's words have a terrible finality about them.

'Declan?'

'They're going to charge me with murder. With murdering my own dad.' I hear the fear in him now, naked and strong. Then his words start frothing and coming apart. 'But you know I couldn't have done that. You *know* . . .'

I feel the lump in my throat. He's right: the Declan I remember couldn't hurt a fly.

'They've got something.'

I hear my own breath hiss down the line. 'What does *that* mean? What *something*? What are you—'

'Nix, I need you to—'

'No, Declan,' I snap. 'What you *need* is a solicitor. You can't just—'

There's a click. An instant later, Declan's voice changes back into Detective Sergeant Jason Scott.

'Mrs Robbins?'

'Still Walker,' I correct him. '*Ms* Walker.' It buys me time to shake away the memories. The monsters in my head haven't had a chance to get their bearings, but they'll come. Tonight's going to be hell.

'Ms Walker, your ex-husband is currently helping us with our enquiries. We're attempting to establish who was at the Mary Shelley public house on the evening of 9th June 1985. Mr Robbins claims you can vouch for his movements that evening until around midnight. Would that be correct?' He sounds amused.

'Yes,' I say. 'I can.'

'And you're sure of that?'

'Yes.'

'Ms Walker, thirty-five years is—'

'I remember it clearly,' I say.

A long sigh crackles down the phone. Then: 'In that case, you'd better come in and give a statement.' Now he sounds bored and irritated, like this is all some prank at his expense. I wonder how old he is, this Detective Sergeant Jason Scott. I'd like to tell him how I can remember what the weather was like on the day he was born, or something like that. I probably can, too.

'Ms Walker?'

I take a deep breath. What I'm about to say is both the easiest and the hardest thing in the world. 'I can head over right now, if you like.' Because if I'm going to do this then I want it over quickly. I want to get back to my quiet, uneventful life.

'Wordsworth Park High Street.' Detective Scott sounds anything but enthused. 'Turn right out of the station and—'

'I know where it is, Detective Scott. I used to live there.'

I'm supposed to be at work until five, but I leave early. It's quiet and I don't think anyone will notice. I reach Wordsworth Park an hour later – an easy walk to Euston Square and then nine stops on the Underground, just like it's always been. Instinct makes me turn left out of the station, towards the park and what used to be home; straight away, a memory jumps me. I'm seven years old. We're on our way back from the Science Museum, the first time I've been into London with Mum and Dad. My feet are sore and my legs are tired and my back hurts and I'm whining at Mum: *Do we have to walk all the way home now?* It's barely ten minutes through the back of the park to Byron Road but I can literally feel the ache in my seven-year-old feet. The High Street ends in a wall of trees behind a wrought-iron fence and a gate, the entrance into the woods at the back of the park, a narrow track leading through . . .

Only it doesn't, not any more, because now I'm sixteen, walking home from school with my best friend, Kat. The trees have gone from one side of the gate, cut down to make way for the new Parklands Youth Centre. I feel a glow inside, hot butterflies in my stomach, the anticipation of seeing Dec somewhere we don't have to pretend there's nothing going on between us. It's early April and we've just discovered each other and only Kat knows, and I want to see him again so much and—

I stop, confused, jerked back to the present by a man who knocks into me, mutters a reluctant apology and walks on. In the here and now, Parklands has gone, a boarded-up building site in its place. The trees on the other side of the gate have become a car park. The gate has gone, too, and the railings, the muddy track transformed into a paved cycle path.

I Know What I Saw

The police station, when I reach it, has the same carved-stone facade that I remember, the familiar solid doors of age-blackened Victorian wood. I go inside and give my name to the sergeant behind the desk. A policewoman shows me to an interview room, offers me coffee and then leaves. When I look round the room, I see the cameras in the ceiling and a recorder on the wall. I feel a lurch in my stomach. I've never been in a room like this and yet it's oddly familiar from all the police series I used to watch on TV: *The Bill* and *Line of Duty*, and so on. It's a place where bad things happen.

I could visit Mum after I've given my statement. She's only ten minutes away, but as soon as I think it, I know that I won't. It's never been the same since Dad died and she shacked up with 'Uncle' Dave. It's the pretence that gets me – the pretence that nothing was going on between them long before. I'll never know what it cost Dad to keep on as though nothing had happened; but that was how he was, the sort of man who'd do anything for his family.

A man in plain clothes enters, carrying two mugs of coffee. He looks me over with practised eyes, assessing me, my socio-economic status, my body language, trying to work out how to get whatever it is that he wants from me. I try to read him back and decide he's annoyed and thinks this is a waste of his time. He's thinking he should be at home with his wife and kids, because how can anyone remember anything useful from so long ago?

'Detective Sergeant Scott?' I get up before he has a chance to sit down. He puts the coffees on the table and we shake hands. His grip is firm.

'Ms Walker?'

I glance at the recorder. 'Are you taping this?'

'Why don't you sit down, Ms Walker.'

It's almost a surprise when I realise that I'm here to defend Declan as much as I'm here to tell the story of that night. I'm not sure why, but I think Detective Scott sees it, too. He must know that Declan and I separated two decades ago, and that I was the one who walked out. Is he wondering why I'm here, why I still care, what I'm trying to hide?

What *am* I trying to hide? That I still loved him when I left him? But I already know *that*. If I'm honest with myself, I never stopped – not because I don't want to but because I can't; because every feeling I ever had for Declan is still as vivid inside me as the day it was made. I can't forget what it was like to be in love with him and I can't forget how it felt to be betrayed. Although maybe that *is* what I'm trying to hide, because I know I'll never be able to explain it.

'It's a formality, really,' says Detective Scott. 'We're trying to put together a picture of Mr Robbins' movements on the night of 9th June 1985. Thank you for coming in so promptly, by the way. It's always helpful if we can keep things moving along.'

'You haven't answered my question,' I say.

Detective Scott pointedly switches on the recorder. 'Could you state your name for the record, please?'

'Ms Nicola Walker.'

'And your address?'

I give him my address in Farringdon. It's not a cheap place to live. I see a slight shift in his face as he recognises this.

'Conducting this interview: Detective Sergeant Jason Scott. Ms Walker, can you confirm that you understand you've been asked here to give a witness statement concerning events in and around Wordsworth Park and the Mary Shelley public house on the night of Sunday 9th June 1985?'

'Yes . . . if that's what you want.'

'And, Ms Walker, can you confirm that you're here of your own volition?'

'Yes, of course.'

'I'm now informing you that this is a witness interview and that you're not under police caution but that you nevertheless have a legal right to representation if you want it. Do you understand?'

'Yes.'

'And are you content to waive your right to representation?'

'Yes.'

'Thank you. Ms Walker, did you know Arthur Robbins?'

'Yes, I did.'

'Do you understand why you've been asked to give this statement?'

I show him my phone, where I typed *body Robbins Wordsworth Park* into the search engine on my way here:

Thirty-five-year mystery of missing father solved.
Police have confirmed that remains uncovered during construction of the Wordsworth Park leisure centre in north-west London last month are those of missing businessman Arthur Robbins. Robbins, who disappeared in 1985 leaving behind a wife and teenage son . . .

Detective Scott gives me a searching look. I tried not to think about it on the way here and so, of course, I couldn't think about anything else: how could Arthur Robbins' body stay hidden for thirty-five years in a place like Wordsworth Park, which really isn't all that big and where a hundred people walk their dogs every day? It didn't make sense until I saw the boarded-up building site as I came out of the station. Thirty-five years ago, the same ground was a different building site. Parklands was about to go up.

'You found him when you pulled down the old Youth Centre.'

'And why would you say that, Ms Walker?'

'You're asking about the night of 9th June. Whatever happened to him, it happened on that night.' 9th June 1985: Arty Robbins had hired the Mary Shelley for a private party. It was his fiftieth birthday and he'd invited half the neighbourhood.

'And how would you know that, Ms Walker?'

'Because they poured the foundations for Parklands the next morning. We stopped to watch on the way in to school. I remember it . . .' I can take myself back there if I want. I can see the site change, day by day as I walk past it every morning and afternoon.

'We?'

'Look, Declan was with me for the whole of that evening, from when his family showed up at the Shelley until after midnight. I know you'd already started looking for Arty Robbins by then because there was a policeman in my house when I got back home, asking about him. Declan and I were together the whole time. So . . . I'm sorry, but he's not the one you're looking for.' I don't know why I'm apologising when it's the police who've arrested the wrong person.

Detective Scott cocks his head. 'What do you mean – we'd already started looking for Arthur Robbins?'

'I just told you: there was a policeman at my house when I got home. He was asking about Mr Robbins.'

Detective Scott pretends to consult his notes. 'Ms Walker, what was your relationship with Declan Robbins in 1985?'

'How do you know Arty Robbins didn't just . . . fall?' I remember that hole in the ground where Parklands was going to be. There weren't any fences, nothing to stop people getting onto the building site if they wanted to – not like there are today. We used to go there all the time. Declan's mate, Gary, used to smoke weed there after dark with his friends. Declan too, sometimes.

'That's not something I can discuss, Ms Walker.' Detective Scott is looking right into me. 'Your relationship with Declan Robbins?'

'I was his girlfriend.'

'Ms Walker, before we go on, I would like to note for the recording that Mr Robbins claims, in his own statement, that you have an exceptional memory and that your account of that night is liable to be more detailed and accurate than his own.' He raises an eyebrow and I see he doesn't believe it. 'A gift, he called it.'

'I wouldn't really call it a *gift*. But yes, I can tell you exactly what happened that night.'

Detective Scott flashes me a condescending smile. I'm about to shrug it off – I'm used to it, get it all the time – but then he says, 'I must warn you, Ms Walker, that fabrication of evidence may be taken as perverting the course of justice, an offence under the—'

'It's called hyperthymesia,' I snap. 'Google it. There are a few dozen of us in the world.' As a matter of fact, there are probably quite a lot more, but it's not easy to get a diagnosis. 'I saw three different memory specialists when I was in my twenties. There's a paper about a group of us in an American medical journal. I can give you the names of the consultants I saw. You can look them up if you don't believe me. I can give you the number for my old therapist, too, if you like. She's the one who helped me . . . come to terms with it, I suppose you'd say. Every day of my life, every detail, they all exist in here.' I tap the side of my head. 'I'm not like you, Detective. I can tell you what I ate for dinner on 17th September 2002. I can tell you what my mother said when I came home from school after I sat my history A-level . . .' I want to go on – to tell him it's so much more than a party trick, that it's the single defining factor of my life – but my words peter out.

Detective Scott's scepticism doesn't change. 'So, what: you just remember . . . everything?'

'Like I'm right there.' With all the baggage and all the feelings.

'So I could ask you what day it was on, say, 11th February 1995?'

I have to think for a moment. Sometimes it's right there in an instant, at other times it can be like leafing through the pages of a book. Dad's one-way trip to the hospital was months away. Things weren't going well with Declan. Valentine's Day was a disaster that year . . .

There it is. Music flurries up in my head – the sound of my radio alarm that morning. Bloody Celine Dion singing 'Think Twice'.

'Saturday.'

'Very good, but—'

'The weather was miserable but Declan and I went out for breakfast at the café down the road anyway. It was called Annabel's. I had poached eggs but they were overcooked and both the yolks were hard. They burnt one side of my toast, too. Declan spilt his coffee. Outside the café window were three blue Ford Fiestas, all lined up in a row. We thought that was funny. The couple at the table next to us sat in silence the whole time we were there. I remember I spent half the morning later thinking how I never wanted Declan and me to end up that way, and how we were already half-way there. If you want something you can double-check, there was a Space Shuttle landing on the news – I don't know which one – and Mark Foster won a gold medal in some swimming competition. I think he set a World Record.'

I take a deep breath. Yes, I can feel it now. The certainty. For all the trouble it causes me, my memory is a rock of surety. I can tell this man exactly what happened on the night Arty Robbins disappeared. I can help Declan, because I know where he was and I know he's no killer.

'I lost my virginity that night in 1985, Detective Scott. I probably remember it more clearly than you remember what you had for breakfast this morning.'

Detective Scott gives me a sour look. 'I didn't *have* breakfast this morning.'

'And I didn't *have* to come here.'

We glower at each other, and then Detective Scott raises

his hands in a gesture of peace. 'My apologies, Ms Walker, but, to be honest, one of the first things you learn in this job is how unreliable memory can be – how two people's recollections of the same event hours earlier can be very, very different. You'd be amazed at how much embellishment we can conjure out of absolutely nothing, quite unintentionally. People convince themselves, after the fact, that something must have been a certain way; and then later, when asked to recall the events they witnessed, they genuinely think that a whole bunch of stuff they made up is what they actually saw. Over long periods of time, memories of different events in the same place can mix together. It can seem like two things happened on the same night when actually they were years apart – just in the same place under the same sort of conditions. You see what I'm getting at, Ms Walker? And you're sitting here telling me that you can remember, with perfect clarity, something that happened nearly thirty-five years ago? I hope you can understand why a jury might have doubts.'

I'm tired and off-kilter and I want this to be over, so I can go home. 'Detective Scott, you may think you know how memory works but you don't. I spent most of my twenties and thirties talking to experts. Would you like me to relate the conversations we had? The explanations I was given? I can do that, if you like, although you'll need a bigger tape recorder. I've had scans and tests until I was blue in the face.

I know about impressionistic memory and embellishment and cross-synthesis. When I got home from seeing Declan that night, the clock on the mantelpiece in the lounge said seven minutes past midnight. I'm perfectly aware that when I see a clock that says seven minutes past midnight, I have no more idea than anyone else whether that clock happens to be stopped or running late, or set to Timbuktu time and—'

'I'm not suggesting that you're—' He's annoyed at me now but I don't care.

'Yes, you are.' I just want to go home. 'At some point you're going to suggest that perhaps I remember seeing the clock on the mantelpiece on some other day; or that when I tell you I saw Declan from my bedroom window, it wasn't that same night; or that the dress Mum was wearing might have been—'

'Are you really *that* confident of your memory?'

What do I have to do to prove myself? 'Would it help if I tell you what everyone wore to the party that night? Mum's dress was a dark purple. It had lines of black spots, long sleeves, big shoulders. Tight at the waist. Dad was in a black polo-neck shirt and a leather jacket, like he thought he was the Milk Tray man—'

'Arthur Robbins,' says Detective Scott. 'What was *he* wearing?'

I picture Arty Robbins in the Shelley that night. 'Pale-blue jacket. Blue jeans. Levi 501s, I think. Some sort of white shirt. I never saw him with his jacket off so I don't know whether it was a polo shirt, but it probably was. Brown leather cowboy boots. They looked old, like he'd had them for ages. They had a design on them. Some kind of snake. A rattlesnake, I think. I remember he had a belt with a big silver buckle, too. I didn't see what it was.' Flash clothes, flash car. He wanted to stand out, wanted everyone to know he was loaded . . .

Detective Scott's face changes. His posture shifts. The bored ennui is suddenly gone and I have his attention. We watch each other in silence and then, very slowly, he nods.

'Well?' I ask.

'Well?'

'Do you want me to tell you about the night Declan's father disappeared or not?'

'Yes, please, Ms Walker,' says Detective Scott. 'I think that would be very helpful.'

2

Saturday 8th June 1985

I'm standing in the alley that runs behind the back of my house, far enough from where it opens onto Shelley Street that no one will see us unless they look. No one ever actually comes down here except me and Dec because it's all overgrown with brambles and ivy and full of insects and spiders. It's a perfect summer evening and Dec's arms are around me, the two of us crushed together and kissing. I feel his tongue flickering over my lips, which is weird but sort of nice, and so I open my mouth a bit too, and feel how that excites him even more. His hand on my back slips slowly downwards as if he thinks it's some sort of ninja hand and that if it's stealthy enough then maybe I won't notice, which makes me want to laugh.

He pulls away just an inch and murmurs 'I love you, Nix!' which I know perfectly well is supposed to distract me from his ninja hand but kind of makes me melt inside anyway. I draw back one arm from where it's draped around his shoulders and reach behind me. I feel him tense as I grab his wrist, the disappointment already building. This time I can't stop myself. There it is, the little giggle.

He pulls back, hurt. He's probably about to say something – almost certainly the *wrong* something – so I don't let him. I step into him and lace my fingers through his hair. I feel a delicious shiver go through him, and then it's my turn as he presses me against him and I know *exactly* how much he wants me.

He tugs my blouse free of my skirt. His other hand slips inside. I feel his fingers on my back, hot and electric. There's a delicious warmth in my belly and I know I ought to stop, but the thing is, I don't *want* to stop. We've been going out for two months now and I think I'm ready. Just . . . not in an alley full of insects and brambles.

The hand on my back is sliding around my ribs. I kiss him harder, like I'm somehow not noticing, and let him cop a feel for a moment, just long enough for him to think he's getting away with it, before I break away.

He doesn't complain. I should hope not, too. He knows perfectly well I've let him go a whole lot further than we usually do.

'I love you, Nicky Walker,' he says again, this time with a cheesy grin. To be honest, it works just as well as it did the first time.

'You *are* a lot better than homework,' I say back, which makes him laugh, and then I laugh too, and then I'm kissing him again before I even have time to think about it, and I have to stop myself before we end up doing it behind a bush at the back of someone's garden. I want our first time to be a better memory than that.

Dec looks sort of sad and distracted when I pull away. At first I think it's because I'm not going to have sex with him, although it's a bit daft to imagine that our first time would be in an alley. But then he sighs and I realise it's not about that at all. 'I've got to talk to you about something.'

'What?'

He shakes his head. 'It's not a big deal, but . . .' He trails off. 'Tomorrow, maybe. At Dad's thing. You're coming, right?'

Dad's thing being a party at our local pub, the Mary Shelley, which belongs to Dec's granddad, Vincent Robbins. My best friend Kat's mum works there on account of Kat's real dad – the one who walked out of her life before she was even born – having been Dec's dad's little brother, and all the Robbinses being so big on looking out for family. My own mum helps out too, sometimes. Anyway, Vincent is throwing a party tomorrow for Dec's dad's fiftieth birthday or something like that, and all their friends are invited, even if – as Dad says – *friends* means everyone in a mile radius. But then maybe they *are* all friends. The Robbinses have lived in Wordsworth Park since forever and they're loaded. Everyone knows Dec's dad. Arty Robbins is a parish councillor and a school governor and all sorts . . .

Arty Robbins has a secret, mind you. And *I* know it.

'Mum's helping out,' I say. I look away and then slowly look back, doing my best at a sultry Madonna come-hither look. 'Actually, Mum and Dad are probably going to be there all night. *Your* mum and dad too, I reckon.' I have *plans* for tomorrow night, you see.

Dec licks his lips. His eyes narrow. 'Reckon so,' he growls. It's about the worst Clint Eastwood impression imaginable but it makes me smile. I hug him and then we're kissing again, and it takes an age before I tear myself away and skip down the alley. When I look back, Dec is still there, watching me.

I'm at the gate into our back garden when I hear a noise from Kat's house next door. I can't see anything, but it's a man's voice, low and throaty, and I know exactly who it is, which makes him the *last* person I want to meet sneaking around out here.

'I'm going to keep these.'

Here's the secret: Dec's dad, Arty, and Kat's mum are having an affair. I've known since I saw him sneak up next door's garden from the alley two weeks ago while I was standing at the bathroom window. I mean, I didn't *know* that was what he was doing there, not the first time, but I've seen him again since, and heard a couple of things, too; and no, I haven't seen them *doing* it, thank God, but why else is Arty Robbins sneaking in through the back garden when he's Kat's uncle and they've all known each other for years and years and he could simply go in the front if there wasn't something he was trying to hide?

Which makes it all really weird, because Kat is my best friend and Dec is my boyfriend, and Kat and Dec are cousins, and I'm the only one who knows about Dec's dad and Kat's mum, and what am I supposed to do?

'And you, sex-kitten, you can go draughty down below until next time, to help you remember what we just did.' Arty Robbins laughs. It's not a nice laugh but then I never liked him. No matter what everyone else thinks, there's something not right about Dec's dad.

And that's the thing, because I don't think *Dec* likes his dad either, but everyone *else* thinks he's the bee's knees and I don't want to cause trouble. It's just . . . I don't know. Should I tell someone about what I know? But who?

He's coming this way. He'll use the alley to sneak away because that's what he always does, and now I can't decide whether to dash for the gate into our garden – which means he might hear me – or go back the other way and hide.

Bloody Kat! She told me her mum was working at the Shelley tonight, which was great because it meant I could see Dec and pretend I was at her place, but it *also* meant I wasn't expecting Dec's dad; and now apparently Kat's mum *isn't* working at the Shelley after all, which means I'd better not tell Mum I've been at Kat's house revising for next week's exams in case she decides to check, which means I have to come up with *another* story about where I've been, and *pronto*.

I go for the gate, open it as quietly as I can and slip out of the alley, holding my breath as Arty Robbins hurries away. I lurk behind the garage for a few minutes, wondering what to tell Mum about where I've been, then head up the garden path. The *best* thing would be if she's in the lounge and I could slip in quietly enough that she doesn't hear.

No dice: Mum's in the kitchen as I come through the back door. She looks up, startled. I'm instantly on guard because her face looks like something really *bad* has happened – either that or she's thinking really hard about something, which probably means it's something to do with me. And now I'm wondering if her secret mum-radar already knows where I've been or, worse, she's worked out my plan to slip away with Dec from the party tomorrow night.

'Mum . . . what is it?' The way she's staring is starting to freak me out.

'Nothing, love.' She turns away. 'Just looking at you, that's all.'

She doesn't ask where I've been, which sets off about another hundred alarms in my head because she *always* asks, and that look was definitely *not* nothing. 'I was in the park with some friends,' I say. There's really no way for Mum to check but I still have this dread that somehow she knows I'm lying.

Mum sighs.

'Mum! *What?*' I'm about ready for the sky to fall in, or for Mum to announce we're moving to the Outer Hebrides or something, but after another moment of staring right through the floor, she turns back to me and smiles.

'It doesn't matter. Do you want a sandwich?'

'Um . . . yes, OK.' I start towards the fridge but Mum stops me.

'It's fine. I'll bring it up. What do you want?'

Now I *know* something's wrong, because Mum's idea of tea these days is either to remind me that the fridge is still in its usual place or to suggest that if I'm old enough to have a boyfriend then I'm old enough to use the bread knife without supervision and to call for my own ambulance if I cut off any fingers. She stole that line from Dad, though she never admits it.

'Have we got any ham?' I ask, waiting for the catch.

'I think so.'

'Ham salad then?'

'Salad cream?'

'Yes, please.'

I head upstairs, slowly, still waiting for the sky to fall, but there's only the sound of the fridge door opening and closing.

Weird.

In my room, I take some books from my school bag so it can at least look like I'm up to something Mum will like, then stare out of my bedroom window. My bedroom is at the front of the house and Dec's house is almost right across the road, which means that Dec and I can stand at our windows and watch each other, if we want to.

He's not there, not yet. He *will* be, though. Later . . .

God! The *last* thing I want is a ham-salad sandwich; what I *really* want is to go over there and hang out and listen to music, and spend the whole evening kissing him and maybe more. The *maybe more* is on my mind a lot because I decided last week that I want him to be my first, and now I can't stop myself from thinking about *it*: how to do *it*, and where, and what it will be like, and most of all how to make absolutely sure that Mum and Dad can't have the slightest suspicion because God help me if they do, even if I *am* sixteen now.

Thinking about things that aren't the revolutions of 1848 and glaciation and the themes in Shakespeare's *The Tempest* is what ended up getting me a detention yesterday, so I move my books around a bit, trying to find an arrangement that properly shouts how there's some positively mental exam revision going on. It's silly, because I don't need to revise – not for history and geography, not for English literature and the sciences, not for any of it. If I was there in the lessons, I remember them perfectly.

It seems like Mum has forgotten about my ham-salad sandwich – no surprise there – so I go and lie in bed with a copy of *Just Seventeen* borrowed from Kat and mostly stare at the ceiling thinking about Dec, which ends up with me so far in my own head that I don't hear Mum come up the stairs. I almost fall out of bed in shock when I see her standing in the doorway.

'Jesus, Mum! Heard of knocking?'

'Revising hard?' she asks archly, which is such a mum sort of thing to say. Sometimes I think she'll never get it: how I don't *need* to revise. Even *I* don't get it, not really, how everything seems to stick in my head.

She's carrying a plate. The sandwich on it looks like it came from the Ritz.

'I was taking a break, OK?' I'm still startled enough for it to come out sounding all snippy.

'It's OK, love, I'm not here to criticise.' The way she says it gets the hairs rising on the back of my neck all over again, because right there is another mum-sentence that always has a huge *BUT* sitting on the end of it. Mums and dads criticising is kind of the point of them, isn't it?

'I'll get back to it after I've eaten, promise,' I say. Two

more and then I'm done. Geography on Monday, history on Tuesday, and that's *it*. O-levels finished. No more school. At least, not until after summer, because Dad's adamant that I'm staying on to do A-levels even though I'm not sure I want to.

'I'm off to the shop,' says Mum. She doesn't move, though, just stands there in the doorway looking around my room like she doesn't quite know why she came up in the first place. Not to tell me she was going out, that's for sure.

'OK,' I say, which is definitely her cue to leave me alone now, please, but she *still* doesn't go away. 'Mum! What?'

'Seems like only yesterday I was putting your hair in pigtails with those pink bows.' She lets out a long, wistful sigh. 'You remember those?'

'Mum, I was seven!' I *do* remember, though, all fresh and squishy. Sitting in the lounge, legs crossed, Mum sitting on the floor behind me, gentle fingers in my hair, *Blue Peter* on the telly. I like the way the memory washes through me, warm and cosy. I feel safe and happy and loved.

Mum shakes her head and takes another deep breath. Here it comes. And sure enough: 'Your father and I have had a talk,' she says, and I *know* this is going to be about Dec.

'I got a detention yesterday,' I say, in a desperate effort to change the subject.

Mum only laughs. 'You? A detention? Well, your dad

34

won't be pleased.' Mum ought not to be pleased either, but it doesn't seem to bother her at all. So much for changing the subject.

'So I'll be late home on Monday,' I say, and then add quickly: 'You can check with the school.'

'I trust you,' she says, which makes me feel all squirmy about the hundred million times I've lied about where I was when I was seeing Dec. 'But promise you'll be careful, love, all right?'

'What do you mean?' I think I know *exactly* what she means but I'm too dazed by this whole conversation to ask whether her idea of *careful* means condoms or a chastity belt.

'Sweetheart, I know it probably seems hard to believe, but I was sixteen too, once. I know what it's like. You think you know it all but you don't. I don't want to see you hurt, that's all. Dec seems a nice enough young man but . . . sixteen is still too young.'

OK, so this is *definitely* about me and Dec. 'Too young for what?' I ask, and then wish I hadn't because the answer's so obvious that it makes me feel ridiculous.

'Too young for making choices that you can't take back.'

I want to shout at her, *Mum! Dec and I are NOT having sex, OK? And even if we were, I'm not stupid!* But then we'll end up having an argument when all I want is for her to go away. So I sit up and smile, and act like I'm a proper grown-up, the way Mum wants me to be.

'I'm not going to do anything stupid,' I say. 'I promise.'

Mum looks lost in thought. 'I love you, Nicky,' she says. 'We both do.' She smiles but underneath is something weird, like she's afraid. She turns away and goes back downstairs and leaves the house so quietly that I almost don't hear the front door as it closes.

I eat my sandwich and remind myself to be extra-careful about slipping away tomorrow night. I'll ask Kat to cover for me, which she will because she's my best friend, and because she doesn't have a boyfriend of her own right now, and because we promised ages ago that we'd cover for each other – mostly because of how Kat's mum is a complete dragon about that sort of thing.

Later I hear Mum come back from the shop, but she doesn't come upstairs. Dad comes home and I hear the TV turn on in the lounge under my room, the same routine as always. Mum joins him. They'll be sitting down to watch Kenny Everett like they do every Saturday, except now I hear the TV turn off again, and then Mum, quiet but not quiet enough.

'Craig, we need to talk.'

Dad mumbles something grumpy. They both get up and go into the kitchen, which they only ever do when Mum wants to talk about something she doesn't want me to hear.

Oh God, this is still about Dec, isn't it – it *has* to be, otherwise why would they be talking in secret? I bet I know what it is, too: Mum's worried about me going over the road because she doesn't trust Dec's mum to 'keep an eye on things', only Mum doesn't want to be the one to be mean so she's offloading it onto Dad.

I feel like I'm full of stones, too heavy to move. I could slip out and listen but what's the point? Dad will come up in a minute or two, half stern, half apologetic, delivering Mum's orders like they're supposed to be his own.

'I swear to God, if you don't stop—' Mum's voice, raised, and then I hear a crash, the smash of broken glass. A quiet murmur as Dad says something, then Mum again. She talks too quietly to understand but I hear the snip and snarl of her words. She's angry – really, really angry; the last time I heard her like this was when Gran got knocked down by some idiot in a car from the estate on the other side of the park, and I want to cry, because I'm actually a little bit scared now and because it's not *fair*. I'm sixteen! It's *OK* to have a boyfriend! It's *normal* and it's not like Dec's some loser. Even *Mum* said he was nice, for God's sake. And his dad is Arty bloody Robbins! Of Arty Robbins Estate Agents. Arty Robbins with the swanky new Audi that Dad pretends not to envy: *Vorsprung durch Technik* and everything. Arty Robbins who was a parish councillor at the same time as Mum and had her blushing like a schoolgirl when she said how charming he was . . .

'Jesus Christ, Susan! Just stop for a moment. Have you thought what this would do to the girl?'

My whole body goes numb. I lie still as a statue, trying as hard as I can not to make a sound. I don't think I've ever heard Dad snap like that . . . but now the voices in the kitchen have gone quiet and I can't make anything out and—

BAM! The kitchen door slams hard enough to shake the whole house. Everything goes so quiet you could hear a mouse holding its breath. I reckon if I looked in a mirror, I'd be as white as a sheet. Mum and Dad never fight like this, not ever. I don't think this is about me and Dec any more.

I creep to the bathroom and crouch down by the window and open it a crack. They're outside by the garage, right below me, and I can hear every word.

'What do you suggest?' That's Mum's no-room-for-argument voice. 'Pretend it isn't happening?'

Dad's voice is hollow. He sounds . . . scared. 'Have you thought about what this would do to Nicola?'

'Of *course* I have. She's my *daughter*!' Mum's voice, on the other hand, is like a bomb about to go off. 'That's partly the point! Some things you can't brush under the carpet, and this is one of them. It can't go on, Craig. It has to stop. It has to stop *now*!'

'She's in the middle of O-levels, for Christ's sake! At

least wait until—' Dad stops abruptly. Mum falls silent, too. I can almost feel them both looking up to see the bathroom window ajar, me lurking in the dark on the other side.

This isn't about me and Dec. It's about *them*. Mum and Dad.

They're getting divorced.

3

Sunday 9th June 1985

It rains all morning on the day of the party and so I mostly stay in my room, dreading another *talk* from Mum about boys and about all the terrible things that can happen to a girl my age, and how important it is for her or Dad to always know where I am. Honestly, the way she goes on – and Kat's mum is even worse – you'd think there was a rapist lurking in every shadow. Although . . . no. I could live with a 'talk'. What I'm *really* dreading is Mum and Dad coming up to my room to tell me that they're very sorry, but our family is falling apart.

It doesn't come. Sunday lunch passes in tense silence and then Mum heads off to the Shelley to help get everything ready for the party. Dad settles in front of the telly to watch the horse racing while I flop around in my room, restless, staring at the ceiling. I try to take myself back to the alley and Dec but the memory that surfaces instead is of Kat; of the two of us sitting in her room talking about boys, Kat complaining at how her mum is worse than Mary White-house when it comes to boyfriends, and also such a hypocrite because she was only seventeen herself when she got preg-nant with Kat; then telling me about Arty Robbins' little brother – her real dad – the one she never knew because he never hung around. She talks about him a lot these days, like she's been asking Dec and maybe Dec's dad and maybe even Vincent in the Shelley. No one's heard from him in years. Kat's real dad. Daniel Robbins, black sheep of the Robbins family. It was that same evening that I told her how Mum and Dad had been arguing a lot more than they usually did.

The TV goes quiet. I hear Dad's footsteps on the stairs and then he knocks gently on my door.

'Nicky? Can I come in?'

I don't answer. Usually Dad won't open the door unless I say it's OK for him to come in, but this time he turns the handle. The door opens a crack, slow and tentative.

'I'm coming in,' he says, and he does, and I guess he can tell what I'm thinking because he puts on his sad face and looks at the floor and comes over and crouches beside the bed and strokes my hair.

'Last night . . . It wasn't about you, kiddo.'

I'm not worried about it being about *me*. 'Are you and Mum getting divorced?' I ask him.

'What? No! Sweetheart, I'd never let anything break up this family. I promise.'

It's the kind of meaningless thing parents say on TV, but Dad says it with such a calm confidence that it actually sort of works.

'Thanks, Dad,' I say. 'Dad? I really like Dec . . .'

'Declan Robbins? He seems nice enough.' He looks a bit sad, then forces a smile. 'He must have something going for him if even your mum thinks you could do a lot worse.'

'Gee, thanks!'

'She worries about you.' Which is sort of good, but scary, too. I want to tell him that he and Mum need to sort it out – whatever *it* is – but I don't know the words, so I tell him I'm going to go next door to hang out with Kat. He nods. 'I'll be round to pick you up when it's time to go.'

I don't go to Kat's. Instead, I walk across the road and knock on Dec's door. His mum answers.

'Hi, Mrs R. Is Dec at home?' Mrs R looks rotten, like she was up all night: puffy face, red eyes, hair mussed up like she only just got out of bed. Not that it bothers me, but I can't imagine Mum being caught out like this. Then she turns a little and I see she's not only puffy-faced; her left cheek is all swollen like she banged it on a cupboard door or something. Mum did that once, in the kitchen when I was small. Turned and smacked into the corner of an open door. It was the only time I ever saw her cry. Then I see Mrs R's right hand, tucked away like she's trying to keep it hidden. There's a plaster cast around her wrist, disappearing up her sleeve, and I remember Declan telling me on Wednesday, after he'd missed school for a day, how she'd had a fall and dislocated it and he'd had to drive her to the hospital because his dad wasn't around.

Mrs R gives me a vague look like she doesn't even see me. I can never tell whether or not she likes me, but that's OK because I don't think Mrs R likes *anyone*, because she almost never leaves the house. I suppose she thinks I'm too young for Dec. But I'm sixteen, thanks, and Dec's only two years older than I am, and everyone knows girls grow up faster than boys. I actually sort of like Mrs R because she doesn't ask all the usual mum-questions, like *Where have you been?* and *Who were you with?* and *Have you eaten?* but today she's blank.

Dec isn't at home – I know that because if he was then I'd hear his music – and so I thank her and leave her standing on the doorstep like an extra from *Night of the Living Dead*. I walk to the end of Byron Road and turn right onto Shelley Street, past the Mary Shelley and through the gates of Wordsworth Park, hoping Dec might be there with his mates. I walk past the playground and the playing fields but he's not there, either, and so I cross the tiny road that splits

the park in half, Wordsworth Lane, and head for the Secret
Car Park. The Secret Car Park isn't *really* secret, but the way
it's almost invisible between the trees means hardly anyone
ever uses it, which is why the boys from the estate hang out
there at weekends. Sometimes Dec is there with his dodgy
mate Gary Barclay. They still hang out now and then, even
though Gary didn't stay on to do A-levels like Dec.

I reach the car park. No sign of Dec, but Gary's van is in
its usual place, Gary lounging beside it with the rest of his
loser friends, the sort who look at anyone my age as though
we're scum. Mum would have a kitten if she saw me talking
to this lot, but it's broad daylight and none of them are as
tough as they pretend.

'Seen Dec?' I ask, casual as I can manage. The estate
boys mostly don't know who Dec is so they all glance at
each other as though I'm some sort of alien. Gary looks me
up and down, then shakes his head.

'You want to hang out with us, darling?' asks one of his
friends. The others laugh but not Gary.

'Not here,' he says. 'Go on, scram.'

I walk away, doing my best to stay all casual. I don't
know where else to look and I'm feeling a bit wobbly inside
now, like I don't fit properly in my own skin. I can live with
Gary and his leering, and with Dec's mum being all weird,
but I can't push away what I heard last night – and all of it
together is turning out to be a bit much. I end up going to

Kat's house, like I told Dad in the first place, and we flop together in her room, kicking our heels and talking about music and telly and who we think is going out with whom and not telling anyone at school. Normal stuff, which makes me feel better. I tell her the creeps were in the park again and Kat tells me she thinks Gary's a bit of a dish. I tell her she can't possibly be serious, and that what *I* think is that wearing a long coat in the middle of summer makes you look like a clown. Kat throws a pillow at me.

'He's cool.'

'Cool? Gary?' I shudder. 'You *know* what—'

'That Susie Cooper is a lying slut! You know she made it all up, don't you? She wasn't going out with him at all.'

Susie Cooper is in the year below me and Kat and I saw her and Gary hanging out at least twice after school last year, but I don't say anything. I sit in silence for a bit instead, thinking about last night until I can't stand it any more.

'Mum and Dad had another row,' I say, and I'm right there in the bathroom again, hearing it all and feeling utterly miserable. 'I don't know what to *do*. I think . . . I think they're breaking up.'

Kat sort of sags and moves to sit next to me, hugging me close. 'You can always come here, if it gets too much.'

'I'm scared, Kat.'

I remember what a mess Kat was when her second dad left, back at the start of fourth year. Still is, really, just doesn't talk about it any more. And then Kat asks me if I've read the bit in *Smash Hits* about Madonna's America tour, and we get back to talking about movies and music; and by the time Dad knocks on the front door, I'm mostly thinking about Dec again, and of the party, and of the two of us slipping away together, and that's all *much* better . . .

There's bunting everywhere when we reach the Shelley, and a great big *Arty Robbins, Fifty Years* banner hanging over the front door. Vincent and Madge Robbins and Mr Crane are all dressed in pristine white shirts and green aprons, pulling pints and lining them up. I spot Mum in a purple dress as she comes out of the kitchen with a plate of sausage rolls, and Kat's mum following with a tray full of glasses, both of them heading for a line of tables already loaded with cheese-and-pineapple sticks and prawn-cocktail glasses and melon balls and egg-and-cress sandwiches, and stuff like that.

'Get you two girls a drink?' Dad asks, then comes back a minute later with two halves of shandy. It's a lovely summer evening, so Kat and I go outside and sit on a wall, swinging our legs and sipping our shandies.

'I saw your Uncle Arty sneaking round the back of your house last night, by the way,' I say. 'And it's not the first time, either.'

As soon as the words are out, I wish I could snatch them from the air and pull them back inside. I mean, I can't believe

Kat doesn't already *know* about her mum and Dec's dad, but even so, I promised myself I wouldn't say anything. I'm already starting to say I'm sorry because I know she's going to be mad; but what actually happens is that she goes as white as a sheet and looks about to see if anyone is watching and then looms in close and hugs me and bursts into tears. It's all so unexpected that I don't know what to do.

'Kat, what *is* it?'

'You can't tell anyone! Please . . .'

So she *does* already know.

Her eyes go wide. 'You haven't told Dec, have you?'

'No!' I've been thinking about it. I mean, it seems like maybe he *ought* to know, but . . . 'It's a bit awkward, really.'

'Oh God, Nicky, you *can't*!'

'OK, OK, I won't. I promise.' I heard what some people at school said about Kat's mum after Kat's second dad walked out. I remember seeing Kat crying when she thought no one was looking. I guess it's been hard for both of them since he left.

'*Promise*-promise?'

I take her hand and squeeze. 'Promise-promise.' I draw my fingers across my lips. 'It's a bit weird, you know? I mean, he's my boyfriend's dad and . . .' And I don't know quite what, but parents aren't supposed to do stuff like this.

'It's over,' Kat says. 'It was just a . . . I don't know. A thing.'

It didn't sound very over last night, but I don't want to upset Kat any more than she already is. I suppose it's not really my business what her mum gets up to. 'Well, maybe mention to your mum how I'm not the only one who can see into your back garden, eh?'

There's a weird look on Kat's face for a moment, like what I said doesn't make any sense. Then she hugs me again, and then Dad comes out and brings us each another half-pint of shandy with a don't-tell-your-mother wink, and everything is back to being OK and we talk about other things until it starts to get dark.

There's a bit of a cheer when Dec's dad finally shows up at half-past nine. Back inside the pub, the crowd breaks out into 'Happy Birthday' and Vincent is all over him with hugs and back-slaps. I sidle over to Dec and we sneak out the back to kiss where no one can see. Or at least, where we *think* no one can see.

'Get a room!' Kat's head pokes out of the kitchen window, one big cheesy grin, and I can't think of anything to say because that's *exactly* what I was planning for later, thanks, and maybe Kat can read my mind because her eyes go all big and wide, and I really *ought* to say something right now but I'm frozen and I can't and . . .

Kat's mum saves me, appearing at the back door. 'Declan, your dad's looking for you. I think he's about to make his speech.' She has a camera on a strap around her neck, a big old Minolta that I think is actually Dad's. Her eyes settle on Kat at the kitchen window. 'Oh, perfect! The Three Musketeers, all together.' She circles to face me and Dec, with Kat leaning out next to us, takes a couple of pictures and then disappears back inside. Kat ducks back, too, but not before she gives me the most exaggerated wink imaginable. A round of applause breaks out inside the pub. Dec tells me he reckons he'd rather be kissing me than listening to his dad bang on; I tell him I think he's got a point and so that's what we do, and when we finally come up for air, I tell him my plan: we're going to slip away in a bit, just the two of us, because who wants to stay here getting bored? I feel the anticipation thrumming off him. It's inside us both, an electric thing that can't wait.

We go back inside. Vincent Robbins is standing on a chair, telling everyone how the Shelley served pints all through the Second World War, even after a stray bomb fell on Wordsworth Park and put the crack in the south wall that's still there. He yells at us all to enjoy the food, all bought and paid for by his son Arty – who, by the way, in case you didn't know, also bought a new minibus for the school at the start of the year and put up a big chunk of money for the new Youth Centre they're building in the park. He launches the crowd into a chorus of 'For He's a Jolly Good Fellow' as he steps down.

I look around for Mum and Dad, trying to work out how

to make a stealthy exit, and spot Mum with Dec's dad. Half the people in the pub are still singing, but the last 'And so say all of us' falters into uncertainty as more and more people turn to look: it's obvious that Mum is livid and giving Dec's dad a piece of her mind because Arthur is all red-faced, and Dec's mum, right beside him, looks like she's seen a ghost.

I shrivel up inside and look away, because what else can this be about except me and Dec, and I don't understand because I thought Mum actually *liked* him. She as good as said so! I see Mr Crane stock-still at the bar, looking on. Kat is standing on her own, staring at them like she's got laser-eyes. Actually, about the only person in the room who *isn't* watching them now is Gary, lurking in the shadows of a corner, and now all I can think of is: what's *he* even *doing* here? But I suppose he's Dec's mate . . .

What Gary's doing here right now is watching Kat, the pervert; but Kat doesn't notice because she's watching Mum and Dec's dad, trying to hear what's being said over the hubbub with an intensity like it's Simon Le Bon talking to Madonna about doing an album together.

'I want to go,' I say to Dec.

Someone turns on the music. Mum twists on her heel and storms away, out the back of the pub, snatching a packet of cigarettes from the bar as she goes. I catch a glimpse of her face. She's furious, her hands shaking with rage.

'What was that about?' asks Dec.

'I don't know and I don't want to hang around to find out.' I start trying to pull him outside. 'Maybe your dad started on the canapés before he was supposed to.' I look again for Kat to tell her we're going, but she's still staring at Dec's dad.

'I see you found him.' I jump, startled, and there's Gary Barclay in his stupid coat even though he's indoors, creeping up next to us like some obnoxious ghost. I open my mouth to say something clever and pithy but my brain comes up empty and so I end up gawping like a sour-faced idiot. Gary grins, like he thinks that's about right. 'Excuse me.' He gives Dec a leery grin and a nod and pushes past, heading for Kat. I'm half-minded to follow, because Kat doesn't want anything to do with the likes of him, but Dec catches my arm.

'Come on,' he says. 'Let's just go.'

Mum will be out the back, smoking. I look for Dad and spot him on his own, staring through the crowd as though he's looking for someone, but his eyes slide right over me and on. I don't know what's going on but I've had enough of this place, and if we don't leave soon then I'm just going to go back home to bed and cry.

Outside, I hear Kat around the corner in the car park.

'It's over.' She sounds scared. 'It's finished!'

'You tell me who he is!' That voice – it's Gary bloody Barclay again. 'Tell me and I'll fucking kill him!'

Dec tries to pull me away but I'm not having it. I'm done with people being stupid and mean; done with this whole rotten party. I don't like Gary and I don't care if he and Dec are mates, because I *really* don't like the way he sounds, and Kat is my best friend. I head for the car park and turn the corner and see Gary with a face full of rage and Kat cringing away, which just goes to show I'm right.

Gary glares at me. 'Piss off!'

'Everything OK?' I ask, not budging an inch. It clearly isn't.

'It was until you got here.'

Music and the muted buzz of conversation waft around us, punctured by raucous laughter. I feel Dec's presence behind me but he's not exactly helping. I mean, it *ought* to be him that's doing something – Gary's his friend, and Kat's his cousin – but he won't. Bit of a wet blanket sometimes, my Dec, but Kat looks really scared, and so I shove right past Gary and grab her by the arm and walk her away before anyone can stop me. We go and sit on the same wall where we sat with our shandies, and Gary doesn't follow, thank God. Maybe Dec is holding him back, warning him to leave his cousin alone. But probably not.

'It's OK,' says Kat. 'Really.'

'You and . . . Gary?' I probably shouldn't ask but I can't help myself. 'Were you *breaking up* with him?'

'No!' She sounds shocked. 'We're not . . . It's not – it's

not like that. Gary's . . . he's all right. Really, he is. He gets a bit—'

'Gary? All right?' I can't believe what I'm hearing.

Kat gets up, obviously still upset. 'Just . . . *leave* it, will you?' She stomps back into the Shelley, and I don't know where Gary's gone but I can't see him. And what the bloody hell was *that* about?

I find Dec where I left him, in the car park.

'He thinks he's so special but he's not,' I snap.

'What?'

'Gary bloody Barclay!'

'He's all right,' Dec says, but he says it very quietly and doesn't look at me.

'Some day the police are going to visit that van of his, and that'll be that.' I can't see Gary skulking out here anywhere so I suppose he's gone back inside. Him and his stupid coat. Honestly, I know Gary and Dec were friends years ago, but I have *no* idea why Dec still has anything to do with him.

I squeeze Dec's hand. 'Think your mum and dad will be here for a while?'

He nods. 'It's Dad's party. They sort of have to be.'

'So, let's *not* go to the park then.'

4

Saturday 1st February 2020

Detective Scott is busy making notes. 'What time was it when you left?'

'I didn't check, but it must have been about ten.'

'And you left with Declan Robbins?'

'Yes.'

'Where did you go?'

'We went to his house. We were there until just after midnight. I was with him all the time.' I hesitate, wondering how much to say, wondering how much Declan has already said. I settle for silence. If Detective Scott asks questions about what happened there, then I'll answer them. If he doesn't, then so be it. It's not really his business.

'Did anyone see you, that you can recall?'

'What: going to Declan's house? No. Everyone was in the Shelley and . . . we didn't *want* to be seen, Detective Scott.'

'And you didn't see anyone else on your way there?'

'No.'

'What about at the party before you left? Anyone suspicious? Anything unusual?'

'No, not really. I mean, I don't know what was going on between Mum and Arty Robbins – *that* was unusual. But . . .'

'Did you go straight from the Mary Shelley to the Robbinses' house?'

'We might have stopped on the way for some snogging, but otherwise – yes.'

Detective Scott shoots me a baleful look. 'So . . . you and Mr Robbins left the Mary Shelley together at around ten. You went back to his house, and no one saw you.'

'That's right.'

'How long were you alone together?'

'As I already told you, I was with him until just after midnight. When I got back home it was seven minutes past.'

'From the clock on the mantelpiece?' He gives me a side-eye. I suppose he can't help himself.

'Unless it was set to Timbuktu time,' I say, which at least draws a hint of a wry smile. 'At which point, your Constable Simmons was in the lounge with Dad.'

'Constable who?'

I look him in the eye. 'I already told you that, too: when I got home, there was a policeman already there, talking to my dad. He was asking about Arty Robbins. They were in the lounge. I didn't hear most of what they were saying but I did hear the policeman mention Mr Robbins. I remember his name from the badge on his uniform. That was when I saw the clock on the mantelpiece. Dad told me to go to bed, so I went upstairs and stood at my bedroom window. Declan had said he was going to go back to the Shelley, so I waited. I watched him come out of his house. He looked up at me and waved, then I watched him walk down the road until he reached the end and turned towards the pub.' I remember it vividly: how I kept watching long after he was gone, thinking about what we'd just done, until I heard the policeman in the lounge getting ready to leave.

Detective Scott makes another note. 'What time was that? Roughly?'

'It was only a few minutes after I went upstairs. Quarter past midnight, maybe? I didn't check the time. But, Detective Scott, don't you see? Your constable was asking about Arty Robbins. Arty Robbins was already missing.'

Detective Scott nods, but something isn't right. I've landed what should be a killer blow and it barely seems to register.

'You've got the wrong man,' I say. 'Declan didn't do it. He was with me. He *can't* have done it.'

'That's for the investigation to decide, Ms Walker.' He

flashes me a look that tells me exactly what I can do with my opinions. 'While you and Mr Robbins were alone, what did you do?'

I wonder: is he deliberately trying to make me uncomfortable? 'I don't know what you mean, Detective Scott. We had sex, but I already told you that so I'm really not sure what else you want to know. Are you expecting me to tell you who was on top? How many times?'

'No, Ms Walker. I mean, was there anything *else*? Did anyone else come to the house, for example, while you were there?'

I hesitate at this. The fact that he's asking must mean Declan remembers some of it. I suppose that's to be expected, given what happened.

'Yes,' I say. 'Declan's father.'

'What time was that?'

'I don't know. There wasn't a clock in Declan's room. We can't have been there for more than ten minutes, though. We were still dressed.'

'What happened?'

'He was . . . he was looking for his wife, I think. He asked Declan where she was. Declan said he didn't know. He was . . . very angry.'

'You're referring to Mr Robbins?'

'Yes. No . . . I mean his father. Arty. Arty was angry. They . . . It got pretty heated. Something to do with Declan bunking off school for a day earlier that week and taking his mother to see her sister. I . . .' I shrug. 'He wasn't there for very long. A few minutes. I was hiding under the bed, so I didn't see much more than his feet. I don't think he knew I was there.' All of which is true, but only touches the edges.

'So, Mr Robbins' father left his own party and went home, and he was looking for his wife, you say.'

'That's what he said. He asked about Dec's friend, Gary Barclay, too.'

'Wasn't his wife at the Mary Shelley, which was where you last saw Mr Robbins' father?'

'As far as I knew, yes. Everyone was.'

'Didn't it seem strange, then, that he was asking after her?'

'It *all* seemed strange. We certainly didn't expect to be disturbed. But, Detective . . . We were young. We had other things on our minds.'

'Can you give me some idea of when Arthur Robbins left?'

'Around half-past ten, give or take.'

'And you stayed there, with Declan Robbins, until shortly after midnight.'

'Yes.'

'You didn't leave the house at all?'

'No.'

'And you didn't see anyone else?'

'No. We talked for a bit and then . . .'

'What did you talk about?'

'Really?' I sigh. 'Fine. We talked about us, and we talked about our parents. The Robbins household clearly wasn't as happy as it seemed from the outside, and my parents had had a row the night before. I thought they were about to get divorced, if you must know. We talked about the future and what we were going to do together. We talked about why there was a porno magazine under Declan's bed. All sorts. What are you looking for?'

Detective Scott frowns. 'Did Mr Robbins talk about his father at all?'

'Mostly he talked about leaving home. We talked about how it would work for us if he wasn't living across the road.'

'Robbins was planning to leave home?' Detective Scott's brow furrows as though I've told him something important.

'He was sitting his A-levels,' I explain. 'If he got the grades, he wanted to go to university in Nottingham.'

Detective Scott nods. He seems to think about this for a long time, then puffs his cheeks and blows air and shrugs.

'All right. After you left, when did you next see Mr Robbins?'

5

Monday 10th June 1985

It's early, too early for a school day, but I don't care. I fling open my bedroom curtains and let the sun stream in. There are storm clouds in the sky to the north but all I'm thinking of is Dec, the beads of sweat on his back, his fingers drifting over my skin, his eyes wide and bright with lust. I stand at the window, lost in the memories, all picture-perfect and glorious as though I'm right there again, until my heart starts doing loop-the-loops. It's like the whole world has changed and everything is brighter, the colours more vivid; but it's not the world, it's me. *I'm* what's changed. I feel like I could move mountains, walk on water, do *anything*.

Coming home last night was weird, what with Mum and Dad both there, Dad in the lounge with a policeman, Mum upstairs coming out of the bath. My heart almost stopped when I saw the policeman because at first all I could think was that Mum and Dad had noticed I was gone and reported me missing, or something stupid like that. But I knew I was wrong as soon as I caught Dad's eye. The air didn't change. There wasn't some big sigh of relief. It wasn't about *me* at all.

'Where have you been?'

'With Kat. It was boring.' I remember putting on as much fake concern as I could muster. 'Is everything OK?'

'Go to bed, Nicola. Your mum's in the bathroom. If you know what's good for you, you'll stay out of her way.'

I wish I was waking up with Dec now, not in my own stupid bedroom, but I didn't want to be there when Dec's dad came back home; besides, Mum would have gone mental if I'd stayed out all night, so it's probably just as well.

I go to the bedroom window, dressed in my pyjamas, and look across the street. The curtains at Dec's window are open now. They were closed last night when he left so he must already be up. I will him to come to the window so I can see him. I want to be with him. I want to phone him right now and talk to him and know he's OK and that *we're* OK, but that means going downstairs, and I'm not going downstairs until the last possible minute this morning. Grab some food and run off to school before Mum has a chance to ask the inevitable *Where were you last night?* and *Who was with you?* and *What did you do?* and all the rest. I'll have to face it sooner or later because it's not like they didn't notice me come home last night, but I'll take later, thanks.

Mum slams a cupboard door downstairs, which sets off all sorts of alarms because no way should Mum be up this early. My heart squirms. I'm in for an inquisition and a lecture for coming home so late, I know *that*, but if she somehow works out that I spent last night having sex with Dec instead of being with Kat then I'll probably spend the next three years locked in my room. I'll have to grow my hair long, like Rapunzel, so someone can climb in and rescue me.

I wonder if she already knows, somehow, the way mums do. Then I try to remember what time it was when I slipped in last night. Past eleven? I saw the clock on the mantelpiece, framed between Dad and the policeman as I stood in the doorway to the lounge. Constable Simmons, that was what his badge said; as for the clock . . .

Seven minutes past midnight.

Oh God! Mum's going to go mental but, whatever happens next, it was worth it. I want to put on some music, maybe 'Slave to Love', which I only got at the weekend and have hardly had a chance to play at all, but then Mum will know I'm awake and come stomping up to yell at me. Anyway, my head keeps going back to that stupid Foreigner song that you couldn't get away from back at the start of January. 'I want to know what love is,' sings Lou Gramm, and I want to tell him that I know *exactly* what love is, and it's wonderful.

I stand at the window but Dec still doesn't show, and Mum's still clattering and banging around downstairs and it's obvious there's no way I'm sneaking off to school without taking a lecture, so I decide I might as well get it over with. I get dressed and go downstairs and then stop as I see Dad's leather jacket hanging from the coat rack by the door. There are streaks of orange mud all down one sleeve and across the back, which reminds me of the policeman again. I heard him saying something about Dec's dad, so maybe there was some big drama at the Shelley. I hope so, because maybe that means Mum's thinking about something that isn't *What time did you get home last night, young lady?*

Fat chance. Mum's at the sink in the kitchen, washing vegetables. The atmosphere as I come in is cold enough to freeze a polar bear.

'Morning,' I say, trying to sound like I haven't noticed.

Mum doesn't even look up, just moves on to chopping carrots. I drop a couple of Shredded Wheat into a bowl and pour in some milk, thinking that the faster I'm out of here, the better. I start to carry my bowl out of the kitchen, and it's looking like maybe my luck's in – but, of course, that's when Mum rounds on me, banging the vegetable knife down hard enough that I jump.

'So?'

'Um . . . ?'

'What have you got to say for yourself, young lady?'

Young lady. I *knew* it.

I tell myself to keep acting innocent. 'That . . . I'm . . . going to have breakfast upstairs? You know? We've got geography today. I was going to do some last-minute revision.'

'I don't think so,' she says, so I stay where I am, resigned to the inevitable. A silence grows between us, each waiting for the other to speak, until we both start at the same time.

'What time did you—'

'Why was there a policeman—'

'What time did you get home last night?' She doesn't look at me and I know she already knows the answer, probably to the exact second.

'Mum! I'm sixteen and it was only *just* past midnight! Why was there a policeman here?'

'Never you mind.' Her hand moves to her throat. An absent-minded gesture but now I see the dark marks on the side of her neck. They look like bruises.

'Mum—'

'Where were you? Because you clearly weren't anywhere near the Mary Shelley last night or you wouldn't need to ask.'

I take a mouthful of Shredded Wheat, part of me wondering what on earth has happened while the rest of me tries to think my way out of this. 'With Kat,' I say when I can't come up with anything better. 'Revising, you know?'

Mum rolls her eyes. 'Nicola Walker, *please*!'

'We lost track of time! Sorry.'

Mum takes a step closer. Her eyes are so narrow you could cut yourself on them. 'Revising, is it? *That's* your story? Funny, because after your dad spent half an hour looking for you, he knocked on the Clarkes' door on the way home and no one answered. Let's try this again: where were you?'

'OK, so we weren't revising. That party, Mum, it was just so . . . boring. There was nothing to *do*. We went for a walk.' Oh God, that's so *lame*.

'A walk? For two hours? Where did you go? India?'

'The park, Mum!'

'You went out into the park. In the dark. For two hours.'

I have a brainwave. I put on my angry face. 'Actually, since you apparently have to know the *exact details*, Kat was really upset because of this boy called Gary who keeps bugging her. He was all over her at the Shelley and that's why we didn't stay. It's kind of creepy, actually. He's well dodgy.'

I expect this to take the wind right out of Mum's sails but for some reason it doesn't even make a dent. 'And do you want to tell me how long you and Kat were in the park together . . . No, actually, don't, I don't want to hear you lie to me again. I'll ask you one more time. Where were you? Tell me the truth this time, Nicola, or I swear you'll spend every weekend from now until the end of summer locked in your room.'

I put a careful edge on each word. 'Why does it matter? What difference does it make?'

'It makes a very big difference if your walk involved a long detour across the road.'

I almost tell her I wasn't anywhere near Dec's house but stop myself just in time. She knows. I don't know *how*, but she does; and she's shaking, she's that angry, and I'm actually a bit scared.

'Were you with him?'

'With who?'

'You know *exactly* who I mean. Your father's going to skin that boy alive.'

'For God's sake, Mum, I'm sixteen! I am *allowed* to have a boyfriend, aren't I?' I can't imagine Dad skinning anyone, but what he *will* do is turn my home into a prison camp – probably with hired guards and everything to make sure I don't go anywhere or see anyone that Mum hasn't decided is OK.

'Where. Were. You?'

'Since you apparently already know, why are you even asking?'

WHACK!

I don't see it coming. I don't think Mum sees it coming, either; but all of a sudden, my cheek is stinging as the bowl of Shredded Wheat flies out of my hands and smashes against the door frame, and there's milk and mushy cereal

67

bits all over my top and in my eyes and in my hair and drip-
ping down the side of my face.

We look at each other, me trembling with shock, Mum
looking like she doesn't recognise who I am. We stare and
stare and neither of us says anything, and then I turn and
leave without a word and go back to my room. Mum doesn't
follow or say anything. I feel tears wanting to come and I
can't quite stop them, but I'll be damned if I'm going to fall
to pieces; and so I take myself back to last night – to Dec, to
being with him, to how it felt to have him wrapped around
me – until the tears go away. Then I change my clothes and
throw the dirties on the floor for Mum to deal with later,
and go to the bathroom mirror to assess the damage.

It's not so bad. The side of my face still has a bit of Shredded Wheat sticking to it and my eyes are puffy, but a quick
rub with a flannel and a few dabs of make-up and I look
almost normal again. Except . . . not quite. The face looking
back at me seems subtly different, more assured. I feel alert
and I suddenly know exactly what I'm going to do. When
Dec leaves home, I'm going with him. There's only another
six weeks before school finishes and then we'll spend the
whole summer together, and there's nothing Mum and Dad
can do to stop me. Maybe I won't come back at all.

It's too early to be leaving to go to school but I'm not
hanging around to have another breakfast thrown all over me
and so I go back downstairs and leave the house, slamming

the door behind me. I go to Kat's house and ring the bell. When Kat's mum answers, there's a moment like she's considering not letting me in, but then she stands out of the way.

'I suppose you can come in.' She doesn't sound keen. 'I take it you've had breakfast?'

'Actually, no.'

She shakes her head and rolls her eyes. 'Help yourself.'

The air is wrong here too, like it's wrong at home, thick with tension. I see Kat at the top of the stairs and there's obviously something she needs to tell me, which is good because I *really* need to tell her how the two of us and Dec were hanging out in the park last night between ten and midnight, if anyone asks. 'Mrs Clarke . . . did something happen last night? At the Shelley?'

Kat's mum gives me a sharp look. 'What happened, young lady, was that no one could find you.' She whips a murderous look to the stairs. 'Or our Katherine, for that matter.'

'I went looking for her,' says Kat, and it's like she's reading my mind. 'We sat in the park for a bit. You know. Because of . . .'

Kat's mum turns her annoyance up the stairs. 'You did, did you? Until nearly midnight? When you knew that Nicola's parents were looking for her?'

'We were with Declan,' I say, because Kat needs to know that part of the story before she goes and says we were on our own. 'We just sort of hung out for a bit. The three of us together . . .' I shoot a glance past Kat's mum to Kat. 'We left because of this boy called Gary Barclay, who's friends with Dec and keeps bugging Kat to go out with him and—'

Kat lets out a high-pitched laugh that sounds more like a cry of alarm. 'Except it turns out he's a poof! That's what Declan said, anyway. Can you believe it?'

I stare at Kat, incredulous that she chose to go with *that* as her story.

'And . . . and I did *tell* Nicky her mum was looking for her.' Kat's staring at me hard, and I'm looking right through them both, thinking *What on earth happened last night?* along with a good healthy dose of *And where were* you, *Katherine Clarke?*

'Did you now?' I don't think Kat's mum believes a word of any of this, but I nod vigorously, and then I sort of put things together, realising that whatever happened maybe had something to do with Mum and Dad, which is a bit of a shock, and so it's easy to put on a show.

'Oh my God! There was a policeman in the house when I got home. Was that . . . ?'

I look from Kat to Kat's mum and back again, hoping one of them will help me out. Kat obviously doesn't have the first idea what I'm talking about, but Kat's mum nods. For a moment it looks like she's going to tell me but then she changes her mind and shakes her head. 'Best talk to your mother about that,' she says. 'Speaking of which, I'm sure she isn't keen on you being on your own with a young man two years older than you are, even if he *is* our Katherine's cousin.'

I make a face – *not keen* might be a new World Record in understatement. 'Dec's . . . having some problems at home,' I say, and I'm ready to say a whole lot more, too, because it's always good to put in as much truth as you can when you're making up a story, but then I remember: Kat's mum and Dec's dad are *doing* it, so I'd really better not talk about what I saw last night. 'That's why we didn't come back when Kat found us,' I say instead. Oh God, *again*! How *lame* does that *sound*?

Kat's mum sighs as she stands aside to let me through to the kitchen. 'None of my business, I suppose. Or yours either, I fancy. Go on. Get yourself some breakfast.'

She doesn't come with me. Kat and I are in and out of each other's houses all the time, so I already know where everything lives. It's like having a spare second home sometimes, which is usually really nice, but not today. Today I grab a bowl of Corn Flakes and some milk and gobble it down as fast as I can and then Kat and I leave for school, early and glad to escape.

'So . . .' I just want to get our story straight, but Kat's having none of it.

'Did you and Dec *do* it last night?' Her eyes are wide and dancing with mischief. 'You did! Nicky Walker, you slut!'

'What happened after we left?' I ask, trying not to go all embarrassed, which is always a dead giveaway. 'There was this policeman—'

'I don't know. I wasn't there. Anyway, never mind *that*—'

'Yes, speaking of which, where were *you* last night?'

Kat grins and starts dancing from side to side. 'Dec and Nicky sitting in a tree, F-U-C-K-I-N—'

I elbow her. 'Shut *up*!' She laughs and starts asking all sorts about what Dec asked me to do and where he wanted to put it and things like that, all of which are a bit of a shock because Kat clearly knows a *lot* more than I thought she did about *it*, and probably a lot more than I do, and some of it is very definitely *not* the sort of thing they talk about in *J17*. And how come she knows all these things unless *she*'s done it too, because from the way she's talking, I'm pretty sure she has, which can only mean that Kat has a secret boyfriend she hasn't told me about even though I'm her best friend.

By now we're in the park, heading for the path between the woods and the building site where the new Youth Centre is going to go. There's a bit of a crowd where two huge cement trucks are parked up, and a whole bunch of people have stopped to watch. Mostly it's kids on their way to school but I see mums and dads there too, and even Mr Crane from the Shelley.

'Kat . . .' I don't know what to say. I want to tell her about what I saw last night but I don't know how. 'Did *you* know that Dec's dad bought the school a minibus last year?'

Kat shrugs. 'Not until last night.'

'Did you know he's one of the school governors, too? Everyone thinks he's so bloody marvellous.' But he isn't. I know that now. After last night, I know *all* about Arty Robbins.

Kat shivers. 'Is this about your mum?'

'My mum?'

Kat looks at me looking back at her, all bewildered. 'Yeah. Something happened last night at the party, after you left. Mum's livid about it. Something about Arty and your mum. I wasn't there either, so—'

'My *mum*?' I remember the bruises, and Arty and Mum arguing at the Shelley. And the policeman, last night . . .

Kat's expression turns sour. 'You're right, though. You could say Uncle Arty stuck his hand up your dress and it wouldn't matter. Short of photographic proof of him murdering Jesus or something, everyone would just say *Nasty little liar*. I keep wondering how much Dad was like him, or whether he was completely different—'

'*That*'s what he did?' I stare at her in shock. 'To my *mum*?' Oh God, is *that* what happened at the Shelley?

Kat looks suddenly alarmed, like she's gone too far or said something she shouldn't. 'No! No, at least . . . I don't *think* so. I don't know. I wasn't there. I'm just saying what it's like. You know what I mean. *But it happened, Mr Wallace! Mr Roberts keeps touching me!* And then Mr Wallace says *And how short was that dress, young lady?* And the next thing you know, he's calling your parents and it's all about *you* and what *you* did, and everyone thinks you're the school tart because obviously all the *other* girls dress like bloody nuns, don't they?'

I stare at her, waiting to see whether there's more. I have no idea where this is coming from, although I *do* know about Mr Roberts, head of the English department. Mr Touchy-Feely, as he's known.

Kat smiles in a way that's sort of sad and angry at the same time. 'It happened to Mum when she was at school, too. Groped by a teacher when she was fourteen. She told me, when she did the *talk* thing.' She makes a sour face. 'That was about it, really. The rest was: Don't do it, never talk about it, and if you do it with anyone before you're eighteen, I'll hunt them down and kill them.'

'She said *that*?'

'The last part is a summary. She was more graphic.'

I look round furtively and whisper, 'So she doesn't know you've already—'

Kat elbows me, hard this time. 'Shut *up*! Anyway, I never said I had.' But she bloody has, the sneaky cow.

I raise an eyebrow. 'Did you leave the party with Gary Barclay last night?'

I Know What I Saw

Kat rolls her eyes. 'Don't *you* start.'

'Well, *did* you?'

Kat shakes her head. I'm not sure if I believe her but I know Kat: if she doesn't want to say then she won't, not even to me.

We reach the path and stop for a bit to see what all the fuss is about, but it's only lots of workmen over on the building site shouting at each other as they pour concrete into the big hole that they spent most of last month digging. It's nothing exciting, and then I see Dec on the edge of the crowd, waving at me. I quickly say goodbye to Kat and then I run to him.

6

Saturday 1st February 2020

I don't know how long I've been sitting here with Detective Scott, talking about that night in 1985. An hour? Two? I've lost myself so deep in the memories that I've almost forgotten why I'm here. That's how it can be, sometimes: I'll let myself follow one memory and a thousand more pop up all around me. Suddenly, I'm not in 2020 any more but 1992, or 2001, or 1985 – every single memory as vivid to me as this morning's breakfast.

'That's it,' I say. 'I saw Dec again the next morning, on the way to school. He was waiting for me.' And this, I think to myself, should be the end of it; because by the time I left Declan and went home, Arty Robbins was already missing.

Detective Scott gives me a look that he's given maybe

half a dozen times now. A part of him still wants to think I'm making things up, but mostly he believes me.

At least I *think* he believes me.

'When you saw Mr Robbins the next morning, did he seem . . . in any way unusual? Stressed? Secretive?'

'No.'

'Did he say anything about what he did, after you saw him leave his house?'

'He told me he went back to the Shelley and that he stayed the night there.'

'Didn't that strike you as a bit strange?'

Not as strange as Detective Scott might expect, but I don't think I'll be going into *that* right now. 'He stayed there because his mum stayed there, too. No, it didn't strike me as strange at the time.' Which is true as far as it goes. 'You *have* talked to Anne Robbins about that night?'

Detective Scott makes a sour face. 'Ms Walker, for the record, how clear would you say you are in your recollection of events?'

'I recall everything about that night as clearly as I see you in this room,' I say. I'm tired of this. I've spent my whole life being told that what's completely natural to me can't possibly be true. I've seen the look on Detective Scott's face a thousand times: that even mix of curiosity and doubt that people have when they start to believe I'm not making it up, that maybe I really *do* have an exceptional memory. A part of him is wondering what the trick is; another part how good it really is – how far back, and how deep, my memory really goes. If we had time, he might ask. I'd tell him, too.

'One more question: was Daniel Robbins there that night?'

It takes me a moment to place the name. Daniel Robbins. Kat's father. Declan's uncle. Arty Robbins' brother.

'No,' I say. And why is he asking about a man who left Wordsworth Park before Kat was even born and who never once came back?

'Are you sure? Would you have known him, if you'd seen him?'

'Probably not. I never met him. I've seen pictures, since, but of him when he was much younger. So no, but . . . Detective, Daniel Robbins had been gone for almost sixteen years. This was his brother's fiftieth birthday party, held in his father's pub. If he'd come back, *everyone* would have known!'

'Thank you for your assistance, Ms Walker.' As he turns off the tape, I can still feel his scepticism. 'We'll be in touch if we need anything more.'

'Can I ask you a question?' I ask.

'Shoot.'

'Has Declan got a solicitor?'

Detective Scott rummages through his pockets and hands me a card. Angela Watson, of Lainton Legal Associates. 'Duty solicitor. As far as I know, Mr Robbins hasn't asked for different representation.'

Declan has used a solicitor twice before, that I know: the first time when we almost bought a house together, the second when we got divorced. I don't recognise the name Lainton Legal.

I thank him and get up to go. 'Do you want references for the medical experts who can tell you about my condition?' I expect him to demur but he smiles and says yes, that would be helpful. As he escorts me to the front desk, I ask when Declan will be released and get a bland can't-talk-about-that sort of answer. As I'm about to leave, though, he stops me.

'Off the record, Ms Walker, he *did* do it.'

I look at him, shocked that he'd say such a thing. Is he even allowed to? I want to tell this Detective Scott that I lived with Declan for ten years; that whatever Declan's faults, violence wasn't one of them. But I've done what I can. I've given my statement. The police will have to let Declan go, and I need to walk away from this.

'You're wrong,' I say, and maybe they'll discover what really happened to Arty Robbins or maybe they won't, but either way, Declan probably won't even call to thank me. He'll put it behind him; Detective Scott will move on to another case; and a few weeks from now, it'll be like none of this ever happened.

Except for me. For *me*, all this will be in my head forever.

It's dark outside the police station when I leave. I walk to the end of the High Street and sit on one of the benches at the entrance to Wordsworth Park and my head is full of Declan. I call Kat but the call goes to voicemail. I leave a message asking if we can meet. I need to unload. I need to talk the memories out. If I don't, next week is going to be hell.

I've always remembered things – that was simply the way it was. I was like a sponge with new words, with stories, with facts and figures. My teachers at primary school thought I was some kind of prodigy. 'Gifted and talented' they'd probably call it these days, but Mum didn't want a daughter who was different, thanks; and certainly not a prodigy, so that was that. Looking back, I think she hoped it would go away if she ignored it. It didn't, of course, but she never really accepted that she was wrong.

It wasn't until secondary school that I understood I wasn't *clever* exactly; it was just my memory, and that wasn't always so great. I mean, it was still *mostly* great because I could remember all the lyrics to every song and never had to do any revision for anything except maths, because most subjects were simply remembering what you'd been told in class . . . But while everyone around me was worrying about how their bodies were changing, and who liked who and who didn't, I had to worry about what was going on in my head, too. It was like living inside an amplifier, where every taunt and jibe stayed as fresh as the moment it was said. Stupid things, but I still remember them even now – like the time in primary school when Justin Moore pulled my pigtails hard enough to make me cry and all his friends laughed at me. Playground nonsense, forgotten in five minutes by the rest of them, but I never wore my hair in pigtails again. Later, I took to keeping a low profile. I tried to fit in. I'd fake answers in tests and mock exams, deliberately not doing as well as I knew I could so I didn't end up getting top marks and being singled out for being a nerd. After the first couple of disasters, I was probably the only adolescent girl in history who spent most of her time desperately staying away from the boys she fancied, killing the crush before it blossomed and then cut me to pieces with months of heartbreak when it inevitably ended.

And then I found Declan, and I was happy. Deliciously, deliriously happy. And lucky, too, because we stayed together through the last years of school. I don't know a single one of my friends whose first true love lasted more than a few months, but it seemed that Declan and I only ever got stronger. When I was twenty-one, I married him. We were going to be together forever.

Until we weren't.

I don't know when things started going wrong. Does that seem odd, given how I remember everything else with such clarity? But it's true, because there was never *one* thing. Even the woman I saw with Declan at the very end – she was just the last straw. I saw him kiss her and it was like a thousand other little things, stretching back for years, all clicked into place. So no, I couldn't tell you when the first crack appeared between us; and believe me, I've looked and looked and looked; but it's memories of the little things that always pop into my head, like those songs from my youth that still get played on the radio again and again. Maybe it was the day he came home from work and went straight to the telly without saying a word. Maybe it was the time I was upset and he didn't come and find me and give me five minutes of his time. Maybe it was the evening I was planning to go out with friends and asked if he wanted me to stay at home and keep him company instead, and he said no, thanks, he had work to catch up on. It was weekends spent in Asda and Tesco and B&Q and never picnicking in a field or by a river. I remember every romantic trip we ever planned and never took. I remember him having a shower one day, and me walking in ready to have sex and nothing happening, because everything was too awkward and uncomfortable; and at the same time I remember *exactly* how much he'd wanted me in those first few years, and how nothing else would have mattered . . .

I went to see Kat a year before I ended it: Kat who was still my best friend then and is still my best friend now. She'd dumped Gary for a second time a few months earlier but now they were back together again, and so I'd gone to try and talk her out of it – as far as I could see, Gary was the same jerk he'd been when we were teenagers – but somehow we ended up talking about me and Declan instead; how nothing was the way it used to be, how everything was bland and mundane, how there was no passion in our lives and how that could only mean he didn't want me any more. I went on and on: how he used to call me at work during the day to say he loved me, and now it was only ever to ask if I could pick up some milk on my way home; how he always used to stop to kiss me on the way out every morning, never mind the bed-hair and the pillow-face; how sometimes it would turn into more and we'd both be late, but now more often than not I didn't even see him before he left; how we always used to eat together in the evenings but now we often ate on our own; how we used to go out two or three times a week, but now it was barely once a month.

'It's the same thing as with Mum and Dad,' I said. 'I remember them from when I was really small: how they used to be with each other, how they used to hold hands all the time. They were always touching each other. Little things. I remember when I was seven or eight, sitting in the lounge, the three of us watching telly together, and Mum and Dad were sat side by side, Mum's hand on Dad's leg and his hand on hers. Now they just . . . sit and do their own thing. Dad's got his bridge club and his golf, and Mum has her Oxfam thing going. They never do anything together any more.' I'd watched it all happen. The disintegration of love into teamwork, into the business of making a family and fitting in; the distance growing between them; Mum's affair with David Crane that year when Declan's dad disappeared, even if she always swore there was nothing going on; Dad finding out, leaving, coming back three days later. The two of them getting on with things like nothing ever happened. As if raising a child was like running a family business . . .

'It's the same thing,' I said. 'Only now it's happening to me and Dec and I don't understand what I did wrong.'

I looked at Kat, hoping she might have an answer, and found her looking back at me like I was some sort of idiot.

'You do realise you're describing every relationship ever?'

'No. I don't.'

'Well, you are. I don't know about your mum and Dave Crane, but whatever it was, it obviously didn't last, and your mum and dad are still together. Look at them. They still love each other. It just changes, that's all. It can't be all . . . teenage passion and hormones forever. God, imagine how exhausting that would be!' She laughed. 'Christ, I'd go mental if Gary was all over me all the time like he was back when we started. Trust me: Dec loves you. It's obvious. Is he sleeping with someone else?'

'God, no!'

'No mysterious late nights at the office? Strange phone calls? Doesn't come home with an unfamiliar perfume on his jacket? Lipstick on his shirt? That sort of thing?'

'Don't take the piss, Kat.'

'Nicky, I've known Dec since I could barely walk. He's a big pussy-cat. You have nothing to worry about.'

Maybe she was right. I couldn't decide then, and I can't decide now. Afterwards, I tried to tell myself that the way things were with Declan was just . . . normal, but it was so bloody *hard* when I could remember every perfect moment, every kiss, every tenderness, every fling of passion. It was all right there in my head – all our past, the intensity of the love we had. When I took all that and put it beside the present, it felt like I was living in a desert.

It got worse. *I* got worse. And I know it was me, that Declan didn't really do anything wrong. He hadn't strayed, not then. He saw my unhappiness and we talked it through and he tried to make it better, but that was never going to work, not when the gulf that I felt between us was a gulf to a past that only *I* remembered.

And then he *did* stray, and that was that.

It's dark and now it's cold. I'm sitting on a bench, staring at the boarded-up building site where Arty Robbins died. If I wanted, I could walk down the cycle path and cross Wordsworth Park to Byron Road. I could visit Mum and dick-face Dave. I could go back to where the rot started – that summer of 1985 – and face it down, but what would be the point? What difference would it make?

Off the record, Ms Walker, he did *do it.*

I Know What I Saw

I don't know what to make of Detective Scott. Why would he declare Declan guilty like that? Does he think I'm lying? Does he think I'm making it all up? But I'm not, and I really did talk to a dozen memory experts in America in the late Nineties. One of them really did write a paper on hyperthymesia, although I wasn't his principal subject. But they were in it for the science; I was their research, not their patient. In the end I stopped seeing them. What I wanted was something to make it all go away. The truth is, I still do. I don't *want* to remember everything, because remembering everything is what drove me from Declan. But there *isn't* a cure, and never will be, and so after all those years in America, I came back to London and settled for the compromise of a quiet existence, innocuous, uneventful and alone.

It's getting late. I head home, trying to shake away the ghost of Arty Robbins and of that summer. We all knew the police were looking for him even before a day had gone by; when they didn't find him, you could see the lace curtains of the front rooms along Byron Road twitching with the talk: *Where's he gone? What did he do? What did his wife do to drive him away? How terrible for the boy!* As far as anyone knew, he'd simply walked out on his family, on his life, on everything. *Done a Reggie Perrin*, Dad said. There were rumours for a while that his estate agent business was bankrupt; but this was the Eighties, when estate agents couldn't walk five yards without tripping over money, so if it wasn't *that*, what was it? Gambling? Money laundering? It had to be *something*, right? This was . . . Arty Robbins. Big-hearted, generous Arty Robbins, who wasn't afraid to splash the cash; who'd bought the school a new minibus and new kit for the Wordsworth Park Juniors football team; whose adverts all but paid for running the local paper; and who'd invited a hundred people to his dad's pub for free food and drink, just because he could. Who, as it turned out, was one of the private investors in Parklands, and whose estate agency was making money hand over fist. There were no secret hidden debts, no criminal gang connections – nothing. No one could understand why he'd simply walked away from his life.

The police suspected foul play and for a while it was a murder investigation, but the rest of us never believed it, and now I wonder why. Because the police never found a body? Because of all the stories that came out after he was gone? I don't know. Back then, I didn't care – all *I* could think about was Declan, and how it might as easily have been my own family coming apart. I think, sometimes, it was only because of Arty Robbins that Dad didn't do the same. Like it jolted him: the idea that families really could and did disintegrate, and that ours was worth saving.

There were plenty of whispers after Arty vanished, mind you, most of them about his wife, Anne. No one could say exactly what she'd done but it became her fault somehow, the Arty-shaped hole in our community. Mum caught a slice too: everyone knew that she and Arty Robbins had had a row that night at the Shelley. I'm sure some people wondered if they'd been having an affair. Mum laughed it off and it went away, but it gave the gossips something to chew on. After a time, the whispers started about the way Arty had treated Anne – the abuse, the bruises, the fractured wrist that week before he disappeared – and perhaps that's why no one else ever put two and two together about Arty and Chloe Clarke. No one ever knew about that except for me and Kat; and Chloe, of course. I kept my promise and never said anything about it, not even to Declan.

Declan. Declan, Declan. He made everything OK when Dad walked out for those three horrible days in August. But it *was* only three days, and afterwards it seemed that everything slowly went back to normal. The neighbourhood adjusted around us. It didn't change the fact that no one ever knew why Arty Robbins had run away or where he'd gone, but the police stopped asking questions, the articles and adverts in the local paper slowly faded away, and everyone quietly forgot.

Almost everyone.

I try googling him but there isn't anything about Arty Robbins on the Internet from when he was alive because he existed before all of that. No social media, no website, no Rightmove page for *Robbins' Properties*, which long ago changed its name to something bland and forgettable. All I find, as I sit on the bus, is what I already know: human remains discovered by workmen demolishing the old Youth Centre in Wordsworth Park, confirmed as being Arthur Robbins, missing since June 1985; a murder inquiry launched and a man taken into custody.

Declan.

I suppose, in a way, the Internet has made my own gift available to everyone. You don't need a perfect memory – facts, history, it's all there if you want it, right up to a record of your whole life, kept in words and images and sounds on social media, without the baggage of *feelings*.

Off the record, Ms Walker, he did *do it*. Detective Scott's words circle like an angry shark in my head, refusing to let me go.

On the Friday before the party at the Shelley, they finished digging the pit for the Parklands foundations. On the next Monday morning, they filled it with concrete. A hundred people saw Arty Robbins at the Shelley. It had to be that night then – whatever happened to him – between some time after ten-thirty and whatever time it was the next morning when the first workmen arrived to fill the hole. When Kat and I stopped to watch on the way to school, my thoughts were all over the place. Certainly not on what those workmen were doing. When I think of it now, it makes me shiver. They had no idea, of course, but still . . .

I Know What I Saw

At home, I sit on my bed with my cat, Chairman, purring on my lap, the two of us staring at the photograph of me and Declan and Kat, which Kat's mum took that night at the Shelley. We'll have some scritch-and-snuggle time and watch something trashy. I'll probably cry a bit and spend tomorrow feeling sorry for myself. And then I'll go back to life-as-usual and all of this will be more memories. I've done my part. I've given Declan his alibi. I'm glad I could help him. I owe him that. I owe *myself* that, but Declan and I separated twenty-four years, five months and one day ago – and, no, I'm not counting, I'm really not, I just can't forget even if I wanted to; and now the same gift of memory that tore us apart is what's dragging us back together.

Maybe I'll go away for a few days. Some bed-and-breakfast, a place to clear my head. Or maybe it's time I started looking for a friend for Chairman. I know cats are supposed to be solitary animals, but Chairman is a Norwegian Forest cat, and Wegies like company.

The words on the screen blur. I force myself to breathe. In and pause. Out and pause. I can probably expect a week of nightmares and flashbacks until I force the memories back into the musty cupboards where they belong. And then everything will go back to normal. Everything will go back to the way it was, as simple as that.

Except it *isn't* that simple.

I squeeze my eyes shut and dive into the past, to the places that always save me: to standing in my window, looking across the street and seeing Declan looking back; to a lazy summer afternoon beside a river; to the rustle of his feet on the carpet and the smell of him: sweat and cigarette smoke and petrol; to feeling him climb into bed beside me, soothing me back to sleep.

That. That's what I threw away.

I still love him. Love him and hate him and miss him, because I can't forget and I can't forgive. There's no pretending otherwise, and nothing I can do to make the feelings go away. I've been trying for twenty-five years but he still haunts me.

Will he call when they let him go? They *have* to let him go. He was with me. By the time I left, his dad was already missing.

Off the record, Ms Walker, he did *do it.*

I barely knew Arty Robbins. It's none of my business what happened to him. Everyone else missed him, but *I* didn't, and I don't think Declan ever did, either.

So here I am, thinking of the past, of the present and of the memories I carry inside me, the good and the bad.

My phone rings. I close my eyes and force myself to breathe. It's been a long, long day and I have a sense that something terrible is coming. I hesitate and almost don't answer. When I do, it's a woman's voice, a stranger.

'Hi. My name's Angela Watson. I work for—'

'I know who you are. You're Declan's solicitor.'

'Yes.' She sounds surprised. 'Ms Walker, Mr Robbins has instructed me to . . . to pass on the news. I'm sorry, but it isn't good, I'm afraid. The Crown Prosecution Service has decided the evidence merits prosecution. They're charging Mr Robbins with the murder of his father.'

7

Sunday 2nd February 2020

It's a miserable afternoon. I didn't sleep well last night. I've been going over in my head everything I told Detective Scott, wondering whether I've said the right thing. That's what you do, isn't it, when it's too late to change anything? It's what *I* do, anyway. Over and over because I remember it so perfectly. I didn't tell him *everything*, of course. I suppose Detective Scott would say it was up to him to decide what was important, but you have to draw the line somewhere, don't you?

That's my Sunday; that and searching the Internet for everything I can find about the body discovered in Wordsworth Park; and thinking endlessly about the years Declan and I were together, which is why I'm lying on my bed still in my dressing gown with Chairman curled up at my feet when my phone rings again.

'Nicky?'

'Kat!'

'*Sorry* I didn't get back to you yesterday. I was out when you called and then, well, you know how it is. I tried later, but—'

'My phone was off.' I don't know why I feel I have to apologise.

'You sounded . . . upset. Is everything OK?'

Everything is very far from OK. 'I don't know where to start. I spent yesterday afternoon talking to the police. Kat, it's—'

'Oh my *God*, the *police*?' I hear the hesitation as her best-friend radar kicks in. 'What happened? God, are you *OK*?'

'I'm fine.'

'But what happened?'

'It's . . . a bit of a long story. Actually, I wouldn't mind some company.'

Kat barks a laugh. 'Come over! It's just me and a bottle of Chardonnay in the fridge at the moment. Gary won't be home until *seven*.'

'He's working? On a Sunday?'

I can positively *hear* her eye-roll. 'It's this deal he's got in Docklands. "Massive and worth a fortune and, blah-blah, make us rich; sorry, Babe" – usual story.'

I Know What I Saw

I tell her I'll be right over. All I'm doing at home is feeling sorry for myself, and I've been here enough times to know that wallowing is best done in company. I tug on a pair of jeans and root through my old collection of faded band T-shirts, stuff that belongs to a time before the different trajectories of our lives pulled Kat and me apart. I pick the white New Order shirt, thirty years old. One of Kat's other cousins did some catering work for Peter Gabriel, back when I was eighteen; New Order came to visit, and she knew I was a fan, so she got them to sign a shirt for me. The whole band. I remember how it felt when she gave it to me, like she was the most awesome friend in the world.

By the time I'm dressed, I already feel a little better. I head out like I'm nineteen again, 'Blue Monday' on my headphones. Unfamiliar streets roll past the window as I ride the bus to Kat's East London flat, leaving me adrift in time. I'm nineteen and I'm twenty-five and I'm all the ages in between – those precious years with Declan when life was a joy and I was happy; so much better than fifty-one, with the weight of a lifetime and all its mistakes on my shoulders. I feel taller and more alive. I feel as though I could walk home after a night of drinks and clubbing and not be a cripple in the morning. I can't, of course, but I enjoy the idea. I have the same thought as I always do when I'm meeting Kat: that we should do this more often, that she's good for me.

My hand doesn't even touch the buzzer before the door flies open and Kat bursts out. She grabs me in a crushing hug.

'Nicky, you look fantastic!' She stares at my T-shirt. 'Is that from when we went to see them at Wembley?'

'Remember that bloke you were with?'

'I do. Richard. Dick.' She curls her tongue around the word. 'Yes. He was a bit.'

'I don't think New Order was quite his thing.'

Kat's dressed the same – jeans and a T-shirt – although a modern fashionable one, not an old rag like mine. She steps back into the hallway and I follow. We were nineteen and Richard the Dick was thirty: one in a string of bad choices Kat made when she wasn't dumping Gary or taking him back again. I'll never understand why she stuck with him in the end, but she did. They finally married a year before I left for America, moved out of London while I was gone, bought a house somewhere in Kent and had three lovely kids. The kids grew up – the youngest is in her first year at university – and now Kat has her own flat in Stratford, built for the Olympics and almost brand-new, and that's where she seems to live, even though they still have the house in Kent. I assumed, when she first told me, that she and Gary had separated, but apparently not. He's still a jerk and yet they're still together; and Kat seems happy, so I suppose it doesn't matter that I don't understand it. With Kat, sometimes it's best not to ask.

'So . . . how's things?' We head up the stairs. 'Gary found this great flat near Canary Wharf. It's *enormous*! He wants us to sell the house and move there. He won't tell me how much it costs but it must be an absolute bomb. Apparently, we can get it for a song if this Docklands thing of his goes through. I'd have to give up this place, though.' She pouts.

'Are you going to?'

'Probably. If it's big enough.' We flop into the lounge. The Chardonnay is already out and I've barely sat down before Kat presses a glass into my hand. 'I'll let him tell you about it. He's quite annoyed with you, actually.'

'*Me*?'

'Turns out we were supposed to be going out to dinner tonight. But it's OK, I'll make it up to him.' She winks and moves to sit beside me, legs folded beneath her, and clinks her glass against mine. 'So . . . the police. What happened? Are you all right?'

'I'm fine.' I'm not so sure that I am, and I know Kat can see it, but it's the line I'm sticking to. My voice cracks a little. 'It wasn't about me.' I take a deep breath. 'Did you know the police arrested your cousin?'

Kat sits a little more upright. 'Declan?'

We've been close since we were teenagers. She's my best friend and I've lost count of the times we've talked about my memory, what it means to me and what it's done to me across my life – and I know she's always *tried* to understand, but I'm not sure you can, not unless you've lived inside my head.

'But, Nicky . . . Oh my God! Dec? What did he *do*?'

'I thought . . . actually, I thought maybe you already knew.' Kat and Dec were never close, even if they were cousins, and Kat stayed my friend after Declan and I divorced. But still, news travels in families, and last I heard, Gary and Declan still go out for drinks now and then.

'I've hardly spoken to him for years. I thought he wasn't talking to you any more.'

'He wasn't.'

'So how?'

'He needed me, Kat. For the first time in twenty-five years, he . . .' I have to stop for a moment to swallow the sudden lump in my throat. 'Do you remember right at the end of O-levels? When Declan's dad disappeared?'

'Uncle Arty?' Kat squints as if peering at something really hard. 'God, how could you forget? He walked out on them, just like his brother walked out on Mum. Only difference was he waited eighteen years to do it. Yes, I remember all right. Mum talked about it for months.' She shakes her head. 'God, what a family!'

'The police found his body. A few weeks ago.'

There's something else then – some other look that ghosts across Kat's face. And that's exactly it: like she's actually *seen* a ghost; like all the memories I already have of that night, of that summer, have suddenly sprung to life inside her. When she speaks, her voice is oddly flat.

'So Arty's dead?'

A part of me is sitting with her nearly thirty years ago. This is how it feels, sometimes, like I'm living in both the past and present at once. In the past, I'm in a different flat, smaller and cheaper. I'm holding Kat's hand. She's crying because, after years of searching, she's found the father who abandoned her before she was even born, who somehow ended up in Scotland; only he's been dead for three years and there are no answers to be had. It was 1991, but I remember it as clearly as I see her sitting beside me now.

'There's more,' I say, as gently as I can. 'They found him in Wordsworth Park. He was right there, under our noses all that time. Kat, that night at the Shelley, his fiftieth birthday party – the police think that's when it happened. They think somebody murdered Arty Robbins that same night.'

'Murdered?' Kat's eyes are like saucers. 'What . . . they think someone *killed* him? And they think it was . . . *Declan*? Jesus! But why?'

'Declan had them call me. Twenty years since the divorce, ten since I've even spoken to him, and there he was, on the end of the phone. He told them I'd be able to remember exactly where he was that night – every detail. I'm his alibi.' I don't need to say any more. Kat knows *exactly* where I was that night.

'Wait. They think someone killed Uncle Arty back in '85? The same night he disappeared?'

I nod.

'But you've *got* to be joking! I mean, they can't be *serious*. They think *Dec* killed his own *dad*? I'm sorry. I mean, that's *horrible* but . . . It's just . . . *Dec*? Presumably you told them how daft that is?'

'It didn't make any difference. I thought they believed me.' Oh Christ, I have to pause again before I burst into tears, and I'm not even sure *why*. 'I told them he was with me and that the police were already looking for Arty before I went home, so it *couldn't* have been Declan and . . . and it didn't matter. They've gone and charged him *anyway*! They really think he did it.'

Kat puts a hand on my shaking arm. 'You're taking this pretty hard, aren't you?'

I sniff back a sob. 'I don't even know why. It's not like . . . It's not fair! I know it's all in the past, but I *know* Declan. I know he can't have done this. I *know* where he was and I thought I could help him but . . . If I can't – if no one even *believes* me – then what's the point? I thought that for once it might actually *help* someone, being able to remember everything whether I want to or not, but no. I just . . . What's the point?'

For a time, we sit in silence. Sometimes Kat opens her mouth as if she might say something, only to think better of it.

'Did they tell you where they found the body?'

'It was on the news. Right there in the park.'

'What? No! So he's been *lying* there all this time?'

'You remember they built Parklands that summer? You remember they dug a great big hole in the ground and . . .' It's like I'm there again, the two of us sitting on the swings in the park and kicking our heels. 'Parklands is all a building site again. They're knocking it down to build a new leisure centre. It's in the papers. They found him when they dug up the old foundations. You don't remember, do you? The pit? They filled it with concrete on the morning after the party. We watched them do it on the way to school.'

Kat has a far-away look on her face now, a look of wonder, reaching back through the years. 'Uncle Arty. I remember the police looking for him for weeks. People still talked about it, years after, wondering where he'd gone. And he was dead all that time?'

I know that look. She's reaching for something in her head, but she won't find it; or if she does, it won't be clear. A connection to some old question in her head that's never had an answer.

'Uncle Arty,' she says again, then shakes herself, as if shaking off something sour.

I show her the news report I found. 'He must have been down there when they poured the foundations. You'd think they'd bother to *look* first, wouldn't you?'

Kat looks distracted. 'I suppose someone covered him up.'

A flash of light in my head. *That's* why the police don't think it was an accident! Someone buried him, or at least covered him. They had to. Kat's right, otherwise how did the workmen not see him?

'You don't suppose he was still alive, do you? When they covered him in concrete?'

'Kat!'

'Sorry.' She grins, then looks distant again. 'Nicky, I promise I'm only going to ask this once but . . . Declan – you don't think—'

I cut her off before she can finish that thought. 'Jesus, Kat! He's your cousin!'

'I know. But—'

'Kat! No! He couldn't have. He was with me until past midnight. Then he went back to the party, and I went home and there was a policeman talking to Dad. They were already looking for Arty Robbins.' I give Kat a side-eye, wondering if she has any memory of the stories we told the next morning.

'Wait! Wasn't that the night when you and Dec—'

'Yes!'

A broad smile spreads over her face. 'God, yes. Mum went mental. I mean, not that she had any reason to because we were all in the park together, right? You, me and Declan, watching the stars or something. That's what we told her, wasn't it? Something like that?'

'I don't think we fooled her for a second.'

'No.' Kat twiddles her thumbs and whistles and lets her eyes wander across the ceiling. 'No, she knew all right.'

At first, I think she's talking about me and Declan, but no, this is something more personal. And, come to think of it, Kat never *did* tell me what she and Gary Barclay got up to that night after Declan and I left the party . . .

'Gary!' I stare at her. 'You *were* going out with him!'

Kat makes a guilty face and grins.

'You told me you weren't.'

'Did I?'

'Bloody hell, Kat! I . . . At the party, I thought you were trying to get him to leave you *alone*. That's why I . . .' The vague look on Kat's face tells me that if she remembers what happened at the party at all, it's in a fleeting kind of way, shapes and shadows and feelings, the detail stripped by time. But I remember the look on her face as she walked away, after I told her what I thought of Gary, and finally it makes sense. 'Christ, you must have thought I was a right idiot.'

Kat takes a large gulp of wine and raises her glass to me. 'I have literally *no* idea what you're talking about.' She tops us both up. 'Uncle Arty. It's weird. I always wondered. The way he disappeared without a word.'

'Did you?' I eye her through my wine. Arty Robbins' disappearance was the talk of the street for weeks, and of course I knew all about everything because I was going out with Declan, but Kat never talked about it back then, not once.

'I used to wonder if someone had done him in. I mean, not seriously or anything, but . . .' She shrugs and dismisses the thought with a giggle. 'So, you had to go and talk to some policeman about how you and Dec sloped off in secret that night to have sex?'

'That's about the size of it, yes.'

'Christ, how embarrassing!'

'It's not like he asked for details. To be honest, he didn't seem all that interested; more annoyed. And frankly a bit of a jerk.' I give her a hard look and try my best to mimic Detective Scott's voice. 'My name is Detective Sergeant Jason Bit-of-an-Arse Scott. Miss Walker, you were observed to leave the party shortly after ten. Can anyone account for your whereabouts for the rest of the night?' The wine is a warm fuzz inside me. I have to snatch my glass away before Kat tops me up again. 'You should have seen his face when I told him about the porno magazine I found under Declan's bed. He went bright red.'

Kat snorts into her Chardonnay and splutters, 'A *what*?'

'I *told* you the next *morning*!'

But she's laughing and coughing both at once, and gives me a helpless look, and I suppose: why *would* she remember, after all these years?

I can't stop thinking about Declan, though, locked up in some prison cell. 'I don't . . . I don't know what to do, Kat. I want to help him, but . . .'

'Nicky, I know he's my cousin and everything but . . . You don't owe him a damned thing.'

'I don't know.' I don't understand it but it's there. 'Because it's not fair. Because . . . because I *remember*. Because I *know* he didn't do it.' I see the look on her face. *How? How do you know? How can you be so sure?* And I can't explain it – I just know. I *know* this man. I know who he was and I know Declan couldn't have done something like this.

Kat doesn't voice her question. Instead, she reaches out and takes my hand. 'If you need anything, anything at all.'

I feel so helpless, and at the same time there's something huge inside me – some great old weight from long ago, something I've buried deep – and now it's starting to stir.

'So.' I wipe my eyes. 'That night. You and Gary . . . I remember you telling him there was someone else. God, for a bit I even thought maybe you were breaking up with him and that's why he went so mental. Then I thought you were winding him up to make him go away.'

'Gary wasn't my first.' An empty look flits across Kat's face – some faded hurt she still carries even after all these years.

I start to mentally catalogue the boys at school. I can't help it, sifting through the ones I saw with Kat, searching for sly looks that I missed the first time which might give them away. I don't think it matters, but it keeps my memory busy.

'No one from school.' It's like she's reading my mind. She smiles and makes a wry face. 'It was desperately embarrassing and he was a dick.' The laughter vanishes from her voice. Whatever this is, it still hurts her after all this time. 'Christ, I thought I'd forgotten all about him.'

I think that's a lie but I'm not going to pry. I know exactly what it's like to be haunted by a memory that I'd rather wish away. 'I never knew,' I say instead.

'All my boyfriends had to be such secrets.' Kat forces a smile. 'You *must* remember what Mum was like. I could literally have dated an angel and she'd be like I was doing threesomes with Satan and Genghis Khan. God! Who'd ever want to be a teenager again?' She sighs and then she laughs, and after a moment so do I, and the weight sloughs off me as the years fall away between us like they always do; and a part of me is sitting in Kat's room in Byron Road and we're sixteen again, whispering about boyfriends, Kat petrified that her mum will find out whenever she's seeing someone.

'Your mum *was* a bit of a nightmare about that.'

'Amen. You know, I *do* kind of remember Gary going all testosterone-crazy alpha-primate on me, wanting to know who it was so he could beat them up or something. I suppose he thought he was being noble. Although it was a long time ago so maybe I'm remembering it wrong. Water very long under the bridge.' She puts down her glass and hugs me. 'Oh, Nicky. It must have been so hard, having to talk to the police about Dec after all this time.'

'I didn't want to leave him,' I say.

'You did what you had to do.'

I want to cry. Not because I'm unhappy but because Kat is simply the best; because Kat knows me well enough to understand exactly what I mean; because I don't need to tell her how much I miss what we had, Declan and I, because she already knows. Because when I asked her once if she thought I was crazy for walking out on Declan, she told me yes, she did, but that she loved me just the same either way, and it didn't matter if she didn't understand. That's why Kat is my rock. The memories I have of us together? All good, every last one of them. That's why I love her.

There's a shuffle of footsteps outside the door. It clicks open and Gary walks in. Fifty-three years old now, with a paunch and thinning hair, tie and tailored suit, and it's so hard not to laugh when I can still see him so clearly at eighteen: half goth, half punk, half biker, with his tough-man facade like he was Adam Ant's dandy highwayman; and that stupid battered old van of his, which always stank of weed. I thought he was such a plonker. Largely, I still do.

He stops dead as he sees the empty bottle of wine on the table.

'Riiiight.' I don't know what it is that Gary does except that he works in banking and makes a lot of money. He cocks his head. 'Cancelling our reservations tonight, are we?'

I get up as he takes off his jacket and puts down his brief-case. 'It's OK. I can go.'

'No, you can't!' Kat beams at him. 'Bring us another bottle, lover. And fetch yourself a glass. Nicola has news, and *you're* going to need one . . .'

Gary looks from me to Kat and back again. 'She didn't win the lottery, did she? Tell me she didn't win the lottery.' He winks. 'She only keeps me for the money.' It's a terrible joke, not even a little bit funny, but I suppose this is Gary's way of trying to be nice by not ignoring me. I don't know why he bothers. He must have worked out by now that I never liked him, and never will.

'And don't you forget it!' Kat goes to him, takes off his tie and kisses him on the cheek. 'There's another bottle of 'donny in the fridge and you know where to find the take-away menus. While you're at it, you can guess who's dead.'

'Please tell me it's Boris Johnson?'

'Arty.'

Gary stands stock-still, looking blank.

'Uncle Arty. Arty Robbins. Cousin Declan's dad. Cousin Declan? Nix's ex? Your mate?' Gary still looks blank. 'Oh my *God*. Uncle Arty who disappeared back in 1985, you lump! The night of that party in the Shelley.'

'Oh! Oh . . . shit!' Gary looks at Kat, and then he looks at me and back to Kat, like he's waiting for the punchline to a joke.

Kat cocks her head. 'The police reckon he was murdered!'

Gary stares. We have his full attention.

'Well, don't just stand there like a lemon!' She drags him towards the kitchen and I hear them whispering, Kat telling him about Arty Robbins and Declan's arrest. When they come back with another bottle, Gary gets out a tablet and starts looking things up on the Internet and telling Kat everything he finds, while Kat sets about ordering food. I'm happy to fade into the background, content to watch them. Whatever I think of Gary, he makes Kat happy, which really ought to be enough.

The first time I saw Gary Barclay – *really* saw him – was a month before the party. It was a Saturday and Declan and I had just had our first proper argument. I was stomping my way home, thinking about what he'd said and what I'd said, and what I *should* have said, the way you do, and then thinking that maybe he didn't really love me after all even though he said he did, because . . . because I was sixteen and you think stupid things when you're sixteen. I remember I passed the Shelley and its smell of stale beer, and turned the corner into Byron Road and heard Adam Ant singing 'Stand and

Deliver', quiet and tinny, coming out of a white van parked up across the street. The window was rolled down and there he was: the infamous Gary Barclay.

Looking back, I suppose he *was* quite handsome, with his Morrissey quiff – this was 1985, after all – and his cheek-bones, and his slightly frilly white shirt with enough buttons undone to show off a few curls of chest hair, and his silver chain with one of those half-a-broken-heart pendants that everyone seemed to have back then. I remember staring at him in his van but he was too busy watching the drama down the street to notice me. Two police cars were parked outside a house at the corner of Tennyson Way. Four police-men were at the front door, two of them wearing caps, not helmets. They were arguing with someone in the doorway. I remember thinking I could keep walking and pass by on the other side of the road and maybe hear what they were say-ing, but then the policemen barged their way inside and that was the end of it. It was the gossip of the street for a couple of days. I never knew whose house it was, and Gary lived on the estate, so it wasn't *his*, but I remember the look on his face, how intently he watched it all.

The memory circles me back to Declan and to Arty Robbins. Someone killed Arty Robbins on the night of 9th June 1985. If anyone knew the dodgy characters who lived around Wordsworth Park, it was Gary Barclay. Then I think of the look I saw on his face just now, as Kat told him about Arty being murdered. Like he knew something that was a secret and didn't know whether he should say. Which gets me thinking: what if Arty was up to something that the police never discovered? This was the Eighties, after all, the decade of music and money and cocaine . . .

No. Arty Robbins had money because the Eighties was also the decade of the estate agent.

The doorbell rings, making me jump. Gary fetches bowls and cutlery from the kitchen while Kat spreads takeaway Thai across the lounge table. They talk about work, the idle chit-chat of a couple who know each other's routines inside and out – a check-up, a catch-up – and then Gary tries to be polite again by asking me what's going on in my life. The answer, as usual, is nothing apart from this whole business with Declan's dad; but for the sake of having something to say, I tell him I'm thinking of finding a friend for Chairman, which gets Gary very confused, until Kat explains that the Chairman I'm talking about *isn't* the Chairman of the Trustees at the British Library.

'The Chairman is your *cat*?' Gary asks this with alarmed relief, which I guess is understandable, given that the last thing I said was how I was thinking of visiting some local shelters to see if I could find him a suitable companion. 'Oh! But he's so friendly!' He looks at Kat. 'You never told me he had a *name*.'

Kat pokes him. 'Of course he has a *name*, you lump!'

'What? His name is Chairman Cat?'

Kat and Gary have never been to my flat, so how does Gary know my cat?

'Chairman Mao, you idiot.'

'You call him Chairman—'

'How do you know my cat?' I ask.

Kat makes a guilty face. 'You remember that time you were away for the weekend and I said I'd feed him? I sort of . . . forgot I had another thing. Gary covered for me. He's an angel. Sometimes.'

I cringe inside at the thought of Gary in my flat, but what am I going to do?

'Chairman Mao?' Gary still looks confused. 'Your cat is called Chairman Mao?'

'Chairman *Mao*.' Kat makes it sound like Chairman's miaow.

'Also, he likes to sleep on chairs,' I say, and try not to wince at how lame that sounds when I say it out loud.

'Nicky, if you ever want to get away again, just say. I *promise* I'll check my diary first next time, and if I come over early, Lump here won't even notice.'

'Thanks,' I say, 'but Mum has a spare key and—'

'What's the new one going to be?' asks Gary, butting in. '*Comrade* Cat? General Secretary Purr?' He smirks, like he's said something clever.

'Cat Jong-un,' I tell him, which makes him splutter into his wine and Kat howl. 'Or Sun Cat-sen. I think I like that one better.'

'Not Miewsolini?' Kat offers.

Gary rolls his eyes. 'You can't call a cat Mussolini!'

'*Miew*solini.'

'Oh! I get it! So . . . Like, Fidel *Cat*stro?' Which I have to admit isn't bad.

Kat gives an appreciative nod.

'Or Adolf Kitler,' says Gary with a snort. 'Or . . . *Miao*schwitz!'

Silence. *There's* the Gary Barclay I remember: the Gary Barclay who always had to cross a line, who always had to take everything one step too far and ruin it for everyone. The Gary that Kat dumped at least three times, and three times I sighed with relief.

We both look at him, stone-cold serious.

'Not funny,' I say.

'You can't name a cat after a Nazi,' says Kat. 'And we'll pretend you stopped there.'

'Oh, right, but Mussolini is fine!'

'*Miew*solini. And she's not calling it that. She just said so.'

I move as if I'm about to get up. 'I should go.'

'I don't know. I mean, looking at it from the mouse's point of view . . .'

The Gary who always had to double down instead of admitting he'd made a mistake.

'You'll be looking at it from a sleeping-on-the-sofa point of view in a minute.' Kat comes over and refreshes my glass. 'I apologise for being married to an orang-utan.'

A part of me desperately does want to go. Gary always sets me on edge, like there's something wrong about him. But Kat is my best friend, and we don't see each other nearly as much as I'd like. I settle back onto the sofa.

'That night in 1985,' I say. 'How much do you remember?'

Gary glances at Kat. 'Not much. Why?'

I should leave it alone. Kat's right, I've done what I can. I should go back to my quiet life and forget about Declan. Only I can't. And I don't want to. And I don't know why, but I think I have to try and help him, despite everything. Is it simply because I know he didn't do it?

'We went for a walk in the park,' says Kat. 'Just after you left with Dec. Talked for a bit. One thing led to another and here we are.' She makes a sweeping gesture at the room around her, then snuggles up to Gary and pecks him on the cheek.

Gary shrugs and looks sheepish. He asks how Declan's holding up, and says maybe it's no bad thing that he finally knows what happened to his dad, but how terrible to be a suspect. Kat rambles through who might have done it – not that she has the first idea – and Gary frowns and shrugs and clearly doesn't care. He asks if Declan needs the name of a good solicitor, and then suddenly Kat bursts back into life.

'Hey, you know what? We saw Nicky's dad on our way back to the Shelley. Don't you remember?'

'Not really,' says Gary.

'I almost freaked! Remember? I tried to hide behind a see-saw.'

'Yes!' Gary goes all wide-eyed. 'I *do* remember. But . . . It wasn't Nicky's dad we saw, it was Arthur Robbins!'

'No, it wasn't.'

'It was! You said so.'

Kat shakes her head. 'You barely knew who Arty was.' She pokes him. 'I *know* it was Nicky's dad because I remember thinking that if he saw us then Mum would hear about it and I'd be *so* dead.'

'I could have sworn you said it was your uncle,' Gary mutters. 'To be honest, all I remember was some bloke in a dark jacket. I suppose it could have been anyone, really. I mean, it was . . . dark.'

'It wasn't Arty Robbins,' says Kat.

I hardly hear, but Kat's right. It wasn't Arty Robbins, because Arty Robbins wasn't wearing a dark jacket at the Shelley that night.

I ransack my memory. I can see it all, as it was, that night inside the Shelley: the table covered in food, the women in their dresses, all big hair and shoulder pads, the prints on the

walls of those stupid paintings of dogs playing poker . . .
Half the men in the pub were wearing dark jackets. It could
have been anyone.

The morning after. Kat's mum in the doorway, Kat at the
top of the stairs. *We sat in the park for a bit. You know.
Because of* . . . Kat's mum looking over her shoulder up the
stairs. *You did, did you? Until nearly midnight? When you
knew that Nicola's parents were looking for her?*

Nearly midnight . . . But it was definitely *past* midnight
when I saw Declan leave his house, which means it wasn't
him at least. And I'm so relieved I could hug them both, and
how stupid is it that I feel this way?

And then I remember the mud on the sleeve of Dad's
jacket.

8

Monday 3rd to Wednesday 5th February 2020

Kat was with Gary while I was with Declan. I never knew but it's so obviously true, and now I can't stop thinking about what else happened that night. I don't even know why it matters so much, but it does. I think it matters to Kat, too, judging from the way she looked, and from the way Gary watched for her reaction. I suppose it's because of her own father, Arty Robbins' little brother. I never really knew much about him because he left before Kat was even born and she never talked about him back then. Her mum married again, long before Kat and I ever knew each other. Stephen Clarke, and *he* left too, just after Kat turned fourteen. Kat never did have much luck when it came to dads.

Sitting on the bus on the way to work the next morning, I let myself float back to the autumn of 1991, to the one day she really talked about him. It was a Tuesday afternoon in September, and Declan and I still thought we were happy. I was working in Streatham at a travel agency and we were between flats, living with Declan's Aunt Eileen. I was watching the rain falling outside the windows at work, when the phone rang.

'Hi. Can you come over later?' Kat's voice sounded wrong and she never called me at work, so I said yes, of course. I called Declan to let him know, left work early and went right over. I found her, red-faced from crying and with a bottle of wine already open.

'Bloody hell, Kat! What happened?'

'I found my dad,' she said.

I sat with her for three hours. We drank the rest of the bottle of wine and then I went out and bought us a cake and we ate nearly all of it, the two of us together, and she told me how she'd always wanted to find her real dad – not Stephen Clarke, who still sent her cards at Christmas and for her birthday, but her *real* dad: Daniel Robbins, Arty Robbins' little brother. I have a strange sense of detachment as I relive that evening. She'd talked about him over the years, but only in passing. I'd had no idea it meant so much to her to find him; and yet here it was, all coming out: how she'd been trying to track him down ever since she turned eighteen.

'I just wanted to know, you know? Why he left. Why he never even stayed in touch. Why he never came to see me, not even once.'

She eventually told Gary, who by then had ditched his quiff and his weed-dealing and was working twenty-hour days in some bank in the City, taking us all by surprise by forging a career for himself; and, Gary being Gary, he'd talked to an investigator who was some friend of his. Tracking down Daniel Robbins, it turned out, had been a simple matter of checking public records. A week later, Kat saw the death certificate. Daniel Robbins had died in Scotland three years ago, in a motorbike accident. She'd never get to meet him, never get to ask her questions, never get any answers.

By the time Gary showed up at eight, I had Kat back on her feet. She was herself again, laughing and a bit tipsy and full of cake. I asked her if she wanted me to stay over and she said no, it was fine, she felt better now. She told me I was the best friend anyone could ever have and I told her that she was wrong; that *she* was the best friend anyone could ever have. And then I went home to Declan.

I like this memory. I did a good thing that evening. I was there when Kat needed me, which wasn't always the way. Kat was definitely the better of us in that regard, but that evening I did it right. I cherish the warmth of how it felt as I left, and on the bus on the way home, and that glowing sense of virtue as I snuggled in Declan's arms later that night, telling him why I was so late.

'It's weird, isn't it?' I said. 'Your uncle pulling a vanishing act and then, fifteen years later, your dad does the same. Like it runs in the family. *You're* not going to vanish on me, are you?' I was laughing as I said it. It was meant to be a joke – with hindsight, not a good one – but I wonder whether there was a grain of real fear there. We were happy and in a good place, and yet I think the first cracks had already been showing.

That memory leads me to another. I find myself propelled forward in time by a few months, to the spring of 1992. Declan and I had been married for twenty months and we were still between apartments, still living in Clapham in Declan's Aunt Eileen's spare room. It's cramped and we've long worn out our welcome and I want to get out. I want it to be just us again. We're both still working, which is good news because unemployment is high, so are interest rates; rents are rising, the country feels ill at ease and an election is coming. I've found a place in Battersea that looks promising – a bit expensive, but I think we can manage. I've made an appointment to see it. I've told Declan to meet me there after work and he's said yes, he'll be there, and now he isn't. I wait until he's half an hour late and then I go and look at it on my own and it *is* perfect. I'm angry, thinking Declan doesn't understand how badly I want a place of our own, so

I say we'll take it and I put down a deposit and go back to Clapham. When Declan shows up, he's full of apologies. He tells me that something came up at work but I can smell the beer on him. He apologises some more and admits that yes, when he knew he wasn't going to make it, he let himself be persuaded to go to the pub for a couple of pints. He listens attentively as I tell him about the flat, and makes all the right noises and doesn't mind that I've said yes without him. He's enthusiastic and excited and seems as glad as I am to know that we'll have a place of our own again. He tells me he loves me and how wonderful I am, and I forgive him, and everything is fine again.

But I don't forget. I can't, and so it never goes away.

I push the memory aside and think of happier times. I think of the day we moved into that flat, how Declan carried me across the threshold and filled the place with flowers; and then I find myself back in bed with Declan that night, after Kat told me about Daniel Robbins.

You're *not going to vanish on me, are you?*

Declan didn't laugh. 'I'm nothing like my dad,' he said, like I'd touched something raw.

'Do you ever . . . do you ever think about where he is? What he's doing?'

'What do you mean?'

'Your dad?'

'Not really.' He twisted away from me and turned out the

light. Later, as I lay there listening to him breathe, I went back through the other conversations we'd had over the years. He always seemed uninterested, like the past was the past and he didn't want to know. I thought about Kat, desperately searching for memories of a father she'd never known. I thought about Declan, walling away the memories he didn't want as though it was as easy as putting up a garden fence. It left me wishing I could do the same. That I could live in the present and not be constantly haunted by the past . . .

Back in the present, I'm so busy being haunted by the past that I forget I'm on a bus on the way to work and miss my stop and end up almost in Regent's Park. It takes me twenty minutes to walk back and makes me late, which earns me a concerned look from Joy on reception and a stare at his watch from Ed, who runs the archive.

'Trouble on the roads?' he asks, and I've been here long enough to know he's already checked Google Maps for a traffic update.

'Not really. I just got engrossed in something and missed my stop. I'll make up the time.'

'You could leave earlier in the mornings,' he says, which is what he always says to anyone when they're late. 'Then it wouldn't matter.'

I give a meek nod, both of us knowing I have no intention of following his advice. For the rest of the morning, I try to look busy, but I can't concentrate because my mind's all over the place. I can't stop thinking about the mud on Dad's jacket – that's the thing – and hearing Dad and Constable Simmons talking in the lounge. I keep seeing Declan from that night, smiling and turning away and walking to the end of Byron Road, the night swallowing him as he turned the corner towards the Shelley and the park. I want to help him – I do – but I don't know how; maybe Kat's right and I've already done all I can, and so what if I can remember things better than anyone else? I was with Declan until midnight but that's all I know. Whoever killed Arty Robbins was probably some stranger I never even met.

Over lunch, I call Lainton Legal. A young woman takes my name and number and promises that Ms Watson will call me back as soon as she can. I tell myself I should go and see Mum and ask about that night. I even manage to call her, but it's dick-face Dave who answers, and I don't know what to say and so I hang up. Maybe I'll try again later.

Detective Scott wonders why Declan staying the night in the Shelley didn't surprise me. But the Arty Robbins that the rest of the world saw wasn't the real Arty Robbins . . .

Why was Dad out in the park shortly before midnight?

Ms Watson from Lainton Legal doesn't get back to me. I stay late to keep Ed happy and then go home to curl up with Chairman. We watch the movies that Declan and I used to watch together – *Cocktail* for me, *Die Hard* for Dec, *Dead*

Poets Society for both of us – letting myself remember everything that I threw away, trying to flush the old feelings out of my system. It doesn't work. I can't stop thinking about him. About us. About the past. I can't turn it off.

On Tuesday morning, I drag myself into work and stare at the screen, feeling completely incapable. I almost forget we have a client coming in that afternoon. I have a presentation to give, and thank God I did most of the work last week. I stagger through it, relying on my memory, hardly aware of what I'm saying. I tell myself Ed doesn't notice. I honestly don't think he does.

Still no call from Lainton Legal. I go home and deluge myself with cream and fruit and sugar. I allow myself half a bottle of wine, which lands me sitting on the doorstep clutching an old half-pack of cigarettes, tugging on my vaporiser like a drowning woman gasping for air, rueing the day that Joy and I made our pact to give up smoking. I knew, as soon as I heard Declan's name, that it would be like this, this storm-surge of memories. I wonder if I should phone in sick for the rest of the week and spend the time going to cat shelters and rescue centres looking for a friend for Chairman – anything that might work as a distraction. My life in Wordsworth Park is ancient history. It's twenty-five years since Declan and I went our separate ways and I need to walk away from this. I don't care. I *shouldn't* care. It's not my business. I've done my duty and I've told the police what I know, and it's not like I haven't been here before with things coming up that drag me into the past. Sometimes it happens out of the blue and I have no idea why.

I tell myself all these things and I know that this time it's not going to work. I can't let this go, even if I should. I'm not sure why, but I feel it: some little piece of steel inside me that won't be moved. I'm fifty-one years old and on a roller-coaster of emotions like I'm fifteen; and my way out is to do what I always do and take myself back to the years in America, twenty-eight, divorced, aiming to make a career for myself; but even that's not good enough any more. I wasn't *happy* then, not really, I wasn't even *content* or *OK*. I was focused. It seemed enough, but if I'm honest, it's simply what got me through each day.

I take an early bus to work on Wednesday morning to make sure I get there on time. When I check my phone, there's a text from Kat: *U OK hun?*

I message a reply: *A bit wobbly but I'll live.* I check my voicemail and my email but Declan's solicitor still hasn't called back. I suppose I'll try again later. I suppose I'll try again with Mum, too. I don't want to, but I think I have to.

My phone pings. Another message from Kat: *Free tonight if you want to come over. G has work thing.*

I get off the bus a stop early and nip into my favourite café to buy coffee and a hot sandwich for breakfast. Sausage, bacon and egg with a touch of tomato salsa. It's a treat, the closest I allow myself to a fried breakfast; and a mistake, because the smell walks me straight into another memory of Declan. I'm upstairs under the duvet, fresh coffee and frying bacon wafting through the house. I hear his feet on the stairs as he comes up and so I pull the duvet around me, pretending to be asleep. He comes in and I hear him put a tray on the table beside the bed. I feel him close as he leans over me. He thinks I'm asleep. I hear him whisper: *I might just have to ask you to marry me, Nicola Walker.* I don't react . . .

And suddenly I'm sitting on a plane to New York, years later, three empty whiskey miniatures on the seat-back tray in front of me. I've actually done it; I've walked out. I've left him, and my whole life should be stretching before me on an endless road of possibilities, but I'm crying and I can't seem to stop, and I feel so damned miserable, and I already know I've made the most terrible mistake of my life, and it's too late to take it back . . .

'Hey, Miss? Are you OK?'

I have to blink a few times to bring myself back to the present. The world is blurry. A waitress stands over me, someone I don't recognise, hardly any older than I was back then.

'Sorry,' I say. 'The father of an old friend just passed away.'

'Oh.' She hovers in that way people do, like they should offer something or do something, despite us being perfect strangers.

'Thank you,' I say. 'I'm fine.' God, I could murder for a cigarette. I still have that crumpled half-pack in my coat pocket, remnants of a twenty bought three weeks ago on a Friday night out with Joy, before we made our pact to quit. Before I heard about Arty Robbins.

I cram the last of the sandwich into my mouth and wash it down with gulps of coffee. Outside, I take half a dozen long drags on my vaporiser and walk quickly to the library, shaking off the spider-web memories of Declan as best I can. Joy waves at me from reception as I hurry past. I flash a smile back, and her own grows wide and bright. I like Joy. She's young and full of an infectious enthusiasm for life. I wave the vaporiser at her. '*Please* tell me it gets better.'

She puts on her *right-with-you-sister* face and clenches a fist. 'Stay strong!'

I used to be like her. I wish I still could find that version of myself. I can *remember* it. But I can't *be* it.

Ed works at home on Wednesdays, thank God. At my desk in the archives, I call Lainton Legal and leave another message for Declan's solicitor. Then I close my eyes and take myself deep into the past: 1983, February, sitting in a Portakabin that passed for a classroom, all of us shivering in the winter cold, Mrs Spare droning on about geography. I turn to look out the window and there he is: a boy I've never seen until now, a couple of years older than me, dressed in the same school uniform as the rest of us but shiny and new.

His hair is in a side parting which would make him look all grown-up, except he's mussed it over. I look at him and he looks back and smiles. And it wasn't like we became friends afterwards or even had anything to do with each other – two years apart at secondary school might as well have been the Berlin Wall back then – but I remember that smile.

Declan. The first time I ever saw him.

My phone rings. A number I don't recognise.

'Nix?'

My heart almost jumps out of my chest. He sounds so distant, so uncertain. 'Declan?'

'Nix?'

'H . . . Hi.' I don't know what to say. I don't know what I *can* say. 'How are you?' I almost ask, *Aren't you in prison?*

'I . . . I'm . . .' I hear his sigh. 'How are *you*?'

'Not dead and not mad and not in hospital, so I suppose I'm fine. What . . . what do you want? Are you—'

'My solicitor says you've been calling her.'

'I wanted to know—'

'They gave me bail,' he says.

'They've – they've dropped the charges?' I can't hide the joy.

'No, I'm . . . They let me out on bail because of Mum. They do that sometimes, even when they think you're a murderer.' *Murderer.* I hear the scorn in his voice, the despair and the loathing. 'I had to give up my passport, and I've got one of those ankle-bracelet things and . . . Well, you know.'

I don't, but I'm not sure what to say.

'There was a cock-up about some evidence they were supposed to have that wasn't ready. There's another hearing next week. That's probably all I've got. But I just . . . Thank you. You know, for . . . for telling them what happened that night. Thank you for trying.'

I could almost hate Declan for the honest concern in his voice. I know he means it, and *I* was the one who walked away, even if *he* was the one who was having an affair; and he knows I wish things had been different, and I know that he wishes it too, but what does he think he's doing, sounding like I'll somehow forget what I saw – like there's a chance we could be friends again?

We could never be only that, not with so much history between us.

'I . . . I wanted to thank you properly. You know, if I can, if you wanted to . . . I mean, I've got this tag on me so I can't really *go* anywhere, but I could cook dinner or something. If you . . . if you wanted to come over.'

Walk away, Nicola Walker, walk away. 'When?'

'Whenever.' He laughs. 'Like I said, it's not like I'm going anywhere.'

I can't do this. I absolutely can't. 'Tonight?'

'That would be great. About seven?'

Why? Why am I so stupid? 'OK.'

'Great. I'll text you my address. I'll see you then.'

'Declan!' I whisper. 'You should know, I . . . I didn't tell them everything—'

Too late. Too slow. A click and he's gone.

I stare at my phone. I can't believe I'm such an idiot. I should call him back. Call back right now and tell him I've changed my mind. Tell him that I'm meeting Kat. Or simply not show up, because otherwise the memories of being in love with him will come in unstoppable floods, and it would hurt less to dive head-first into the bloody office shredder.

I need to calm down. I need to call him and tell him I can't do this. No, what I *need* is to go back in time, to something calm and neutral – a memory from before I ever knew about Arty Robbins being dead—

PING!

I jump and almost drop my phone as Declan's text comes through, giving me his address. In my head, I'm already right back to the last time we spoke before he called on Saturday, sobbing down the phone, telling him how sorry I am for everything that happened and begging him to see me again, and of course he says no because I'm drunk, and he knows it.

I feel Joy's eyes on me as I pass her desk. I go outside and sit on the library steps, off to one side, out of the way of the steady ebb and flow of people. I can't get that memory out of my head. How he told me to leave him alone. How he told me to go to hell. How I chain-smoked my way through a whole packet of cigarettes after he hung up.

I look at the address he's given me and it's not even all that far away. Finsbury Park. Not far from the Emirates stadium. Christ, I could almost *walk* from here.

I have to tell him what I told Detective Scott. What I *didn't* tell Detective Scott.

No! No, I don't! What I have to do is walk away. I have to get my life back the way it was. I have to call him, or text, or . . .

I go back inside. Joy catches my eye and gives a little nod and asks if I want to go out for a quick drink after work tonight, and I think *Why not?* We could go out and eat. Make a night of it. I could do the sensible thing and not go to Declan . . .

'I'm going to see my ex-husband,' I say. 'His dad died.' Why am I even talking about this?

Joy winces in sympathy; and I'm thinking how we could still go for a drink, we could talk – maybe that's what I need; I could ask her what she thinks, if she thinks I should go.

All the way back to my desk.

At half-past five, I pack up and head out, and in my head I'm six years old and lying in the dark, terrified because of something I saw on the telly while Dad was watching *Doctor Who*; and I'm sixteen and hiding in Declan's room under his bed; and I'm twenty-three and in love; and I'm twenty-six and he's out late and he hasn't called and I don't know why; and I'm sitting in the kitchen with my head in my hands, remembering what Kat said about mysterious late nights at the office; and all I can think about is how we never seem to talk about *us* any more, and I can't remember the last time he said *I love you*; only of course I *can* remember and it's been seven weeks and five days and is that really such a long time, and why am I even counting, and dear *God* I need a cigarette . . .

And at the same time, over and over, nagging in the back of my head: if Declan didn't kill Arty Robbins, who did? Did Dad do it? Why? But if he didn't, why was there mud on his jacket the next morning? Were those really bruises I saw on Mum's neck? How did they get there? Why were the police already looking for Arty?

Three stops down the Victoria Line and then a short hop on the bus or a ten-minute walk. My hands are shaking. Declan. It's been ten years since we exchanged more than a few sentences and I'm nervous as hell, and the butterflies in my stomach are like that evening in 1985 as we walked away from the Shelley back to his house together, with no idea of the drama we'd left to play out without us.

Who could possibly have wanted Arty Robbins dead?

I fumble the packet of cigarettes from my coat pocket. I'm so nervous that I almost drop them. I tap one loose and put it between my lips, light it and draw hard. The hit is immediate, the memory that was about to overwhelm me knocked sideways. I take another drag and then crush what's left on the pavement. I feel giddy and sick and my mouth tastes horrible. I won't tell Joy. It wasn't a whole cigarette. It doesn't count.

Thirty-four years, seven months and twenty-seven days since Declan's dad disappeared. I remember every single one. I barely knew him but I was glad he was gone. He had his secrets, Arty Robbins: his affair with Kat's mum, and that wasn't the end of it. Some of the truth came out after he left, but was there more? Something that none of us ever knew, even after he was gone?

One glimpse of what he truly was and I hated him.

I'm five minutes from Declan's flat and an hour early. I look about for something to do. There's a coffee shop, bland and faceless – lattes and cappuccinos and toasted paninis – the sort of place that could be anywhere in London these days. Its only tie to the past is that Panini used to have something to do with the collectable footballer cards that the boys at school used to trade. I look at the menu and then leave, because what am I going to do? Drink coffee for an hour and think about how stupid I am to be here at all? I left work early because I thought I'd need some time to get myself together, and all I've done is left myself with nowhere to go but the past. I should have called Kat, taken her up on her offer or asked her to come with me. Apart from Kat, there's no one who knows me, not really . . .

I turn down the path to Declan's flat. In my head, I'm in the kitchen of the house we used to share, years later, wondering what's happened to us, how we've drifted apart; and I'm sixteen and in the alley behind Byron Road, waiting for him even though I know he's not coming; and then a week has passed and he's back, and I don't care what Mum says, and I'm seeing Dad's face and the twinkle in his eye that Mum doesn't notice as he tells me *I'd better not catch you with that Robbins boy again.*

That was after the party. After Mum did a complete flip and suddenly Declan wasn't acceptable any more.

Catch you. I knew exactly what he meant.

Was it really Dad that Kat saw that night? Why was he out in the park so late? Why was there mud on his jacket?

And now I'm hunched against the wall of Parklands on my twenty-sixth birthday, and it's the middle of the night and I'm sobbing beyond hope of comfort because Dad is dying and I saw Declan with that other woman, and I know it's all going wrong because I've seen it all before, at home that summer when Declan's dad disappeared, and I remember it perfectly and I know what it means . . . Finally the spiral takes me to where I always end, to the worst memory of them all: to being with Dad and watching him die of the cancer inside him, actually *watching* him leave, right there in front of me, there and then gone; and how, even in that moment, I wasn't living in the present, because I'm sitting through my father's last moments and remembering Declan sitting with that woman, too close, holding hands, kissing; and all I can think of are the thousand and one things that have gone before, the little disappointments, the let-downs, the taking for granted of things that were once a delight. I didn't know who she was but what difference did *that* make, for God's sake? It wasn't about *her*, not really. She was just the last of a thousand cuts; and so I buried Dad and took careful aim at the best thing to ever happen in my life and blew it to pieces because I was so scared that whatever happened to Mum and Dad was happening to me and Declan as well.

Oh, Declan. Why didn't you try harder?

I'm outside his flat and my eyes are full of remembered tears. It's easier to keep walking, and so I do.

What if I'm the only person who can help him? Does he even *deserve* my help? But that's the wrong question. Do I *want* to help him?

Yes. Even if I don't know why, I do.

The path is a dead end. I turn back and pass his flat a second time. I'm a mess. I should go home, but then I'll kick myself because I've come this far and I should see him, even knowing how this ends, because the month of misery is coming whether I like it or not; and maybe I *can* help him, maybe that's how I finally make my peace over what happened between us and put an end to it for good . . .

But how? By remembering the clothes that people wore at a party thirty-five years ago? I wasn't even there when it happened! I don't have the first idea who killed Arty Robbins.

Oh God, Nicola Walker, *why* did you say yes to this?

I walk back to the main road. Deep breaths, deep breaths. There's a fast-food kebab shop across the way and they have a few seats inside. I sit down and nurse a cup of tea and force myself to think about the good times, sipping on it long after it goes cold; even then, I'm still a quarter of an hour early when I'm back outside Declan's flat and ringing the bell.

The door buzzes at once. I push it open and head up the stairs. I hear footsteps from above. A giddiness hits me and I have to stop and steady myself and . . .

There he is. Ten years and he's hardly changed. A little more weight on him, his hairline a little further back so he looks a bit like a budget Tony Soprano. I fish a hanky from my bag, blowing my nose and dabbing at my eyes as he bounds down the last set of stairs and stops right in front of me, awkward like he doesn't know what to do. He wants to hug me but he doesn't know whether that's OK. And it *shouldn't* be, it really shouldn't, but it is. I fall into his arms and it feels so good, because I'm twenty again, and in love, and the world is full of colour and the future is bright . . .

Was full of colour. *Was* bright.

I pull away. 'Sorry,' I say. 'Memories.'

He smiles, wary. I see it in his face – the old love we had still there, somehow still alive. It breaks my heart and I have to turn away so as not to burst into tears.

'Come on,' he says. 'Let me put the kettle on.'

He leads me to the third floor, through a solid-looking door into a spacious open-plan lounge-and-dining area separated from a kitchen space by a waist-high partition. The furniture and the size of the apartment tell me he's done well for himself. He might even be rich, in a London sort of way. I look around at the Simon Marsden prints on the walls, the neatly stacked cabinet beside the television, the big plush moose toy I bought for him thirty years ago. It's all the Declan I remember, gone upmarket. It feels strange and out of place and puts me almost on edge, until I realise . . .

It's all us. Me and him.

Declan follows my gaze. 'I'll put the kettle on,' he says again. He turns away, pointing down a narrow hallway with three doors, two on one side, one on the other. 'Bathroom's at the end on the right. Mum's room is on the left but she's not here. She's been staying with Aunt Eileen while I was – you know . . .'

'Your mum lives here?'

He doesn't say anything. He doesn't need to. Anne Robbins was diagnosed with MS a year before I went to America, and that was two decades ago.

I sit on the smaller of the two sofas, arranged at right angles with a glass-topped coffee table between them. The table is a mess of clutter: half a dozen photography books under a handful of travel magazines and some loose sheets of paper that look like local council forms. I don't mean to pry but I can't help myself. They're about his mum, about putting her into care.

When I look up, I see him watching me from the kitchen.

'How bad is it?' I ask.

'She's a bit wobbly but she can still look after herself for now. It's just – I need to make arrangements in case . . .' His face twists into a wry smile. 'At the bail hearing, my solicitor made it sound like she needs constant care, but really . . . But she does struggle with the stairs. And it's not fair to leave Aunt Eileen to pick up the pieces if . . .' He looks away. 'You know.'

On the corner of the table is a tourist guide to a place on the west coast of Scotland. I pick it up and look more closely. When I look inside, I realise why it feels familiar. The brochure is new, but I've seen this place before. Harris Lodge. Declan picked it out before Dad fell ill. We were going to go on a second honeymoon. One last effort to find our way back to the passion and the romance, and all the things I remembered which it seemed we'd lost.

We never went. Dad's cancer saw to that.

Declan comes over with our mugs of tea. 'I was thinking

of taking Mum. Before all this. Drive around, take in the scenery. You know, that sort of thing.' He puts my tea on the table and flops into the other sofa. 'Mum and Dad went there for their honeymoon. I don't think I ever told you that.'

He must see the surprise on my face. 'No. No, you didn't.'

'I thought she might . . .' He shakes his head, struggling to explain himself. 'Dad's family came from that part of the world. She still talks about him. Even after – you know. After everything he did.'

I *do* know. I remember it.

'He used to say it was the most beautiful place in the world: standing on top of the cliffs, watching the sun set. He never wanted to live in London, but that was where the money was. They were going to retire there.' He shrugs. 'That's what Mum says anyway. Uncle Dan went back after he . . . I've got a couple of cousins up there somewhere, too. We're not really in touch.'

'You never said anything about that before.'

'I know. I thought it sounded – you know, weird. I just . . .' He sighs, and it looks like he's about to say something more, but it doesn't come.

'Declan, I don't know how much you remember, but . . . The police didn't ask about what happened back at the house so I only told them we were together, and what time it was when I left.'

'Thank you. I suppose that must have been hard for you.'

I want to tell him he has no idea of *hard*, but maybe that's unfair. Of everyone I ever knew, now or then, Declan was the one person who seemed to understand what it was like to be me.

'I don't get it!' It bursts out of me. 'You were with *me*. I *told* them! You were with me and then you went back to the Shelley and I saw you go. And there was a policeman in our lounge when I got back, and he was talking to Dad about – about *your* dad. They were looking for him, so he must already have been missing. Why do they think it was you?'

'Apparently, someone saw Dad out in the park near midnight.' He shrugs. 'I don't know who. And then, apparently, I went out looking for him after I went back to the Shelley. It's all stuff they got from the investigation the first time around. The search, you know? When they were looking for him.'

'You told me you stayed at the Shelley all night!'

He shrugs helplessly. 'Did I? I don't remember.'

'And anyway . . . That's *all*? They can't—'

' "Hard forensic evidence linking Mr Robbins to his father's death." That's what the prosecutor said. They cocked something up, so whatever it is, they couldn't release it. They've got something, though, and they won't tell my solicitor what it is until it's ready. On the bright side, they can't keep me locked up while they sort themselves out, so here I am. There's another hearing a week from now. Then we'll know.'

'Oh, Declan.' I have to resist the urge to reach out and touch him. 'That must be horrible.'

He shrugs. 'It's all bullshit. I didn't do it. I *know* I didn't do it. But it's the waiting, you know? The uncertainty. The way everything goes on hold.'

We sit in silence, each of us staring at our tea.

'How . . . how are you keeping?' he asks.

'Still working in the library,' I say. 'I have a flat not far from work, now. It's nothing grand, just a bedsit really. But it's enough.'

'Not far from work?'

'In Farringdon.'

'Christ, that must cost a bomb!'

No point arguing – prices in central London are insane. 'I'm only renting,' I say, which is technically true. 'It's tiny.' I make a show of looking around me. 'You're doing all right, by the look of things.'

'All the money from Dad's business after he . . .' He stops. 'And the house. Mum should have kept it and rented it out, I reckon. Do you know how much those houses go for in Byron Road these days? It's daft.' I hear the note of scorn, the same note I remember hearing whenever he thought someone was putting on airs. 'You go back there much?'

'Not really.'

'Me neither. It's all changed. Gentrification, the local paper calls it. It's ridiculous, if you ask me; makes me glad that I don't have kids. I don't know how they'd ever afford a place of their own.'

Kids. I look for any trace of bitterness and don't find it. 'I saw,' I say. 'When I was at the police station, I saw what they've done to the park.'

'And what they've done to the High Street.' He snorts his disdain. The High Street, when Declan and I were teenagers, was a Co-op, a couple of TV repair places, three charity shops, three banks, Omar's Kebab Palace, the chippy, a dry-cleaner's, a fruit-machine arcade, three estate agents – one of them Robbins' Properties – two hairdressers, some place that sold sofas and stuff like that: all with a constant traffic jam running through the middle. Now it's a massive John Lewis and the rest is restaurants and coffee shops and mobile-phone outlets, and the whole place has been pedes-trianised.

Silence stretches out between us again.

'I'm sorting things out for Mum,' he says after a bit. 'I mean, she can mostly look after herself but it's only going to get worse.' He looks away and I see the weight of what's happening to him, crushing him. 'To be honest, I was going to do it anyway. I can't keep looking after her, not forever.'

I got on OK with Declan's mum until I walked out on him. I suppose she hates me for that. If she does, I can't blame her. I never told her about seeing Declan with another woman. I never told anyone except Kat.

'Is there . . . anything I can do?' I ask.

'Not really.' He looks away. 'Christ, Nix. I'm past fifty and what have I got to show for it?' He shifts on the sofa and I glimpse the tracker locked above his ankle. He catches my eye. 'I didn't have to wear this. Could simply have walked out, but my solicitor said it would make a good impression. You know, show I'm trying to cooperate.'

I sniff the air. 'Something smells good.'

'That'll be the fennel. Don't get too excited. It's nothing special.'

'You remember when I tried to boil an egg and ruined the pan?' Declan was always the better cook, much to Mum's horror.

'Four *minutes*.' He laughs. 'Not four hours!'

I smile too, because that's exactly what he said on the day it happened. 'I just forgot, OK?' That's what he thought was so funny. That *I* forgot.

He brings two bowls of pasta from the kitchen, layered with fennel-spiced sausage, tomato and mascarpone sauce. It smells delicious, and I have to remind myself that this isn't my life any more. It's a step back in time for a few hours, that's all. I close my eyes and slide into memories of Declan in the not-so-Secret Car Park, sitting in his Capri . . .

Declan nods. 'Thing is,' he sighs and looks distant, 'they're saying I went back out, after I got to the Shelley, but if I did, I don't remember it. I remember being in my room, the two of us. I remember *you* so clearly. But the rest – all the stuff before: going to the Shelley with Mum and Dad, the party, even what happened between me and Dad when he nearly caught us – it's all just . . . scraps. Flashes. Impressions. And after . . . it's a blur. I don't remember that night at all, after you left. Nothing.' He takes a deep ragged breath. 'I suppose that means I could have done it. I mean, I'm sure I didn't, because how could I forget something like *that*? But everything I did and everywhere I went after you left? I honestly don't know.' He sighs and shakes his head and gives up. 'It was almost a relief when Dad disappeared, you know? And now here he is, fucking up my life again. I suppose *you* remember it all like it was yesterday.'

I nod.

'I wish I had your memory.'

I look away. 'No, Declan.'

'I can't even picture him any more.'

I put my bowl back on the table, half eaten.

'Too spicy?' asks Declan.

'I'm not that hungry tonight. You really don't remember anything at all?'

Declan takes our half-finished bowls back to the kitchen. 'I remember thinking about you, about seeing you. The party itself? Not really.' His words dissolve into the scrape of cutlery on china and the clatter of the dishwasher. 'Afterwards, I remember seeing you at the window. Then at the back of the Shelley – I have this sort of sense that I hung out for a bit with Gary, maybe?' There are tears in his eyes when he comes back to the sofa, and yet he's smiling. 'It was all so stupid. We were all so fucking stupid.'

'We were young.' I don't know what else to say. The young don't have a monopoly on stupid.

'Nix . . .'

'Declan, something happened at the Shelley after we left. Do you remember, I told you about the policeman who was at my house?'

The way he looks tells me that no, he doesn't remember it at all; but there's something he wants to ask, and it's a struggle, which means I don't think I want to hear it.

'I remember seeing you there.' He's smiling, lost in a memory; has to force himself back to the present. 'I don't know. The only thing I remember about the rest of that night, to be honest, was thinking about us. What we'd done.'

He gets up and leaves the room for a minute and then comes back with an old faded photograph. I recognise the faces from the party. Arty Robbins is in the middle. His dad beside him, Vincent Robbins, and his stepmum, Madge. Dave Crane has his arm around Arty Robbins' shoulders, giving a big thumbs-up to the camera. Mum lurks in the background, wearing one of Vincent's aprons. Her smile is forced, like she really doesn't want to be there.

'Kat's mum took pictures. She gave them to Mum. The police took most of them but I found this stuck behind a drawer. Look at them. Arms around each other, all smiling for the camera. One big happy family.' He laughs bitterly. 'What a charade! Vincent and Aunt Madge couldn't stand each other, and Aunt Madge hated Dad, too. Blamed them both for Uncle Daniel running away. Dad was always Vincent's golden boy.'

'The police asked me about him,' I say. 'Your Uncle Daniel. Whether I saw him at the party.'

'Uncle Daniel? Why?'

'I don't know.' I pick up the picture and look at it. I didn't see this moment that Chloe Clarke caught forever; it was obviously taken before the party started: people seen across the room, the roar of a hundred voices far too loud for me to hear what any of them were saying. Like seeing Mum talking to Arty Robbins, spitting fire, telling him to keep his son in check . . .

If that's what it was.

Back in Declan's flat, we watch each other now. Another silence, but this one feels dangerous in a different way. I want to kiss him.

I should go.

'I've got ice-cream in the freezer. Home-made gooseberry-and-elderflower.'

I should say no, but I nod. 'Yes, please.' He goes to the

kitchen and rummages in the freezer, then comes back with two bowls, each with three perfectly formed scoops.

'Electric ice-cream scoop.' He grins as he puts them on the table and then goes back to the kitchen, fetches a bottle of sherry and pours a drizzle into each bowl. 'Just a touch.' He sits beside me and I feel how close he is. 'I keep thinking about who could have done it. I can't stop. I suppose that's what happens when . . .' He makes a face, then suddenly he crumbles and all the bravado falls away, and he's scared and small, a middle-aged man with nothing much to show for himself, staring into the abyss. 'Dad was an arse. You know he was. Other people knew, too. It was all coming out, what he really was. Could have been – I don't know. Could have been anyone, for all I know. But everyone was in the Shelley. I don't know who it could be, Nix.'

Not everyone. Not Kat and Gary, for example. 'Declan—'

'They sent someone to take a statement from Mum. While I was locked up.' He seems to shrink into himself, clutching the bowl to his chest. 'Nix, the thing is . . . she told them I was at the Shelley all night. She told them I never left the party. Like, at *all*. I don't know why she said that. Maybe that's what she remembers, I don't know. But the police know it isn't true and . . . I remember Dad coming back to the house and . . . and I think there was a fight and you were hiding and . . . But I don't *remember*!' He's almost in tears.

'You really don't?'

He shakes his head, and I want to hold him, hold him tight and never let go and make it all like it was. I put down my bowl and take his hand. 'Hey.'

He puts his other hand on mine and squeezes. 'I'm sorry, Nix. I shouldn't have asked you over but I'm desperate.' He pulls free and pushes the photo from the Shelley towards me. 'I was hoping you – well, with the way you are . . .'

I turn towards him and he slumps into my arms. I hold him, stroking his hair. 'You didn't do it, Declan.' Inside, I'm melting.

'I *know*! But . . . I was hoping you'd remember something.'

I don't. That's the thing. Nothing that helps. I remember so much. I remember everything and I still don't understand what happened that night. I can't piece together the fragments and I don't know which bits matter and which bits don't. It's like having a head full of jigsaw-puzzle pieces, but not *all* the pieces; and there's more than one puzzle, and I don't know which pieces go together, and whenever I try, the picture doesn't make any sense.

But I can't say that to him – not now, not like this.

'I'll help you. I promise.'

'Then tell me what really happened that night. Tell me what you remember.'

So I tell him.

9

Sunday 9th June 1985, 10.15 p.m.

Standing outside the Shelley, I have to spell it out in small, simple words before Dec gets it: *Let's go to your place.* So that's what we do, because half of everyone in Byron Road is at the party right now and I can't see any of them going home any time soon, particularly Dec's mum and dad, which means we'll have Dec's house to ourselves for ages. We go up to his room and I forget all about Kat and Gary and about Mum and Dad. Dec's hands are all over me, making me tingle on the outside and molten in the middle, but when he starts pushing his way up under my shirt, I stop him and pull back, even though by then I really don't want to.

The curtains on the bedroom window are open. I close them, feeling his eyes on me, how intently he watches me.

'What did you want to talk about?' I ask.

'Huh?'

'Yesterday. In the alley. You said—'

'Oh. Yeah.'

He looks crestfallen and starts glancing around his room, although I can't imagine what help he thinks he's going to find in the unruly scatter of clothes on the floor or the shelf cluttered with its handful of ragged-edged books, or the poster of Ian Rush, or the old record player with its careful stack of LPs propped against the wall beside it.

'Thing is . . .' And I think: *Here it comes*, and the butterflies that are already filling my stomach are fluttering for all they're worth. He takes a deep breath and then looks me in the eye and out it blurts: 'I've got to get out of here. I can't stand it any more. I can't live here. Not with . . . I don't know where I'm going to go and – Jesus, Nix, I don't know what to do, because I can't stay, I just can't, but you're the best thing I've ever had in my whole life and . . . and I want you to come with me.'

I reel away, bewildered and hurt because I know something's been brooding away in there for ages, but Dec's never said anything like *this*, not even slightly. 'What do you mean you can't stay? What's going on?'

'Everyone thinks my dad's so great, like the sun shines out of his arse with his minibus for the school and his open house at the Shelley, but he's not. He's fucking not. He slaps

Mum about. He always has, but last week he put her in hospital. It's been going on for years. You remember that time I was off school for a week with a broken arm? He did that.'

I shake my head, speechless. This isn't how I saw the evening panning out.

'He didn't like the way I talked to him and so he broke my arm. Last week, when I had to take Mum to the hospital because she'd dislocated her wrist? That was him; and she won't do anything, just says it was an accident and he didn't mean it and he's sorry. But he *isn't*, and I don't want to be here when it happens again – I just don't. I have to get away, Nix. Before I go crazy!'–

He swallows hard and looks at me with eyes full of hope and tragedy, like he's sure I'll say no, because what he's asking is completely mad; and because, sure, I don't get on with Mum and Dad like we're best friends, because who actually does, but they're not *that* bad, not run-away-from-home bad, nowhere near, and it's not like they hit me or . . .

I remember the bruise I saw on Mrs Robbins' face this afternoon. I can't say I'm even surprised. It's shocking to hear, but now that I think about it, it's not at all surprising. Despite his whole respectable-businessman lifestyle, there's always been something a bit wrong about Dec's dad.

'Bloody hell.' It's all I can think.

'I know it's stupid.' He looks away and there's a space

between us that wasn't there before, and I don't like it, not one little bit.

'I can't just . . . go!' I can't believe I'm saying no.

'Yeah. I know.' He tries to smile.

I reach out and touch him, trying to close the hole between us.

'I told you I was out of school because Mum hurt her wrist and I had to help her out. Truth is . . . my Aunt Eileen called. She said she was having some sort of emergency and needed Mum's help, and Mum couldn't drive, so she asked me to take her; except when we got there, Aunt Eileen wasn't having an emergency at all. She knew what had happened. She knew all about Mum and what Dad was doing. She told Mum that if she didn't get away then he'd put her in the hospital again, sooner or later, because that's what men like him do. Or worse. Mum wouldn't have it. She got angry, and she and Aunt Eileen had this huge argument and . . .' He shakes his head. 'I can't stay here, Nix. I just can't.'

I lean across the bed and wrap my arms around him, holding him tight, but he's not there, not really. It's like hugging a dead thing.

'I don't want to lose you,' he says.

'But couldn't you stay at the Shelley? With your granddad?'

Dec breaks away and looks at me like it's the most absurd,

ridiculous, preposterous idea ever – like I've suggested that he live on the moon. 'Last place I'd want to go.'

'Or . . .' I don't want to say it because I don't like it, but better than him running off to Kathmandu or something. 'Your aunt lives in Clapham, right? It's still London. We could still see each other.'

He shrugs. 'At weekends and stuff, I—'

He stops, because right then we hear the front door open downstairs and the clomp of heavy boots across the hall.

'Crap! Dad? *Shit!*' Dec's eyes turn wild. 'Hide! Shit! What's he doing back *here*?'

'Oi!' A shout from below. 'Where are you?' Footsteps on the stairs now.

I look around the room, flailing for where to go. The wardrobe looks flimsy enough to collapse if I climb inside, so I drop to the floor and start to wriggle my way under the bed. As I do, I see a moment of sheer panic flash across Declan's face. 'Not there!'

Too bloody late. The footsteps have reached the top of the stairs and there isn't time for anything else. I squirm as deep under the bed as I can go, until I feel something scrunch on the carpet beneath me. An exercise book or a magazine or something. Then the door opens and all I can see are an angry pair of boots and a scared pair of feet by the bed.

'What the *fuck* you doing back here?' Arty Robbins spits the question with enough violence to make me flinch.

'I got bored.'

'Who else you got here?'

'No one.'

'No one?' The boots step into the room. 'Seen your mother?'

'Dad, she was with *you*—'

The boots move again, another quick step forward and jerk and I hear the wet *CRACK!* of a slap. Dec cries out. His feet disappear and I feel him crash onto the bed on top of me.

'Liar!' Dec's dad bellows and his boots stomp to the bed. They look like cowboy boots, old brown leather, a little scuffed. There's a design carved into them, some sort of snake. If I had to guess, I'd say a rattlesnake. 'Vincent saw you last week. You took her to Aunt fucking-can't-keep-her-nose-out-of-other-people's-business Eileen, didn't you?'

The bed heaves. I see Dec's feet as he's dragged off the bed and slammed into the wardrobe.

'Where is she?'

'I dunno, Dad! Maybe she's gone, OK? Maybe you finally did it. Maybe she's finally had enough, you know?'

Another *CRACK!* as the wardrobe shudders. Dec cries out again. Then a second time, *WHACK* – like Dec's dad gave it a quick thought before he decided that one smack in the face wasn't enough. Dec crashes onto the floor and I can see him now, blood running from his nose, his dad pinning him, both hands pressed over Dec's face as though trying to crush his skull, and I don't think I've ever felt so scared in my whole life.

'You tell me where she is or I swear to God—'

'I don't know! She said Aunt Madge—'

'Madge? Fucking *Marjory*?' Arty grabs Dec by the collar, hauls him up and throws him back onto the bed. 'Your cousin and that trash-mate of yours. Barclay. What about them? Where are they?'

Gary? What on earth does Dec's dad want with Gary?

'At the party? I don't fucking know!'

'Not here?'

'No!'

'No, I bet I know *exactly* where they are.' He idly opens the wardrobe door and slams it with enough force that the whole room shakes. 'You'd better be here when I come back or I will put you in a fucking *hole*, you ungrateful little shit!'

Arthur Robbins, parish councillor, school governor and pillar of the community, stamps out of the bedroom with his son's blood on his hands. I hear him clomp down the stairs. The front door opens and crashes shut. I'm shaking, too scared to move in case he comes back. I count slowly to ten and he doesn't, but I still don't want to even breathe.

I'm half lying on some magazine, so I shuffle it out from underneath me, an excuse to stay hidden for another few seconds. On the cover, a naked blonde with perfect teeth and sunbed skin and pumped-up boobs smiles back. A *Penthouse*, which sort of breaks the spell, especially when I think of the look of panic on Dec's face as I started shuffling under here. I ought to be mad at him, because really? A porno mag? But I can't be, not after what just happened.

I squeeze out into the open and leave the magazine behind. Dec's on the bed, curled up, fists clenched so tight that the skin over his knuckles looks like a balloon ready to burst. He has blood smeared across his face where his nose is still bleeding. There's a bloody hand-print on his shirt. He's not crying because boys don't do that, not in front of girls, but I can tell that he wants to. I sit beside him and reach out a hand. When he turns to look, I see he's got a busted lip, too.

'Jesus, Dec.'

I suppose I thought he didn't really mean it about running away. I know plenty of girls at school who talk about it. They say they hate their parents but that's just for a day or two because they've been told they're not allowed to go with their best friend to the Montreux Festival in Switzerland or some-thing. It's not . . . not this.

Dec gets up. He opens the wardrobe and looks at himself in the mirror there, as though he's not quite sure who he is. There's blood all over his face.

'I'm going – I've got to clean up,' he says. 'You can . . . you know. Go back, if you want. To the Shelley.' The way he says it, like it's nothing special, like his dad has done this before.

I feel my heart tripping along. I get up and go to him. Touch him again, as though trying to make sure he's still real. 'It's OK – well, not, but . . . we'll make it work. Whatever happens. I promise.' The words seem clunky and awkward as I force them into sentences but they feel true, too, odd and deep and powerful.

I watch him walk out, then hear the taps in the bathroom as he cleans himself up. I want to run away and be with him because I love him, and love is all that matters; except my parents love me too, even if they're not very good at it some of the time, and I can already hear Dad telling me how stupid it is, and Mum saying how I'm throwing my life away. And of course, I'm *not* going to run away, because it *is* stupid and I have no reason to, except . . . Except that I love him, and everything at home is shit and . . .

I start to cry. It takes me by surprise. One moment I'm standing by the edge of the bed and then the next I've started to shake, and it actually takes a moment for me to realise there are tears coming out of my eyes. It won't be the same if Dec goes, and so I want to go with him, but I can't, I just can't.

I won't let this happen. I *won't*.

His face doesn't look as bad when he comes back. His nose and lip are swollen and he has a twist of toilet paper shoved up each nostril, which makes me giggle.

'Nose-voles,' I say. Dec looks at me like I'm mad, so I guess he never used to watch *The Goodies*. He comes and puts his arm around me.

'I want us to be together,' I say. 'That's all.'

'So do I.' He squeezes me and holds me tight.

'I can't leave home. I can't run away.' I know this. There's no point pretending it isn't true. I know I'm sixteen and all grown-up, but I'm scared and I'm not ready. 'I don't know what to do.'

'There's the weekends,' he says. 'It's still London. I can get on a train.'

We both know it's not the same.

He squeezes me. 'Thanks for staying.'

'I'm going to tell the police,' I say.

'What?'

'I'm going to tell the police. And so are you. Then he'll be arrested and you won't have to go. You can stay—'

'No.'

'Dec!'

But he shakes his head.

'Dec, I don't want you to go! I don't want *either* of us to go *anywhere*! *He's* the one who should go, not you. I want to be with you! All the time.' And I do. I don't want him to be in Clapham where we can only see each other at the weekends. I want him to be *here*, where I can walk from his house to mine, from his house to school, where I can see him every night from my bedroom window . . .

'Nix—'

'No! He can't do this to us.'

I press into him. I feel his hand on my hair, stroking me, and then his other hand on my face, turning me towards him as he leans in to kiss me. I kiss him back and it's odd at first, because I can feel his misshapen lip and the dry, hard tips of those two twists of toilet paper, and taste an iron tang of blood. I feel a surge inside me and take his head in my hands so he can't get away. I feel his fingers on my cheek slip to my shoulder and then inch further, still thinking they're some sort of ninja hand. I pull away and for an instant I catch in his face how desperate he is, how much he wants me. It's hard not to dive on him.

'There's blood on your shirt,' I say. 'You should probably take it off.'

While he does that, I slide to the floor, down on my hands and knees, reach under the bed and pull out the *Penthouse* and drop it in front of him. It's delicious how embarrassed he looks. It's not like he can pretend it isn't his.

Dec gives me a sheepish look. His mouth opens as if maybe he's about to say something, but then it stops and hangs there, because I'm standing in front of him, undoing the buttons of my blouse and feeling really, really smug that I had the foresight to put on the sexy bra and knickers, the ones which would give Mum a heart attack if she knew they were what I'd bought with this year's birthday money.

10

Thursday 6th February 2020

I don't stay the night with Declan. He would have let it happen, I think, but I make my excuses, go home and spend the night staring at the ceiling instead. My heart is thumping. I keep telling myself how I only want things back the way they were a week ago but I know that's not true. I want more, so much more. I want to go back to when we were young. Both ideas are stupid, I know, because no one can go back in time, but I can't seem to let it go.

I try to imagine what it must be like for him, not being able to remember that night. He remembers his dad giving him a beating, and how it wasn't the first, not by a long shot. He claims he remembers the *Penthouse*, too, but not the blood; and I don't understand how he can remember the one and not the other. When I finished telling him what happened that night, he said the rest was sort of coming back to him – the stuff that happened in the Shelley before we left – but I'm not sure how much of that was wishful thinking. I wonder how it feels to be at sea like that. He's got a story now, but I'm not sure how much of it is really his. And, of course, I can't tell him what *really* happened after I left, only what he told me the next day.

As I lie in bed, unable to sleep, I think about Declan's photograph – the lie of it, Declan saying how his Aunt Madge and Grandpa Vincent hated each other even as they lived under the same roof. I think of Kat's mum taking pictures at the party. If I looked through them, would I find Declan looking back at me? Was she still taking pictures after midnight? Does she still have them?

I try to sleep but it doesn't really work and so eventually I give up. I get dressed before it's light outside and have an early breakfast. I fuss with Chairman for a while and think how there must be other witnesses, people who saw Declan at the Shelley when he returned. Even if the police know his mum lied about him being there for the whole night, there *has* to be someone else. I suppose Kat went straight home after she and Gary did whatever they did ... But Gary would have stayed for as long as the drinks were free, and Kat's mum was there right to the very end. One of them has to remember, don't they? I go through the faces in my

memories, one by one. I never had names for most of them –
only the ones who were parents to people I knew.

I check the time. I've got plenty before I need to leave for
work, so I go through the whole evening again, from the
moment I got there, writing down the names I knew and
what everyone was wearing. I know it was a long time ago
but there must have been a hundred people at the party that
night, and it only takes one of them to remember.

Dad's jacket, streaked with mud . . .

If Dad was out in the park close to midnight then maybe
Kat was right and it *was* him that she and Gary saw. But why
was he out there? And how did he get mud all over his jacket?

Mum, livid with fury . . .

I saw her giving Arty Robbins a piece of her mind before
we left. I assumed it was something to do with me and
Declan. Later, I thought maybe she knew about what he was
doing to Anne.

Good riddance to bad rubbish. Dad's words. He never
told me what happened that night or why there was a policeman in our house, but I remember the bruises on Mum's
neck the next morning.

Lingering behind all this is the thought that maybe I
should have stayed with Declan last night, if only to treasure
the memory of it.

I check the time again and suddenly I'm running late. I
grab my jacket and my bag and rush for the door, and as I do,

a memory swallows me like a shark from the deep, dragging down a seal. It's early autumn. I can feel it in the air: the slight nip of a chill that says summer has finally gone. It's 1990 and I'm about to get married and I'm with Kat, in a hotel room, staring at myself in the mirror, at a dress that doesn't seem real – the dress I'm going to wear when I marry Dec in about forty minutes – and a part of me is wondering if I'm supposed to be scared or feel full of doubt, but I'm not and I don't. I can remember our relationship from the start to the present and there's not a single thing I'd change.

I tell this to Kat and she laughs. 'Not even that time he abandoned you at that service station?'

'That was an accident!'

'That's what *he* says.'

'He's your cousin. Aren't you supposed to be telling me how great he is?'

'I don't think you need *me* for that.' She smiles, that big honest smile that seems like it's only for me. 'You could do a lot worse, though. A *lot* worse.' The smile turns into a grin. 'And since we're cousins, he has to treat you right or I'll thump him, and he knows it.'

I relive it as though I'm right there, minute for minute, talking to Kat, feeling the butterflies in my stomach, almost tripping over on the stairs down to the lobby, fumbling my way into the Bentley that Dad insisted on hiring for us. I climb out when we reach the registry office and I'm so light-headed that Kat has to hold my hand, and at first I can't see Dec, only Mum and Dad: Dad beaming like he's won the lottery, Mum looking like she's trying very hard but can't quite hide how she doesn't want to be there.

And then I see him. Dec in his top hat and tails, emerging from a cluster of friends. For the next ten minutes, even *my* memory fails me, breaking into fits and starts, flashes of this and that. Dad and Dec shaking hands. Standing with Dec as we made our vows, putting the ring on my finger. Kissing him. Signing the register. The banquet back at the hotel – Dad again. It was a wonderful day and so I linger there. I don't want to leave, even though I know I should. I want to stay here, before it all went wrong.

When I finally come back, it's because my phone is ringing. I'm sitting on the sofa, eyes full of tears, and I should have been at work an hour ago but I can't seem to move. I remember the wedding dinner. I put Mum next to Mrs R. It seemed the right thing to do, but I don't think Mum said a single word to her all evening.

When I answer my phone, it's Ed from work.

Shit!

'Nicola! Where are you? The Orien Trust people are here and I can't find you anywhere! Are you even in?'

Shit, shit, shit!

'I . . . Sorry. I . . . I'm at the doctor's.' It's the first thing that comes into my head.

'*What?*'

'I'm really sorry. It's just that I was on my way in and I suddenly felt really sick. I had to get off the bus and then I started throwing up.'

'What? Fuck! Are you OK?' There must be something in my voice that rings true for Ed to actually show some concern.

'Probably nothing serious. One of those twenty-four-hour things. I'll probably be fine by tomorrow, but you know – better safe than sorry.'

'I hope so. What am I supposed to do about the Orien Trust?'

'You'll have to ask them to come back. Tell them I'm so sorry.'

'Right. Can you let me know a bit earlier tomorrow, if you're not coming in?'

'Yes, of course. Sorry.'

It's not unusual, slipping into memories so deep that I lose all sense of time, but usually it's for five or ten minutes, not two hours. And I don't skip work for a day simply because I feel down, that's not who I am. But I can't go in now, not after what I just said to Ed.

An hour later, I step out of Wordsworth Park station. To the right are the shops and the High Street. To the left is the park with a couple of benches by the entrance. If I close my eyes, I can see it change as the years pass. I can see a path of muddy brown earth swallowed up by trees to either side. I can see a track covered in gravel, trees on one side, Parklands on the other: my daily walk to school. I see it as it is now, a tarmac cycle path warded on one side by the high wooden boards of the construction site, and on the other by the fence around the car park, the trees all gone.

I'm going home. I'm going to see Mum. I'm going to ask about that night.

I walk to the end of the High Street and onto the path into the park, and I'm twenty-six; and behind the boards that cage the building site beside me, another me is hugging her knees to her chest in the dark and the rain, and the despair is a black pit from which there seems no escape. Another dozen yards and I'm seventeen, and it's a summer night and I'm too drunk to stand, and there's a bench and I'm slumped on it, my head in Declan's lap, and I feel so ill that I want to die. That was the night I discovered I could drown my memory in alcohol, if I wanted, because to this day I don't remember much of what happened.

I walk on and I'm six years old, Mum on one side of me, Dad on the other. I'm holding their hands and everything is bright and brilliant and I feel safe and happy, and then – SNAP! – I'm twenty, and Mum and Dad have turned into Declan, but we're still holding hands and the feeling is the same, and I don't know whether that was how I felt when I was with him or whether it's still the feeling of a small child, or whether it's both . . .

On the other side of the building site, I cross Wordsworth Lane, the playing fields on one side and the woods on the other.

. . . and my sixteenth birthday is only weeks away and I'm sitting on a swing, watching the field where Declan is playing football in the snow with a dozen other boys whose names I can remember, every single one; and Andrew Fisher is coming towards me, and Declan is with him, so I wait and smile, not at Declan but at Andrew Fisher, and Andrew Fisher smiles back and notices me, and everything is perfect and I barely see the look on Declan's face and . . .

I shake myself back to the present. A miserable February morning. I came this way to school every day for years, but everything is different. I remember an ice-cream van in the summer, where the coffee shop stands; I remember a slide, a see-saw, a roundabout and a climbing frame, all set into unforgiving tarmac, but now some adventure-play wooden fort-thing stands in their place and everywhere is covered in bark chippings. My memory is like the sea in a storm today, waves crashing over me one after the other, knocking me down with barely time to get back on my feet. Sometimes it feels like I'm going to drown.

I don't know what to say to Mum. I haven't known since Dad died and she married Dave Crane, throwing away her old life as though none of it mattered. I wonder, sometimes, if it was actually a relief for her when Dad was diagnosed.

It's a mean-spirited thought, probably unfair, but I think it anyway.

Kat and Gary saw someone in the park that night. I need to know if it was Dad. I think what happened that night is that Mum left the party with Dad's best friend Dave, not with Dad. I think Dad couldn't find her and so he went looking. I think he saw them together. I think he already knew something was going on because things weren't right between them even before, but it all got worse after that night. I don't think Mum will ever tell me if it's true. But I have to try.

Do I? Why does it even matter? It won't save Declan. Arty Robbins had nothing to do with the triangle of Mum and Dad and David Crane . . . And yet it *does* matter. To me.

The park gates open onto Shelley Street past what used to be the Mary Shelley. It's got a new name now, part of some bland family-friendly chain. Vincent put it up for sale the year after his son disappeared. He was never the same after that night.

It's closed – too early – which is just as well because I'd murder for a shot of something strong to steady my nerves, or to sit at one of the tables outside and smoke. But if I were to do either of those things then I'd turn around and go home, because I don't want to be here. I don't want *any* of this. It's only been a few days since Declan called but it feels like a month. I wouldn't say I was *happy* before, but at least I'd found a way to be at peace. Now? Now I need to know what really happened that night. All of it.

I walk past the Shelley and Tennyson Way and glance towards the house where Andrew Fisher used to live. We went out for exactly three weeks and one day before I dumped him and started seeing Declan. If I want to, I can picture everything as it was back then: the roads half empty, only a handful of cars parked on the street, green front gardens with their little patches of lawn, flower beds that turned into bursts of colour in the spring and summer. Now the road is rammed, cars and vans parked on both sides, the front gardens mostly paved over, the terracotta red roof tiles cratered by dormer windows and loft extensions. I turn the corner into Byron Road and it's all more of the same. It's been ages since I came back here.

Mum almost sold up three years ago. Fed up with the street being constantly a building site, she said.

I stop across the road from the house that used to be my home. The windows have changed, old wooden frames replaced by glaring white uPVC. The front door is new, too, and the drive has been re-laid and there's a new garden wall. The old flower beds and rose bushes – Dad's pride and joy – have all gone. Replaced, just like Dad himself.

Why do I need to do this? Am I still trying to get Declan back, after all this time?

Not that. I *saw* him with that other woman.

Then why?

In my head, I'm at my window, looking out into the dark, and Declan is looking back, and the yearning is inside me. I feel it now as I felt it then – a blooming, the most beautiful feeling I've ever known. I feel myself falling in love with him, over and over again. Young and strong, my heart already carrying its first few shallow scars, but really only scratches . . .

I want to make it right. I just don't know how.

Across the street, the door opens and Dave comes out. He's starting to show his age at last, hair mostly silver. He's seventy-three years old, a couple of years younger than Mum, but he wears it well, looks and moves more like a man in his fifties. He doesn't notice me at first, not until he opens the car door and feels me staring. When he sees me, it takes him a full two seconds to recognise who I am.

'Nicola?'

I take an instinctive step away. I used to like 'Uncle' Dave until that summer when Arty Robbins disappeared. Then I hated him, and I never stopped.

The feeling sparks a memory. I still see the streaks of mud on Dad's jacket. Dark leather, the mud almost orange. Dad *was* in the park that night . . .

'Are you here for Susan?'

Why else would I be here? I wish he'd just get into his car and go wherever he's going. When he doesn't, I force myself to cross the road. Dave leads me to the front door and opens it and calls, 'Sue! You'll never guess who's here!' When he turns to me, his smile is guarded. 'She'll be delighted to see you. It's been ages.'

As if I can't remember that for myself.

Mum emerges from the lounge and it nearly breaks my heart the way her face lights up. She almost runs at me to hug me. 'Nicky! What a lovely surprise.'

'I'll make some tea.' Dave slips diplomatically to the kitchen while Mum drags me to the lounge, sits me down and flutters around as though she doesn't know what to do.

'Dave was about to go to the shops. I hope you don't mind.'

'Of course not.' The sooner he goes, the better.

She asks about work, which hasn't really changed since I started at the library ten years ago, and about Joy and a few other friends I've mentioned over the years. It's what she always does, skirting around the edges of my life, looking for meat where there isn't any. My world is quiet and simple because that's the way I like it. At least she's given up on grandchildren.

Dave brings in a tray with a teapot and a pair of cups, a little jug of milk and a bowl of sugar. He leans over Mum and kisses the top of her head. I have to look away as my eyes fill with tears. It's what Dad used to do.

'I'll come back with some biscuits,' he says.

I turn back to Mum once he's gone. She's watching me,

and I know what she's thinking because I can see it in her eyes: *Dad passed more than twenty years ago, love.* The thing she doesn't understand is that, for me, Dad is still alive. He lives and breathes in every memory I have of him. I want to ask, right now, about her and Dave back in 1985, but the words are stuck, clumped together in the back of my throat.

'I'm sorry, Mum,' I say. 'I just . . . I can't – I can't forget him the way you can.'

'We were married for almost thirty years, love. No one's *forgotten* him.'

My memory flashes to that picture of me and Declan and Kat from the Shelley: not the picture itself but the box where I keep it. I got it when we went to Clacton, a month after the party at the Shelley. The search for Arty Robbins was in full swing and Mum thought a day by the sea with the sun and the sand would help shake away the blues. That's what she called it. The blues, like it was some passing illness. In the car on the way there, she told us all about her first crush when she'd been fourteen, some boy at her school that had lasted two weeks; how, when he dumped her, she'd thought it was the end of the world. I realised, eventually, that she was telling the story to me, not to Dad. She thought I was upset because I wasn't allowed to see Declan, but it wasn't that, because we never stopped. I was *upset* because home felt like the bloody Cuban Missile Crisis.

All the way there, Dad never said a word. We got to the seaside and Mum bought me that tin full of toffees, like that was supposed to make it all better.

'I don't mean . . . What I mean is . . .' Mum never understood what it was like to be me, never even tried; and I should know better but I can't stop myself, in case maybe today's the day I finally make her see? 'Mum, another year and I'll be the same age Dad was when he . . . when he passed. I know that. But for me, it's still as though it was only yesterday.'

'Oh that's . . . But you *know* that's not true.'

I want to shout and scream: *Obviously* I know it's not true but that doesn't change how it *feels*. Dad got it eventually, somehow – what it was like to remember everything as though it only just happened – but Mum and I have had this conversation about a hundred times and it's like she doesn't *want* to understand.

'You heard about Arty Robbins?' I ask instead.

'Oh yes.' A little gleam lights up in her eye. 'The whole street's been talking about it. Well, those of us who remember him. I was talking to Chloe yesterday . . . You remember Chloe?'

'Kat's mum. Of course I remember.'

'She said they arrested someone.' Mum shakes her head as though it's all terrible, but that gleam is still there, that little shard of malicious glee. It did come out eventually, the truth: how the sun didn't shine from Arty Robbins' backside like everyone wanted to believe. Mum made sure of that.

'The someone they arrested was Declan,' I say. Mum never liked Declan after that night in '85 and didn't try to pretend otherwise, but she still managed to act disappointed when I left him.

'Well,' she says, 'I can't say I'm surprised.'

'Mum! For God's sake!'

Mum makes an *I'm-just-saying* sort of shrug. 'I'm sorry, love, but you know what they say.'

I do, because I've heard it all before. *Like father, like son. The apple doesn't fall far from the tree.* That kind of thing. 'He was eighteen!'

'Pushed him into the pit where they built Parklands, according to Chloe. Good riddance to bad rubbish is what your dad would have said.'

'It's what he *did* say, Mum. I remember him saying it.'

Mum waves a hand as though trying to waft away a bad smell. 'I don't think one single person on this street was sorry when Arthur Robbins took it upon himself to disappear. The way he treated poor Anne . . .' Which is such utter rubbish that I literally have to bite my tongue. It was *years* before people stopped talking about him as though he was the bloody Second Coming.

Except . . . not Mum and Dad.

'Declan didn't do it,' I say.

She looks away.

'I know you didn't like him but he's not a bloody *murderer*, for heaven's sake!'

'Language!' snaps Mum.

I just stare.

'I'm sure the police will sort it out.'

'Yes.' I could tell her about talking to the police, about Declan's alibi, but we'd only get into another fight.

'Sorry, love,' she says. 'I need to make a quick call.' She gets up and walks out of the lounge; when I hear her talking, I know she's speaking to Dave. I can't quite make out the words but it's in her tone. It's her private voice – the one she only used for Dad when she thought they were alone.

Two days after the party, Declan went with his mum to Clapham. It crushed me to nothing. At home, the tension was as though a nuclear missile had gone missing. I thought about killing myself in that stupid never-going-to-actually-do-it teenage way. The next weekend, I packed a bag, all ready to follow Declan to Clapham. Dad caught me. I thought he'd yell and tell me I was stupid but instead he took me out to the park. We walked, just the two of us, and he talked and talked about how love wasn't a flash of lightning – something that came and went – but an ocean, deep and vast and always there; and if what I had with Declan was really love and not some passing crush, then it would survive and last; and yes, he understood how I'd put up with anything, *do* anything, to keep it, but there would be harder tests than this. It all felt painfully embarrassing at the time, but hindsight long ago showed me the care behind those words. He asked whether I knew where Declan was staying and I told him yes, I had his aunt's address. Dad took me to the station and bought an *A–Z* and we looked it up, and then he bought me a Travelcard and made me promise, on pain of death, to be home before dark and not to tell Mum. And then he let me go.

Arty Robbins never did come home. A week later, Declan was back in Byron Road. We saw each other every day. I'm sure Dad knew about it, but he never said a word to Mum. At the end of that summer, Declan went to university and, when he came back, it was like he never left. We held hands and talked about music and television and films and everything. We stopped pretending. I took him home. When I left school, I followed him to Nottingham and the best years of my life. We married a few months after I graduated. Mum never approved, even then, but Dad was always kind. *As long as he treats you right, love.* We were going to make a life. Together. Forever . . .

Mum comes back into the lounge now, looking a little flustered. 'Sorry, love. Just needed to remind Dave of a couple of things I wanted him to get.'

I talked to a therapist once. Anja. I told her about that summer, me and Declan, the mystery of Arty Robbins;

about Dad walking out and for three days thinking he'd never come back. She listened politely and then told me how it was normal for couples in long-term relationships to have periods of crisis – a birth, a death, one partner losing a job, moving house; that what defines the strength of a relationship isn't that these crises never happen, but how they're addressed. Then she asked whether I resented Mum for moving on, after Dad died. I walked out right then. Years later, I understood why: I don't resent Mum for moving on. I resent her because she can.

'What really happened between you and Arty Robbins that night?'

'Oh, Nicola! It was such a long time ago . . .' She bats the question aside but I see the shock in her face, how uncomfortable it makes her. A long time ago, yes, but she remembers . . .

And I'm in the kitchen again, the morning after the party, about to get my breakfast slapped out of my hands, staring at the bruises on Mum's neck, and I can't keep the shock from my face.

'You were arguing. I thought it was about me and Declan, but . . .'

'Yes. Well, teenagers *are* prone to think that everything's always about *them*.' Mum gives me a dark look.

'But it wasn't.'

She slowly shakes her head. 'Someone had to say something. It had to stop.'

I see Declan's mum with her swollen cheek on the day of the party. 'What—'

'It really doesn't matter now, does it? I gave him a piece of my mind, that's what happened. Everyone thought Arty was such a saint!'

'I saw the marks,' I say. 'On your neck. The morning after. Was that . . . was that him?'

'I'd really rather not talk about it, love.'

'The police asked.'

Mum closes her eyes. She bows her head and doesn't say anything for so long that I think she's not going to answer; but when she looks back at me, her face is quite different, old and tired and sad. 'I told you, love. I gave him a piece of my mind. About all his . . . goings-on. Then I think I must have gone outside for a cigarette to calm down. I don't remember how we got there; just being there, out the back of the Shelley, the two of us, Arty shouting and swearing how it was none of my effing and blinding business. I remember I told him I'd set the police on him, and he could explain to *them* how it was none of *their* business.'

'Mum?' Back then, and she already knew about what was happening in Declan's house?

Mum seems to shrink. She takes a deep breath. 'I suppose he only had his hands on me for a second or two but I'll never forget it, and I'll never forget the look in his eyes, either. I don't know what would have happened if Dave hadn't come out. Your dad was right. Good riddance to bad rubbish indeed.'

The tea sits on the table, untouched. I pour a cup for each of us, lukewarm now.

'What I remember most is his smell. Sweat and stale beer.' Her voice trails away. 'Chloe took pictures. Vincent was going to decorate the pub with them . . . She showed them to me, afterwards. She had this one of Vincent and Arthur, glasses full and roaring with laughter, like Chloe had caught them at the punchline of some joke. They looked like they were having the time of their lives. It was minutes after Dave pulled him off me. Arty didn't care at all.'

'Does . . . Do you know if Kat's mum still has those pictures?'

Mum shakes her head. 'The police took them when they came asking questions. Poor woman. She doesn't remember it, of course.'

'The argument you had?'

Mum looks away. 'Nothing that matters now he's gone, love. Let's just say I'd seen enough to know he wasn't the devoted husband he liked us all to think.'

The front door opens: Dave back with a bag from the corner shop across from the Shelley. I hear him rustling in the kitchen and think of the photograph Declan showed me. Arty and Vincent Robbins and Dave, all smiling. Everyone was welcome at the Shelley. That was the kind of place it was – the sort of people we were.

The sort of people we *thought* we were.

Dave comes back from the kitchen and plops a plate of chocolate digestives on the table. 'You talking about Arty Robbins? The police were here—'

'I told her,' says Mum. 'You remember how Chloe said the police arrested someone?' She gives him a look that I can't decipher. 'Nicola says it was Declan.'

Dave looks bewildered and then horrified. 'Oh, Susan! Jesus!' He turns his attention to me, not that I want it. 'There must be some mistake. Weren't you two . . . weren't you two already seeing each other back then?'

'I was with Declan until midnight that night,' I say. 'I've already given a statement.'

'Thank God for that! So he's going to be OK? They'll let him go?'

I look hard at Dave but his concern seems real enough. 'No,' I say. 'He's *not* going to be OK. They charged him. They had to let him go for now, but they took his passport and he's got to wear one of those trackers and report to his local police station every—'

'Jesus bloody Christ!' Dave looks truly shocked. 'They can't—'

'Language!' snaps Mum.

'Sorry, but . . .' He turns back to me. 'But *why*?'

I get up. 'Look, I should probably go.' I know I haven't asked what I came here to ask. I don't think I can, not while Dave is here. If I'm honest, it's freaking me out a bit how he's taking this. It's like he actually cares.

'Nicola was asking what Arthur Robbins did that night,' says Mum. 'I told her you were my white knight.'

Dave gawps and makes a face. 'Only because I happened to be by the open kitchen window.' He looks right at me. 'If it had been your dad, he would have punched Arty. And Arty would have deserved it, too.'

A glance passes between Dave and Mum, intense – some shared meaning I don't understand. And it makes me wonder, because I remember that summer after the party so clearly. I remember a tension between Mum and Dad that was more than simply me and Declan; closer to home than Declan's missing dad. Should I ask straight out if they were having an affair? It's so easy to picture: Mum terrified, Dave her saviour. Carried away by the moment, Dave takes Mum in his arms to comfort and protect her; Dad hears the commotion and comes out. He sees and he knows . . . But he can't do anything because he loves them both, because Dave is his best friend. But it has to go somewhere – that anger, that betrayal, that helplessness . . . And then he sees Arty Robbins, and it's *his* fault, all of it.

'Mum, what did you and Dad do after . . . ? Before you

came home?' I don't take my eyes off Dave. I see the corners of his mouth tighten.

'I honestly don't remember, love,' says Mum. 'I don't think we did anything. Just . . . came home.' She looks around the room as she speaks – anywhere but at me. I feel the lie and the tension between her and Dave; feel the stare he gives while Mum carefully doesn't look at either of us.

'So, you and Dad were together for the whole night?'

Mum shakes her head. 'It's such a long time ago, Nicola. But yes, I think so.'

Yes, it is, but she remembers. I know she does, and I know she's lying. 'So, Dad didn't go out again that night?'

'Honestly, Nicola, I don't remember.'

I feel the walls closing in. I need to get out, but Dave is in my way and I *need* to know. I meet his eye. 'What about you?'

'Me?'

'Declan went back to the Shelley after I came home. Did you see him?'

Dave takes a step back, caught by surprise. 'I . . . I don't think so. I think I spent most of the evening with Anne. She was in a bit of a state.' He shakes his head and glances at Mum. 'Arty was cheating on her. Your mum called him out, right to his face – right in front of her.'

'What?' I don't understand. 'The fight you had, I thought you said it was about Anne. About what—'

Mum lays a hand on mine. 'That's what *you* said. No,

Arthur Robbins was having an affair, if you must know. That's what it was about. I didn't know the rest until later.'

Arty Robbins and Kat's mum . . .

Dave makes a sour face. 'Madge knew about the rest of it, though. Vincent said he'd sort it out, which we all knew meant pretending nothing had happened.' He moves aside to let me pass.

I get as far as the front door and then turn back. 'So, you were in the Shelley all night?'

Dave nods, but he can't look at me as he does so. Lying bastard.

'But you didn't see Declan?'

He shakes his head. 'I really don't remember. I'm sorry.'

I look to Mum. 'And you were here with Dad?'

'Yes, love.' Her face is full of a where-is-this-coming-from concern, but I *know* she's lying, because Dad was wearing his leather jacket that night – the jacket I remember seeing hanging on the coat rack by the front door – which means Dad wasn't with Mum at all, which means that Mum was with Dave; which means they're lying, both of them, even now, even after all this time, and I can't stand it!

'There was mud on Dad's jacket the next morning,' I say.

Mum looks bewildered. Dave looks confused.

'The next morning. When I came downstairs to go to school. His jacket was hanging from the coat rack we used to keep at the bottom of the stairs. There was mud on it.

From the park. If he was with you the whole time, how did it get there?'

'I . . .' Mum shakes her head. 'No, that can't be right. You're confused, Nicola.'

My own mother, gaslighting me. And I'm none the wiser, and I've got nothing left to say.

I leave.

'Wait!' Dave follows me out. 'Nicola, wait. Stop!' My head is full and memories are coming at me from every-where, all out of sequence: me and Declan, that night in the Shelley; Dad and Uncle Dave and Mum in the park together when I was much younger; Dad when I was in my twenties. Everything . . .

I round on him. He's a big man, even if he's old. I suppose he could be frightening if I wasn't so furious. 'What?'

'Your mother's probably forgotten all about this, but . . . she's wrong. We didn't go straight back into the Shelley. We went into the park. To get away. Just for five minutes. You have to understand. She was scared. Anyway, someone must have told your dad something about what happened because he came out looking for your mother and saw us and—' He shakes his head and looks away and shivers. 'We had a bit of a tussle. The mud could have been from that. I remember we both went over, and it had been raining and the path was muddy.'

'A tussle?' I can't imagine Dad in a tussle with *any*one.

'He . . . he got the wrong end of the stick. Thought I was the one who'd hurt Susan. We sorted it out quick enough and then they went home, but . . .'

I look him in the eye. 'Were you and Mum already having an affair before he died?'

'Nicola!' He even has the audacity to look hurt. 'It was just a misunderstanding.'

'You didn't answer my question.'

'He was my friend.'

'I know.'

Dave bows his head and looks away. 'No. We weren't.' But from the way he says it, I know there's something there – something so guilty he can't bring himself to look at me.

I turn away. Do I believe him? I suppose I have to, as far as it goes, but there *was* something between Mum and Uncle Dave that summer. Dad never talked about it, he was too bloody English for that, but you had to be blind and deaf not to see that something broke in our house that night. It seemed obvious – when Dad left for those three nights – that it was Mum and Dave, and that Dad had found them out. And yes, he came back; and he and Dave somehow stayed friends, and things at home almost went back to the way they were but . . . Something had changed, something invisible, intangible, impossible to pin down. Dave had been in and out of our lives for as long as I could remember, and he worked at the Shelley, and so did Mum until she and Vincent had their falling out; and it never *did* make much sense, Mum doing part-time bar work, unless it had been about Dave right from the start – all of it.

My two favourite men. I hear the words. I heard them a hundred times when I was young. I can see them, if I want to: Mum, Dad and Uncle Dave, Mum in the middle, an arm around each of them. Thick as thieves, the three of them.

Whatever makes you happy, sweetheart, as long as he treats you right. I feel as though I could turn round and Dad would be standing there behind me, smiling. Is that what he said to Mum, too? Was that how he made peace with whatever he saw that night?

I'd never let anything break up this family.

I miss him so much.

I turn and walk away. I spend the journey home looping through memories of that summer, looking for answers and finding only questions; and it's only when I'm on my doorstep, thoughts turning back to the present and to Declan, that understanding crashes in.

Either Dave is lying or it couldn't have been Dad in the park an hour later.

So who was it?

11

Friday 7th February 2020

It's 4th August 1985. I'm in my room, thinking about my next secret meeting with Declan. It's almost two months since Arty Robbins vanished. Mum and Dad are in the front garden, weeding the flower beds. My bedroom window is open to the summer breeze and they're right below me. I can hear every word, even though they're being quiet.

'We can't go on like this, Susan, we really can't.'

'I know, love,' says Mum. 'But, Craig . . . it's not what you think.'

'Susan, if you think you made the wrong choice—'

'Oh, for *fuck*'s sake, Craig! It's not *that*! It's . . . it's . . . Fine! You want me to be honest? You just remember you said that.'

I still feel the sense of utter shock. *That* word. From *Mum*! I remember how the rest of that day passed, taut as piano-wire. In the evening, they went out. Dad said they were going to the pictures but Mum came back two hours later on her own and Dad didn't come home at all. I thought that was that: the end of our family. The next three days were like living with an unexploded bomb. Mum barely said a word; when I found the courage to ask, she told me that Dad had to think about some things, and so did she. Four nights later she went out again, something she almost never did on a weekday. She had Dad with her when she came back. They were both half drunk. They practically fell up the stairs and into bed and had noisy sex – now *there's* a memory I wish I could forget – and, after that, everything went back to normal.

Almost to normal.

Do I believe Dave about the fight? Yes, I think I do. About them not having an affair, though . . . No. There's something there. There was something in his face, in the way he couldn't look at me.

'Nicola. Hey! Wakey, wakey!'

I'm at work, and Ed is standing by my desk, and everyone is looking at me.

'You saw the email, right? The Orien Trust people are coming in this afternoon. You *are* ready for them, yes?'

I nod. I'm not sure what time it is. The middle of the

morning? I don't remember what I've done since I sat down at nine o'clock. No, that's wrong, of course. I *do* remember. I've done nothing except stare blankly at my screen as I rake through the past.

'They were happy enough to reschedule under the circumstances.' He frowns, looking at my screen and not at me. 'Actually, can we have a chat in my office?'

'Yes. If . . . Why?'

'I just want you to run through what you've got.'

I follow Ed back to his office, which isn't really an office but a poorly partitioned corner of our tiny open-plan workspace. I remember how it was when I first came to work here and it hasn't changed at all. The desks, the chairs – none of it. We've had our work stations refreshed and a few of the lights have been replaced; other than that, it's exactly as it was ten years ago. I like the stasis. The timelessness of this place.

'Sit down.' Ed points to a chair. I do as I'm told, thinking of the day he first took over. That's the one thing that *has* changed. Ed joined us six years ago, taking over from old Trevor Arnold, who must have been nearly seventy and had put off retiring for as long as he possibly could and spent all day, every day, sitting at his desk reading history books. I remember we bought him signed copies of *Wolf Hall* and *Bring Up the Bodies*, which we all thought he'd like but which instead launched him into a thirty-minute diatribe on how the real Thomas Cromwell wasn't the way Mantel had portrayed him at all and the only decent thing she'd written was *The Assassination of Margaret Thatcher*. He got into a huge argument with Rose Wilkes about it; she told me later that Trevor was bitter because he'd written a historical novel of his own once and no one had bought it—

'Nicola? Nicola!'

Shit! Ed is talking to me and I've got no idea what he just said. 'Sorry?'

'Are you OK?'

'Yes. I'm fine.'

'You zoned out. Am I boring you?'

'I . . .' I don't know. *Is* he boring me? I don't know what he said. 'I'm sorry. I'm a bit distracted at the moment.' I could tell him about Declan's dad, about Declan being arrested for murder, but if I do that, he'll tell the others and it's all I'll hear for months. It won't ever go away because it can't, and this place where I work won't be safe from the memories. I don't want that. I force a smile. 'Still recovering from yesterday, I think.'

Ed gets me to run through the presentation I'm supposed to give this afternoon. I don't know who the Orien Trust are or what they're trying to do; all I know is that they want information on the expansion of the London sewer system throughout the twentieth century. I have it all in my head and I can talk until there's nothing left to say, but apparently that's not good enough.

'It's not exactly a presentation, is it?' Ed looks baffled. 'I know you were off sick yesterday, but still . . .'

Ed's idea of a presentation is a stack of PowerPoint slides. I've known this for exactly five years and eleven months.

'I'll get one ready for this afternoon,' I say.

Back at my desk, I stare at my screen and try to concentrate, but all I can think of is what Dave said, and of Mum, and of the mud on Dad's jacket, and how they're lying to me and how I'll never know the truth.

We can't go on like this, Susan, we really can't!

I slide out of that into a different memory: the first time I brought Declan back home, around six weeks before Arty Robbins disappeared. Mum knew him, obviously, because he'd lived across the road for years. I think she knew we were going out from the moment she saw us together, but she didn't say anything. She let us go up to my room together and left us alone, and then a little later she came knocking on the door, very careful, doing what Dad used to do and not coming in until she was invited, asking if we wanted something to eat or drink. She seemed almost happy about the two of us being together.

I sit at my desk and go through every moment Mum saw us, every conversation we had. She liked Declan right up until that night. And then she hated him, and I never understood why or what he'd done, but what if it wasn't because of something *he* did? What if it was because of his dad? What if it was because of what Arty Robbins did to Mum and to his wife, and to everyone around him?

Like father, like son. Was that it? Was *that* why she hated him?

When Ed comes to see how I'm doing just before lunch, I haven't made any progress. He sits at my desk for the next hour and I'm like a walking, talking Wikipedia, telling him the information he needs while he's the one putting together the slides. He wants lots of pictures, because everyone likes to have pictures, which means going through the newspaper microfiche archives that haven't been made digital yet, which always feels to me like going through the negatives of an old set of photographs. When Zoe, Adam and Kris from the Orien Trust arrive in their expensive suits, we do the presentation together, Ed running through the slides while I stand there, lost in memories of 1985, every now and then jerking back to the present to regurgitate some facts and figures. At the end, I hand out the information packs I made last week. They seem pleased as they leave.

'Whatever's going on with you, you need to sort it out,' says Ed after they're gone. 'You're no use like this.'

No use like this? Don't I know it. I've been here before. With Declan, towards the end. I was no use to *him* like that either, as it turned out.

I push a hand into my jacket pocket as I head home,

fishing for that ragged half-pack of cigarettes. That's when I discover I have Declan's picture of Vincent and Arty Robbins still in my coat pocket, and that's when I have a bit of a brainwave. In a way, I have Ed to thank.

The police may have Chloe's photographs but I bet they don't have the negatives.

12

Saturday 8th February 2020

I feel sort of stupid, heading back to Byron Road. I don't want Mum to see me heading next door, so I walk up Keats Row instead and come back from the other end of the street, all so I don't have to pass our front window. I stand on the doorstep of Kat's mum's house, hand poised to ring the bell. I don't know why I'm so nervous, but I am. A part of me is locked in a memory. It's the summer of 1989. I'm at home on summer break and I'm sitting with Kat in her front room. Kat has a job in London now, working for *Private Eye* magazine, of all things, which is great because she's an absolute mine of stories and I love listening to her. She's telling me how there's a rumour the magazine might start its own TV show next year – some satirical news programme, which could be really amazing – when the doorbell rings and I see the look in her eye, like she knows what's coming. She jumps up and runs to open it and there stands Declan, and I can't make sense of it, because Declan works in Nottingham and told me he couldn't make it back this weekend because of some work he had to do; and yet here he is, and he's dressed in a morning suit and carrying a huge bunch of flowers, which he hands to Kat, and right then and there in the hall he gets down on one knee.

'Nicola Walker, will you marry me?' he says.

And I remember lying in bed all those months ago, pretending to be asleep. *I might just have to ask you to marry me, Nicola Walker.*

I almost have to force my way back to the present. I'm standing before Kat's old front door. I have no idea how long I've been here.

I ring the bell and—

SNAP! I'm six years old, sitting at the dinner table, boiled egg with little toast soldiers to dip into the yolk, for tea. The doorbell rings. Uncle Dave has come to visit, and I'm happy because Uncle Dave makes Mum and Dad happy too. He's funny and we play games while Mum clears up. Later, he sits on the edge of my bed while Mum reads a story. I go to sleep but then I wake up again because I can hear Mum in the kitchen and she's crying. I get out of bed and pad down the stairs. Mum is in the kitchen and Dave is holding her tight and she's shivering with tears. When they see me, Mum beckons me to join them and so I do, the three of us all hugging each other.

'I'm a bit sad, little mouse,' said Mum. 'About Grandpa.'

Grandpa was poorly and it seemed right for Mum to be sad about that; and right that Uncle Dave should give her a hug, because hugs help people to feel better. Even with adult eyes looking back at what a six-year-old saw, maybe it didn't mean much. They weren't kissing. They didn't spring apart with guilt or shame. Mum was upset, that was all, and Dave was a friend. But it's the sum of those small things over years and years that tells me it was more.

If there's one person who knows the truth about what happened at the Shelley that night in 1985 – one person who isn't Mum or David – it's Chloe Clarke.

The door opens. 'Hello?' It takes a moment, and then a smile of recognition spreads over Kat's mum's face. 'Nicola Walker!'

That's the difference between a place like Wordsworth Park and where I live now. When I grew up here, everyone knew their neighbours; and even now, decades later, we greet each other with smiles and cups of tea. I've lived in Farringdon for years and I don't think a single one of my neighbours even knows my name.

'Hello, Mrs Clarke.' Thirty years of being an adult and I still call her that, out of habit.

'Come in.' She steps back and closes the door behind me. 'Can I get you something? A cup of tea?'

'I don't want to impose,' I say, knowing it won't make any difference. 'I'm on my way to see Mum, so . . .' I feel stupid, lying like that. But what else am I supposed to say?

Mrs Clarke ushers me into the lounge, which in this house is the back room, not the front, which means I can see into our back garden and the conservatory that Dave built while I was in America. I can't help but stare. It seems alien. I have so many memories of looking out from these windows with Kat, years before it was there.

'Susan said you came up only a couple of days ago,' calls Mrs Clarke from the kitchen. 'Asking questions about Arty Robbins. Is that what this is about? She misses you, you know. You really should try and visit her more often. Milk and sugar?'

She comes back with the tea I don't really want, asks what I'm doing with myself, then asks after Kat and Gary – the same questions she used to ask when Kat and I were in our twenties and she was desperate to know what was going on in her daughter's life because Kat wouldn't tell her. It's a mum-thing, I think. I tell her that Gary might be about to buy a flat in Canary Wharf. Kat's mum chuckles.

'Katherine did all right for herself with that one, didn't she? You wouldn't have thought it back then, would you?'

I have to smile. 'No, you wouldn't.'

'Oh, I couldn't *stand* him at first.' She gives me a shrewd look. 'I wasn't the only one, either, I think.'

I never understood why, but Kat's mum actually *likes* Gary now. Sure, he doesn't prance around in that stupid coat any more, but he's still the same Gary underneath.

'Susan tells me the police arrested Declan,' she says. 'That's why you're here, isn't it?'

'He didn't do it,' I say.

'I remember you two at the Shelley. I took a picture of you with Kat. And then you all . . .' She raises an eyebrow. 'Disappeared.'

I lean forward and rest my hand on hers. 'He was with me, Mrs Clarke.'

'And you were both with my Katherine in the park for half the night, if I remember it right, the three of you looking at the stars and talking about the meaning of life,' she scoffs. 'I remember *that*! Like butter wouldn't melt in your mouth, you two, and what a right pair of liars you were. Teenagers. You always forget that *we* were that age once. Kat got the rocket of a lifetime, I can tell you. I imagine you got one from your mother, too.' She almost laughs; distant memories that seemed so desperate at the time but now so utterly trivial. 'Still, you both turned out all right, I suppose.'

'A slap in the cereal bowl actually,' I say, but Mrs Clarke only looks confused, so I guess Mum never talked about that. 'You remember that night then?'

Mrs Clarke makes a face. 'Only bits and pieces, I'm afraid.'

'I wondered if you could tell me about Arty Robbins and what happened in the Shelley? I left with Declan after the speeches.'

Mrs Clarke shakes her head, and I can't tell if there's anything more to the name *Arty Robbins* than a distant haze of memory. If I'm right, they were having an affair before he disappeared, and maybe that was what Mum threw at Arty at the party that night, although Mrs Clarke never seemed more bothered than anyone else when he vanished. I suppose she didn't know the *real* Arty Robbins any more than the rest of us did – not until after he was gone.

'Mum says Arty attacked her.'

'Oh yes, well, we all heard about *that*. Your dad was fuming. David overheard it all through an open window and had to rush outside before—'

'Before . . . ?'

'You should ask David, love, not me. He was the one who saw it. He was even more worked up about it than your dad, I think. They were very close back then, all three of them.'

'Afterwards . . . did you see Arty?'

She nods. 'I took a picture of him with Vincent.' She shakes her head. 'I don't think I saw him again after that. But, Nicky, I've already been through it all with the police. I've told them everything I remember.'

'Mrs Clarke, do you know where Mum and Dave went, after it happened?'

'You know you're not fourteen any more. You can call me Chloe.'

'Chloe.' I force a smile. 'Sorry. Old habits. So, did you see Mum and Dave?'

Mrs Clarke shifts a little. 'All I really remember is having to run the place on my own for half the night. It got a bit frantic.'

'What about Declan? Did you see him after he came back? It would be a little after midnight. Mrs Clarke, it's really important.'

Her face scrunches up with the effort of trying to remember. 'No, love. But I'm afraid that doesn't mean very much. I don't really remember anyone in particular.'

'You said you were taking photographs. Official birthday photographer, wasn't it?'

She smiles and nods.

'I was wondering, did you have any photos from later? From after midnight? Ones that might show who was still there?'

'I don't know. The police took all—'

'I know. Mum said. But' – and this is why I came back, because Mrs Clarke was never one to throw things away – 'I was wondering, did you keep the negatives?'

'I . . .'

'Did the police take them?'

'Oh.' A strange look flits across her face. 'No. I didn't think . . .'

'So you *do* still have them?'

'I suppose. Yes, I suppose I do.'

Mentally, I whoop and punch the air. 'Could you check? And could I see them, please?'

Mrs Clarke lifts herself from the sofa. I remember her so much younger, Kat's mum, full of energy. She's not even twenty years older than me and yet she seems as fragile as a shadow. Is this what I have waiting for me, when I grow old? I suppose it is. I thought I was OK with that but now I'm not so sure.

She leaves the lounge and I hear her upstairs, rummaging in Kat's old bedroom. I've been in this room so many times. The earliest I can remember, I must have been five, I think. It does blur a little, going back that far. But, yes, five. It all seemed so big and strange and different and a bit frightening. I remember the smell, how strange it was, not like home at all. It smelled of other people, not *my* people. Mum gave me a book to read while she and Dad talked to Mrs Clarke. I remember Mum and Dad sitting on the sofa next to each other. I remember how they were constantly in contact, touching each other, little gestures of affection.

Mrs Clarke comes back. She puts a shoebox on the table. 'It's all here.' Inside are dozens of envelopes, dated and

labelled. I catch a few words: *Kat's graduation, July 1991.*
Brittany, summer 1982. I remember that Brittany trip. Kat
came back so brown that I thought she must have gone to
Egypt or India or something. It was her last holiday before
her dad left.

She passes me an envelope labelled *Arthur Robbins' fifti-*
eth, June 1985. There are four packets of negatives inside.

'Do you mind if I take these? I'll bring them right back. I
just want some copies of my own.'

'Oh.' She looks surprised and not at all keen. 'Can you
still do that? Isn't everything pixels these days?'

'Boots will do it!' At least I *think* they will.

'I should really give them to the police, don't you think?'

'I can do that for you if you like,' I say. 'I've got to talk to
them again anyway.'

She holds the envelope, weighing up a choice I don't quite
understand, and I have a sense that I'm seeing who she really
is for the very first time; not *Mrs Clarke* or *Kat's mum*, but a
person who existed before Kat or I was ever born. I see the
way her nervous eyes cling to the envelope of negatives and
wonder how many of those dreams survived. I know she
was seventeen when she had Kat. I know Kat never met her
real father, Daniel Robbins, and that the man Kat called
'Dad' walked out when she was fourteen. I never thought
about it when I was young, but it strikes me how they never
had any children of their own. I wonder whose choice that

was and I want to ask, but it's not my business, and Mum always taught me it was rude to pry.

I think I understand why she hesitates. The past is important to Chloe Clarke. Maybe more so than the present. Something we have in common.

'I'll make a second set for you, too,' I say. 'Then you don't have to worry about getting the others back. And I promise I'll look after them.'

'It's just . . .'

'I know. They're what you have left of people.'

Her anxiety dissolves into gratitude. 'You're an angel.' She hands me the envelope and reaches for her handbag. 'I'll pay for them, of course.'

'Don't be silly!' I stuff the envelope into my bag and look at her and smile. 'I'll take care of them. I promise.'

Her eyes glisten. 'Kat says you remember everything. Is that right? Like you have a photograph of every moment in your head?'

'That's not a bad way of putting it. Unfortunately including all the things I'd rather forget.' I see, from the way her eyes dart, that she's got a few of those moments too. Then her look settles back on the envelope in my hand and I see the question she wants to ask, even before the words come out.

'Nicky, if you're carrying around a set of photographs in your head, why do you need mine?'

'I wasn't in the Shelley for long that night,' I say. 'I

remember what I saw but . . . it's not enough. I know Declan didn't kill his dad. I *know* it, but I need to see more if I'm going to prove it's the truth. I need another . . . point of view. Mrs Clarke – Chloe – were you at the Shelley for the whole time that night?'

'From start to finish, yes.'

'And you didn't see anything? Anything that seemed . . . unusual? About Arty?'

She shakes her head. 'Only what you already know: that row he had with Susan. I'd think that was quite enough, wouldn't you? As far as I remember, he left quite soon after. I don't think I saw him again at all.'

'Mum said he was having an affair.' I watch closely, but Chloe Clarke doesn't bat an eyelid.

'I can't say I'm surprised.'

'I need to ask you about . . . something else. About Mum and Dave. Was there something going on between them back then?'

Her guard snaps up. She looks away, which seems an answer all on its own. I'm about to thank her for the tea and leave, but then she looks back at me.

'I don't . . . think so.'

Her words are slow and careful. I wait. Sometimes a silence is all you need.

'Nicola, you *did* know that David and your mother were together before your dad came on the scene?'

I blink. 'No!' Not just didn't know; I never had the first suspicion.

'She told me the story, once. Your dad was David's friend, and he whisked Susan off her feet and that was that, but . . . They were always close, all three of them, so I suppose I could be wrong, but no, I don't think so.' She licks her lips. 'I know things were tense between your mum and dad that summer. Mr Robbins disappearing like that, it . . . rubbed everyone up the wrong way, but honestly? If something had happened between your mum and David, I think I'd know.' She smiles and I see a hint of the mischief I remember: the Mrs Clarke of thirty-five years ago. 'Susan was always far too clever to give anything away, but David . . . He was never very good at keeping secrets, bless him.'

Mr Robbins? Not Arty? It seems oddly formal between two people having an affair.

'I . . . I need to ask you something else. Something . . . I'm sorry. It's a bit rude of me, really.' But I saw Arty Robbins sneaking out of Kat's mum's house. I *saw* it and I heard what he said. Is it possible to be in love with a monster and not see him for what he is? Maybe it is. They say love makes you blind, after all. 'Are you sure you didn't see Arty Robbins again that night – after the thing with Mum?'

Chloe shakes her head. 'After I took that picture of him with Vincent? No. At least, if I did, I don't remember.'

'Didn't it seem strange that he'd just leave? Without saying anything to you?'

'Why would he say anything to *me*?'

'Weren't you and Arty Robbins . . . ?' I leave the question hanging.

'I'm sorry?'

'Back then, I sort of thought . . . you and Dec's dad were – well, I thought there was something going on between you. If you know what I mean.'

She gawps at me. From the shock on her face, I might as well have called her a Nazi. 'Good heavens! Where on *earth* did you get that idea?'

But why else was he sneaking around the back of her house? I heard him. I *saw* him.

'You didn't see him the night before the party?'

'Well, I *suppose* he might have come into the Shelley.'

'Not at the Shelley. Here.'

'*Here?*' Mrs Clarke raises her eyebrows so high they almost fall off her head. 'Love, it was a long time ago and I don't really remember, but you're talking about a Saturday night, so I'm sure I would have been working. We had the party to get ready for, as well as the regular crowd.'

'It doesn't matter. Really.'

Mrs Clarke either doesn't hear or doesn't listen. She gets up and leaves the lounge, and I hear her creak up the stairs back into Kat's old room. I feel stupid for bringing up this poor woman's past. I wanted to ask about Mum and Dave, about Declan, about the photos, that's all.

There they are, right in front of me. Another set of photographs. *Nicky and Dec wedding*. I should know better but I can't help myself. I take the packet and open it and look inside. There are no pictures, only the negatives, but it doesn't make any difference: she gave the pictures to Declan afterwards and we looked through them together, so now they're all in my head. I see him. I see *us*. We look so radiant. So young and so happy—

Mrs Clarke comes back with another dusty shoebox. She opens it and pulls out an old diary from 1985. For all I know, Arty Robbins treated her as badly as he treated everyone else; but I see from her face that she's determined to prove her memory is as good as mine.

'I kept diaries after Stephen walked out so I didn't end up promising to do an early shift when it was parents' evening or a school play, or things like that. It was so complicated, suddenly doing everything on my own. There you go.' She thrusts the diary at me, open at the page for Saturday 8th June.

Shelley 3–12. Party prep!

'I had a shift at the Shelley from three in the afternoon until midnight.'

I scan the page. She was at the Shelley every night that week except the Tuesday.

'Sorry,' I say. 'My mistake.' I should leave this. It's not why I'm here. Maybe she had a last-minute change of shifts that night, or maybe she skipped out for a bit. It's not exactly far from here to the Shelley. But . . . why would she hide it, after all these years?

Chloe puts the diary down and takes my empty teacup. 'Do you want another one?'

'Yes . . . yes, please.'

She goes and then calls out from the kitchen, 'I know you girls all thought I was some sort of party animal, but really? Me and Arthur Robbins? *One* Robbins was quite enough, thank you, and Arty was a married man! And Vincent . . . can you imagine? The Shelley was all I had, and I'd spent quite enough time living off benefits and the kindness of strangers. I didn't much like Arty, to be honest. I suppose I shouldn't say that, but after the way his brother never even acknowledged that Kat was his daughter . . . Poor Vincent. *He* wasn't so bad, not really. I think it broke him when Arty disappeared.'

But I *know* I heard Arthur Robbins talking to someone at the back door of this house on the Saturday night before the party. I *know* I saw him from the bathroom window the week before, and the week before that, coming up from the alley, all furtive and in a hurry. I *know* I heard someone let him in. I remember all these things with the same perfect clarity as I remember everything in between and everything since.

The truth hits me like a thunderclap.

I skim through Chloe Clarke's diary. Three visits. Three dates. And on all three of them, Kat's mum's diary says she was working. But if it wasn't Kat's mum letting Arty in . . .

Kat.

Jesus Christ! Kat and Arty Robbins.

I don't wait for Chloe Clarke to come back. I can't. I run outside and stab a number into my phone, hopping from one foot to the other until a voice at the other end picks up.

'Hello?'

'I need to talk to you.'

13

Monday 10th June 1985

I sit through assembly, impatient for the day to finish. My morning exam is geography and so I stare at the page, trying to make myself think about the water cycle and mountains and rivers and the effects of glaciation, but all I can think about is seeing Dec after school and whether I'm the only girl in my year who isn't a virgin or whether I'm the last to lose it. I know it's all completely stupid even as I'm thinking it, but that doesn't stop it from happening. Ann Cox reckons she's done it with Mark Clatcher in the second-year sixth, which is rubbish, but Alice Cook and Tracy Watson have been going steady with boys from the sixth form for months; and after this morning, I'm pretty sure that Kat's already done it, too.

Am I the last? I can't be, but who even *cares*. And oh my God, Nicky Walker, *concentrate*!

I do the question on map-reading, which is easy because all you have to do is remember what the symbols mean. Then straight back to last night with Dec, and then this morning with Mum in the kitchen; and then back to the policeman at our house, and what on earth happened at the Shelley last night?

'Fifteen minutes.' Mr Houghton prowls between the desks like a hungry panther, scowling eyes roving for people with tiny secret diagrams of the nitrogen cycle drawn on the palm of their hands like they're members of some secret geography society, even though that would be about the lamest secret society ever. Thinking about last night somehow spirals into a fantasy of Dec coming to live with us, which is completely preposterous because the only way that would ever happen is if Mum got hit by a bus and Dad spontaneously exploded . . .

A glance at the paper in front of me reminds me that the only people I ought to be thinking about are the children Bob Geldof is trying to save with his Band Aid thing, all over the news and dying of starvation because of desertification; and that *I'll* be the one who's dead if I don't get at least a B in this exam. Or grounded, which is as close to dead as makes no difference. I draw a labelled diagram of the water cycle exactly as Mrs Spare drew it on the blackboard eight months ago. I don't have to think about it really; the diagram is there in my head like I'm back in the classroom, complete with its soundtrack of Giles Friedrich, the biggest jerk in our year, whispering to Gordon Wills, who back then I quite fancied. I can only make out half of what they're saying but I hear Katie Spencer's name, which makes it immediately far more interesting than whatever Mrs Spare has to offer about the formation of clouds.

'You have five minutes.'

I force myself to focus and write out Mrs Spare's summary of the effects of desertification from memory, word-for-word, and wonder if anyone will notice. Probably not. I suppose if anyone thinks I cheated then I'll just do it again, right there in front of them, and prove that I wasn't.

The buzzer sounds. Mr Houghton collects our papers. After lunch is double history, aka double revision, aka double staring into space. I'm thinking of Dec, and I have that butterflies-in-the-stomach feeling of excitement and trepidation and a sort of hunger – the one that comes when you're nerving yourself for something really scary. It feels like the time Kat and I went up onto the top diving board at the swimming pool because Kat's friend Liz, who can do somersaults and stuff and still hit the water straight, said it wasn't nearly as bad as it looked; so we went up and discovered that Liz was right, it wasn't as bad, it was actually a lot, lot *worse* and from the top it looked like we were about a *mile* above the water. That's the feeling I have, thinking about seeing Dec after school.

I head right out when the bell goes, skipping detention. I'll go and see Mr Wallace first thing tomorrow morning and be all contrite, and I'll get away with it because I'm one of the 'good' girls who does well in her exams. I'll get an extra detention but I don't mind. Dec's waiting for me. His face breaks into a huge grin as soon as he sees me and, the next thing I know, I'm kissing him. I hear whistles and hoots and I know everyone is staring and I don't care . . .

'I love you, Nicky Walker,' he says when we come up for air.

I drink him in like he's a cold glass of lemonade on a hot summer's day. I can't stop thinking about last night. I feel unstoppable, like I can do anything.

Over his shoulder, I see Kat coming towards me.

'You can walk with us if you like,' I say as she arrives, disentangling myself from Dec.

She shakes her head and nudges me. 'I'll see you tomorrow,' and then she pokes Dec gently in the ribs. 'And, Dec, if you're going to take her home again, better check under the bed first, next time.'

She heads away and we watch her go, too shocked to speak.

'You bloody told her!' Dec's all horror on the surface but I feel something else underneath. Pride, is it? Anticipation?

Or is it straight-up lust? I think it's all of them, and I love him so much I might burst.

We cross the park and I tell him about the policeman in the lounge when I got home, and he tells me how he and his mum stayed at the Shelley last night.

'Sort of wish I'd stayed at home,' he says. 'I don't know *what* happened last night after we left but *some*thing did. Some big bust-up. You saw what Dad was like. Anyway, that policeman of yours was at the Shelley, too. Apparently. I mean, he was gone before I got back there, but that's what I heard. Something about a fight, I think. Mum was a mess.' He takes a deep breath and then lets out a long, heavy sigh. 'You see why I just want to get away from this place?'

After what I saw last night, he really doesn't need to say more. I remember the bruise on his mum's face when I knocked on the door yesterday and she hadn't had time to hide it under her make-up. And it's hard not to tell Dec what I know, but I made a promise to Kat last night never to say a word about Arty Robbins and Kat's mum.

'Was she . . . ? Did he . . . ?'

'Did he hit her again? Is that what you mean?' Dec turns to look me squarely in the face and I can't help staring at his black eye and his swollen nose and the bruises on his cheek and his busted lip. 'No.' He shrugs. 'Got it out of his system on me this time.'

I shiver. What I saw last night – I would never have imagined it.

'What . . . what's going to happen now?' What's going to happen to *us* is what I mean. Is Dec going to move away, like he said?

'Don't know. Dad didn't come home last night. Got the house to ourselves, if we want it.' He smiles, only half serious.

'What if your dad comes back while we're there?'

'Your place then?'

I make a strangled-badger noise. I should probably tell him how Mum has guessed about us having sex, so there's a good chance she's hired an international hit man or something. 'Best not. Mum went mental this morning about me getting back so late. Also, she thinks I'm in detention.'

'All right,' he says, as we reach the Shelley. 'Stay here. I'll be back in five minutes.'

I wait by the road, knots and clusters of other pupils from the school drifting past in shoals as they cross the park. I look for Kat. I don't see her at first; but then I do, not on the path through the park but a little further down the road by the entrance to the Secret Car Park. I don't know how she got there without me seeing but there she is, and she's with Gary – I know it's him because of the coat – and I can tell they're arguing because I've seen Kat angry plenty of times and she gets so animated, with her hands waving all over the place. I'm about to go and see if she needs help, but before I can move, she's turned away and is heading across the park towards home. Gary doesn't follow, so I decide she's OK.

Five minutes later, Dec pulls up next to me in the lime-green Ford Capri that his dad bought for him on his eighteenth birthday. He winds down the window and wiggles his eyebrows.

'Want to go for a ride?'

Teenagers have sex in the backs of cars all the time, if you believe the movies. It doesn't look very comfortable, so I'm a bit nervous when I get in, but he doesn't try anything. When I sit beside him, I feel happy and safe.

'Where are we going?' I ask. Not that I particularly care.

'Anywhere, as long as it's away from here.'

Ten minutes later we're heading out of London. I ask him again where we're going and, if we're running away together, could I at least pack some clean underwear first, and he laughs: no, nice thought, but we're not running away, not yet, but there's this place he wants me to see, and does it matter if I'm home late? He fishes out some cassettes from the glove box and we listen to Tears for Fears' *Songs from the Big Chair* album, and he tells me that even if I *think* I don't like it, I have to listen to the whole thing anyway because he thinks it's the best album ever; and of course it isn't, but it *is* better than I thought. I even like some of it, although I make sure that all Dec sees is me making faces like I'm dying.

A few songs later and the world outside is green and full of trees and fields. I wind the window down and lean my head against the door and let the air rush into my face. I don't know where we're going and I don't care. We pass through a village with a quaint name and an old Tudor pub and thatched-roof cottages, and it feels like the first time I've ever properly been away from home on my own.

Dec stops before the album finishes. I have no idea where we are except that we're not in London any more. He buys us each a can of Coke and comes back and asks if I'm OK, because we both know that I'm not, and neither is he.

'Sometimes I think about going to Europe,' he says. 'Go to Italy maybe. Or Spain or Greece. We could get one of those Interrailing cards and head for somewhere warm and sunny, and we could sleep under the stars.'

I laugh. 'The furthest we've ever been on holiday is bloody Bournemouth.' Europe sounds great. Romantic.

We drive for another few minutes and then Dec stops again, this time in a lay-by in the middle of nowhere. A public footpath sign at the edge of the road points across a field to some woods. He gets out of the car and beckons me to follow.

'I want to show you something.'

The sun comes out as we walk together. The air under

the trees is still. It's so peaceful. My hand brushes his. Not deliberately. We flinch away and then reach for each other, fingers lacing together. We reach a clearing beside a river, with an old weathered picnic table and a tyre on a rope hanging from a branch over the water. We bask in the sun and neither of us speaks, and it's a perfect silence because we're both here, the light streaming down, dappled shadows of leaves and branches dancing on rippling water.

'Thank you for this,' I say at last.

'Thank you for . . . for being you,' says Dec.

My head is full of crazy thoughts. I want to reach across the old wood of the table and take his hand and kiss him and never mind where we are – nothing matters except that we're together. I don't want to lose this feeling. I don't quite understand but it's beautiful and it's precious. Is this love? I think it must be, but I was already in love with him last night and this feels even bigger and brighter.

'Mum's really going to do it,' he says. 'She told me this morning. We're going to move out and stay with Aunt Eileen in Clapham. It's all over.'

I lean into him and pull him close. 'It's not your fault.'

'Everyone thinks Dad's so great.' He shakes his head. 'But you know, I'm sort of glad.'

'It's *not* your fault,' I say again. It's what I know he needs to hear because it's what *I* need to hear. I have no idea, really. It must be *someone's* fault, right?

'You sure about that? Because apparently everything that went wrong in Dad's life *was* my fault. He told me that when I was twelve. My fault for being born and screwing everything up. Said my uncle had it right, leaving Kat's mum the way he did. Said he should have done the same – how he regretted it every day that he didn't.'

'Well . . . fuck him,' I say, surprised at myself.

Dec looks at me in shock. 'What?'

'We deserve better. Both of us. Kat, too. So yeah, *fuck* him! Fuck both of them.'

The tragedy melts off Dec's face. He starts to laugh and so do I, harder and harder, until we're both clinging to each other, tears in our eyes, and I'm not sure whether I'm laughing or crying and I'm not sure about Dec, either.

'You know, you're really sexy when you're angry.' He takes a step back, goes to the tyre swing and grabs the rope dangling from under it. 'We used to come here when I was a kid. I'd always end up soaked.' He grabs hold, teetering for balance, gets one foot inside the tyre and then swings out over the river. I'm sure he's going to fall, but instead he hoists himself up and waves his arms, gripping the tyre between his knees as he arcs back towards the bank. Now I know he's just showing off . . .

'Easy!'

I watch as he swings and I start to laugh. 'How do you get off?'

He laughs back and leers. 'Give us a tug, love?'

I go over and pick up the rope he used to pull the tyre to the bank. It's wet and rough and slimy and horrible. I pull as hard as I can, dragging Dec back to the shore. I feel my feet about to slip. Any minute now, I'm going to go over on my backside, and either I'm going to let go or we're both going into the water – and that is *not* happening, not in my school clothes!

'Come on, Nix!' He's laughing at me. *'Pull!'*

I lean back and heave, knees bent, heels dug in, remembering a sports-day tug-of-war from when I was seven, Mr Lambert yelling at us like it was the Battle of Iwo Jima. *Come on, girls! Dig your heels in! Get your weight behind it. Bend those knees and pull!* I grit my teeth and then the rope kicks in my hand, pinging free as Dec jumps and flies straight into me and we both go over in a tangle of arms and legs, and about the best that can be said is that at least he doesn't land on top of me. He's laughing and laughing, enough for both of us, which is just as well because I've landed on a root or something, which means I'm going to have a massive bruise tomorrow, and my hands hurt; and I've got mud all over my blazer, and I really ought to be angry with him, furious, and I want to be, but also I want to kiss him . . .

'You're mad,' I tell him.

He staggers up and offers me a hand. I take it and pull hard, enough that he loses his balance and falls on top of me. And I can feel him, the weight of him, the warmth of him, pressing me down from my knees to my chest, and I can see the shock in his face and the desire, too. His eyes are wide like they were last night, and I'm still furious, but there's something else – a voice in the back of my head that doesn't want him to get off.

'Move, you oaf!' I snap.

He gets up, still laughing. This time I let him help me to my feet. 'You OK?'

'I'm fine.' I *really* want to kiss him. 'But *you're* a bloody idiot.'

Dec nods to the tyre. 'Want a go?'

'What, so you can drop me in the bloody river?' Why am I even thinking about it? I tell him again that he's an idiot, and he grins and shrugs and says yes, he *is* that, but I should let myself go a little, and he really, *really* won't let me fall into the water. I point out that I did a fair bit of letting myself go only last night, if he happens to remember back that far; and who says I *want* to let myself go? And then somehow my blazer is on the table and he's holding the tyre in place and I'm trying to climb onto it, and I've probably put enough ladders in my tights to equip a legion of window cleaners, but like they say on *Mastermind*, I've started so I'm going to finish.

'Stop looking up my skirt!' I try to get one leg around the top of the tyre.

Declan laughs and doesn't look away. 'You're gorgeous, you know that?'

Another pang in my belly. I get one leg over the top and lever myself up, and the rope's pushing my skirt up round my bloody knickers. I squash it down. Why am I doing this? 'If I end up in the water,' I tell him, 'I will bloody well murder you. You and your bloody Capri, too.'

Dec makes like I've shot him, staggers like he's mortally wounded and lets go of the rope, and suddenly I'm swinging out across the water, and it's a lot further and a lot faster and a lot higher than it looked; and there's a noise something between a squeal and a scream that turns out to be me clinging to the rope like it's the only thing saving me from a pit full of angry alligators . . . but I don't tip over and I don't slide and I'm not about to crash into the river and die, and my heart is pounding and I can't remember the last time I ever felt so alive and . . .

'I am going to kill you,' I shout. But I'm not, because Dec's grinning like a clown, and he's not laughing *at* me, he's laughing because I can't hide that I'm loving this. He's laughing because he *sees* me – the *real* me – and because that's what makes him happy; and when he reels me back to the river bank and I have to jump free, he catches me and we stagger back, locked together, and I have his face in my hands and I'm kissing him and kissing him, and I don't stop him as his hands slide up under my blouse, because I love him, I love him *so* much.

It's almost dark when we get back to Byron Road. My

hair's all messed up and there's mud all over my clothes but my heart is singing. Mum's not simply going to murder me, it's going to be murder squared; but she'll murder me a little less if I sneak in and clean myself up before she realises I'm back, so I have Dec drop me on Shelley Street and use the alley to sneak into the back garden. The kitchen door is locked like it always is, but Mum keeps a spare key hidden under a flowerpot behind the garage. The dining room and the back bedroom are dark, which probably means that Mum and Dad are in the lounge watching telly, so maybe all I have to do is let myself in and avoid the creaky boards as I creep up the stairs . . .

I hear them as soon as I crack open the door. They're in the lounge but the telly isn't on. They're not exactly shouting at each other, but I can tell straight away that it's another argument. Dad sounds exasperated: 'That's exactly the opposite of what you said at the weekend!'

'I know what I said, but . . . Look, I really don't know what the right thing is here any more and I still think we can't ignore it. I'm just saying that we shouldn't turn people's lives upside down without—'

'So now she *is* old enough to make her own decisions. Is that what you're saying?'

Oh my God! They're talking about *me* again. They're talking about me and Dec, because Mum's worked out that Dec and I are having sex.

'No, she *isn't*. That's exactly my point! But, Craig . . .' I hear Mum sigh. 'You're right: it's her life that's going to get ruined, too. There's no getting away from that. Old enough or not, it has to be her decision.'

I close the door and slip back outside. I'm sixteen. *Sixteen!* It makes me so angry, because I know they'll never stop thinking I'm a child, even when I'm a hundred. I want to run inside and shout at them: *We used a condom, OK? Is* that *what you want to hear? We're not stupid!*

All I want to do is run. I go back to the end of the alley in case Dec is still there, but he isn't. I sit at the end of the garden for a bit, wondering what to do. When I finally go inside, Dad's in the lounge watching telly and there's no sign of Mum, so I guess she's gone out. I creep upstairs and change into my pyjamas and stuff my dirty school clothes under the bed. Then I sit in the gloom, not bothering with the light, waiting for Dad to notice I'm home or for Mum to come back from wherever she's gone – for one of them to tell me that I'm grounded for the rest of my life and I'll never see Dec again, because did you know that his parents are separating and he's moving to Clapham with his mum; and, by the way, *we're* breaking up, too, and your dad's going to keep the house, but *we're* moving to Mongolia: won't that be fun?

I go to close the curtains and see the light on in Dec's room. He's at the window. My heart jumps. Is he looking at me? I can't tell. I lift my hand and wave but he doesn't wave back, and then I realise that he can't see me because it's dark in my room. I turn on the light and lift my hand again. *Hi.*

Dec does the same. *Hi back.*

I point to him with one hand and touch my heart with the other. *I love you.*

We watch each other. Then Dec blows me a kiss and steps away from his window. I don't move, waiting for him to come back, but he doesn't. I'm about to burst into tears, then the phone rings and I know it's him, and I thunder down the stairs and almost crash into Dad coming out of the lounge.

'Jesus, Nicola! Where the hell have you been?' He looks terrible, like someone died.

I grab the phone. 'Hello?'

'Nicola, I asked you a question, young lady.'

'I love you,' says Dec on the other end of the phone. 'I always will.'

'I love you, too.'

'Nicola!' shouts Dad.

'I have to go,' I say.

I put the phone down and turn to Dad. I know what's coming. The end of the world, that's what. But I don't care, because Dec and I will be together, no matter what Dad says. And we're going to stay together, forever, and there's nothing Mum and Dad can do to stop us.

14

Saturday 8th February 2020

'So now she is old enough to make her own decisions. Is that what you're saying?'

'No, she isn't. That's exactly my point! But, Craig . . . You're right: it's her life that's going to get ruined, too. There's no getting away from that. Old enough or not, it has to be her decision.'

Oh God. Oh God, oh God . . .

I don't even close the door behind me as I leave Chloe Clarke's house. Everything crashes into place. I thought they were on the brink of separation. I thought they were talking about *me*. But it wasn't *our* family they were talking about at all. They were talking about Kat. Kat and Arty Robbins. They *knew. That's* what it was.

And the way Kat talked about him that morning. That wild tirade that came out of nowhere as we were walking to school. *You could say Uncle Arty stuck his hand up your dress . . .*

And two nights earlier, the night before the party.

'Have you thought about what this would do to Nicola?'

'Of course *I have. She's my* daughter*! That's partly the point! Some things you can't brush under the carpet, and this is one of them. It can't go on, Craig. It has to stop. It has to stop* now*!'*

It wasn't about *them*. It wasn't about me, or about me and Declan.

Oh God.

I walk through Wordsworth Park in a daze, replaying everything in my head over and over. Kat and Arty Robbins. *That's* what Mum and Dad were arguing about. Mum knew the truth, all the way back then, when it was happening. She already knew the night before the party, and Kat was fifteen. *Fifteen. That's* what it was all about at the Shelley – why it all blew up like it did. *That's* why Mum was so incandescent, and why Arty went for her. He wasn't just having an affair; he was sexually abusing a schoolgirl, his own brother's daughter, and Mum threw it in his face in the middle of his fiftieth birthday party, in front of everyone. Never mind murdering Jesus; that was one thing the lace curtains of Byron Road would never forgive, no matter how many minibuses Arty bought.

Kat and Arty Robbins. All this time and I never knew.

He was a dick. Kat's own words, a few days ago.

She wanted a way out.

Oh God, no. Not Kat . . .

What was Arty Robbins doing out in the park that night in the first place? Did someone lure him there? Who could have done that? I don't think I know *anything* any more.

Kat?

Jesus Christ, what am I thinking? We were teenagers, for God's sake! She was *fifteen*. She was my best friend. She *couldn't* have done something like that. I'd have known . . .

Wouldn't I?

All my boyfriends had to be such secrets. You must *remember what Mum was like . . .*

Shit! And what was it Arty said, while I was hiding under Declan's bed? *Your cousin and that trash-mate of yours. Barclay. Where are they?* He was looking for *her*. He knew about Kat and Gary, more than even *I* did, and he wasn't looking for *him*, he was looking for *her* . . .

I bet I know exactly *where they are.*

Where did a pair of teenagers go to be alone if there wasn't an empty house they could use?

The park.

I play it out in my head, as much as I know, then filling in the blanks with guesswork. Mum confronts Arty in front of everyone. Maybe she doesn't name names but she makes sure he understands that she knows *exactly* what's going on. Arty flips. Goes after her. Outside the back of the pub, he attacks Mum. Tells her . . . I don't know, tells her that if she doesn't keep her mouth shut, he'll kill her? I don't know, I don't know. Dave comes out and sees it and breaks it up. He and Mum go out to the park to get away from it all; Dad comes out and now *he* sees *them*, and it's all messed up, and they get into a fight that's nothing to do with Arty Robbins, not really.

But what does *Arty* do? He looks for Kat, that's what. After what Mum's said, he needs her silence, needs to threaten her or bribe her, or whatever it takes – except he can't find her, because Kat has left the party with Gary. So Arty leaves too, and goes to the obvious place; he goes to see if she's home. And she isn't, but when he gets there, he sees the light on in Declan's window, and he knows Kat's my best friend, and that Declan is my boyfriend, and Kat is Declan's cousin, so what if *that*'s where she's gone?

And so in he comes; and what happened, happens. Arty Robbins – school governor, parish councillor, all-round pillar of the community – beats up his son while his son's teenage girlfriend hides under the bed. But that wasn't why he went there, and he still needs to find Kat; and he knows about Kat and Gary, and maybe someone saw her heading out into the park, or maybe he just knows . . .

He goes out after her. He finds her.

Kat was fifteen. Am I seriously thinking she lured Arty

Robbins to the edge of that pit and then pushed him in –
twice her size? And then went down after him and buried
him? Could she really have done all that and then kept it a
secret for decades? I didn't see a trace of it in her the next
morning. Christ, we walked to school together! We were
right there when they started to fill the hole and she didn't
bat an eye . . .

'It's over. It's finished!'

'You tell me who he is! Tell me and I'll fucking kill him!'
Gary.

Arty goes looking for Kat. He finds her with Gary. He
tells Gary to get lost, that he needs to talk to his niece, but
what if Gary already knows? What if Kat already told him?

I hail a taxi. Ten minutes later, I'm outside Saint Joseph's
church. I walk round the back and pick my way between
the graves until I find Dad. A wilted bunch of flowers lies
against his stone, from when I came here last month for his
birthday. I still try to make that little pilgrimage, and on
the anniversary of the day he died, too. It's cold and miserable, a light February drizzle falling like dead, damp
cobwebs. There's no one else here. I squat beside Dad's
grave, running my fingers over his headstone.

Last night . . . It wasn't about you, kiddo.

'You already knew,' I say. 'Mum told you, that night
before the party.' Kat and Arty Robbins? It's like trying to
grasp hold of something perfectly smooth and covered in

oil. Dad was a gentle man. Not particularly big or strong. A sparkle of wit and a gleam in his eye, and he could cut you to pieces with clever words if he wanted, but I never heard of him raising a hand to anyone. Arty Robbins, on the other hand, was a designer thug in an expensive suit. He would have punched Dad in the face as soon as blink, and that would have been that.

Good riddance to bad rubbish.

I wish I could talk to him. I wish he could tell me what happened that night. I know he would, if he saw how much it meant to me. I wish he could explain it and tell me it was all nothing.

Does it *have* to be Kat? The police search went on for weeks. For months, it was all up and down the street. And for all that time, Kat never said a word. Never talked about it. Kept her secret . . .

She's been my best friend for more than thirty-five years.

Tears run down my cheeks, mingling with the whispering rain. I should let this go, but I can't stop remembering – that's the trouble. I can't stop remembering what it was like to be in love with Declan. He's in my thoughts every day now: the swing over the river; kissing him in the alley behind our house; the feeling when I stood in the window and watched him watching me; how I felt so full of something I didn't understand that I thought I might burst . . . And then squatting in the dark in the trees on my twenty-sixth birthday, hugging my knees to my chest and crying like it was the end of the world because I knew it was over – sure that the emptiness I felt was how I was going to feel for the rest of my life. And because of all that, I *can't* let it go. I have to help Declan, no matter what it costs. I know he didn't do this thing, and if the only way to save him is to find out who really—

But . . . *Please*, not Kat.

She saved my life once. Almost literally. I was in America. Two years had passed since I'd left Declan and I think I'd regretted every single day, and yet I couldn't go back because what would that change? Nothing. I was miserable and coming to understand not only that the memory researchers I was working with didn't think there was a cure for what I had, but that they weren't even looking for one. It was sinking in: this was my future. A constant torment from a past I could never escape.

Declan and I hadn't spoken in months. I knew the divorce papers were coming but I still wasn't ready for the shock of reading them. They paralysed me. I couldn't leave the apartment. I was drowning in memories. I thought about killing myself as the only way to make it stop. The thoughts grew stronger; and then, two days after the papers came through, Kat arrived on my doorstep.

'What are you doing here?' I asked.

'Moral support,' she said.

She'd taken a week off work and come all the way to

America. Declan was her cousin, so she knew the papers were on their way, and she knew how much I'd need her. She was pregnant, too, around the end of her first trimester, although she never told me until later. She picked me up and took me out and made me eat, and drove us to the cinema and even to a theme park, and insisted that we went on rides like we were still teenagers, and talked to me and talked to me until I started talking back. She stayed until she'd pulled me through.

The drizzle has turned to rain now, cold and heavy. I'm soaked through. My knees feel like they've fused solid. I lean on Dad's headstone to haul myself up.

'I'm sorry, Dad. I wish . . .' The words crack into sobs. 'I wish I had your faith.'

I know, deep down, that I was already thinking of leaving Declan before Dad fell ill, but the memory I can't escape is the day I needed Declan at the hospital and he wouldn't answer his phone. I went to meet him outside his office. I saw him emerge with a woman I didn't know, and something about them felt off. Was it the easy way they were laughing and joking? The way they walked side by side just a little bit too close? He didn't see me, so I followed them. They went into a pub and Declan ordered two glasses of wine. I saw the way she looked at him and how he looked at her, and I knew that look because that was how he'd once looked at me. Then she kissed him. I saw how he sank into that softness, the unguarded bliss on his face. He never saw me watching and I never told him.

It wasn't why I left. It was the last cut, not the first. Somewhere along the way the fire died, and passion slipped out of our lives without saying goodbye. The shine just . . . wore off. It happened so quietly that I'm not sure I'd have noticed if I couldn't remember our days as teenagers as though they were only yesterday. But I *could* remember, I *did* remember, and I missed it. And the more I missed it, the more I wondered what had gone wrong. That's when I started to see all the little things – the thousand cuts that killed us.

Is that how it is for everyone? Was Kat right, and that's simply the way it always goes?

Dad died two days after I saw Declan with that other woman. I was gone by the end of the month. Mum and Dave waited a full two years before they tied the knot. I don't know why they bothered. I didn't go to the wedding.

Not Kat. Please. She's all I have left.

I sink to my haunches. The rain is a steady oppression, the sky a dull slate-grey. I want to burst into tears. Relationships evolve. The passion of first love transforms into trust and friendship and loyalty, dependability, quiet things that never set your heart ablaze but which leave you with gaping holes when they're gone. I know that now. But I'd seen him with another woman. I wasn't going to let there be a Dave. Leaving was self-preservation. I could survive, if I was the one to go. The other way round . . . I wasn't so sure.

I left. I never gave Declan a chance to explain. I didn't think he deserved it. At least, that's what I told myself, but the truth is always more complicated. Is that why I've got to save him now? To make up for never giving him that chance? Do I have to destroy the one friendship that's lasted all these years for the sake of some decades-old memories?

'Nicky? Oh my *God*!'

I blink. Kat stands over me, an umbrella held up against the rain.

'Kat?'

She puts on a stern voice full of drama. 'The phone! You dialled it. We came. It is a means to summon us!'

I look at her, blank, uncomprehending.

'*Hellraiser*? Pinhead?' She shakes her head. 'Never mind.' She crouches beside me and tries to help me to my feet, somehow managing to hold the umbrella over us both as she does so. 'Oh *God*, Nicky. You're *soaked*!'

I look up at her, blurry through the tears and the rain. I forget, sometimes, to come back to the present.

'I need to talk to you,' I say, desperate to ask the question I need to ask in a way that won't sound awful, even though I know it's not possible.

'OK.' I feel her tension. 'But, you know . . . twenty-first century: we have telephones and emails and texts and

Skype.' We struggle upright. 'Gary was going to take me to Ikea this afternoon.'

'That summer. You know I kept telling you how I thought Mum and Dad were going to get divorced?'

'Yes . . .' It's the cautious *yes* I've come to recognise from Kat: a yes that means no, not really, but she trusts my memory to be right. She looks around the churchyard and then up at the rain. 'We also have cafés and pubs and coffee shops.'

'I think . . . I think it might have been something else.'

Another long pause. She's waiting for me to explain. And now I really need to ask the question and I don't know how.

'OK.' She laughs but I hear a wariness. 'This is all a bit *Wuthering Heights*, though, isn't it? Can't we at least go somewhere dry? You're drenched!'

A deep breath and I take the plunge. I have to. 'The night before the party, I heard Mum and Dad arguing. And then again, the night after. I thought it was about me and Declan but . . . I told you I saw Arty Robbins sneaking around your house. Do you remember? How I thought he and your mum . . .' I can't do it. I can't ask, even though she must know by now what's on my mind.

A silence hangs between us, getting longer and longer.

'Kat, did you have anything to do with . . .'

Another blank silence. I can't say it.

'With?'

'With what happened to Arty Robbins?'

Kat stares at me, too stunned to answer.

'It's OK if you did. I won't tell. It's just that we need to find a way to save Declan, that's all. He didn't do it.'

The shock on her face sears me. Shock and horror and – is that fear? 'I . . . Jesus! What? Nicky, I . . . No, I absolutely did *not* have anything to do with what happened to Arty. Why would I?'

'Because he was abusing you, and you wanted it to stop and he wouldn't.'

I'm right. And in a stroke, I've sucked all the joy right out of Kat and stripped her back to some bitter old memory.

'Kat?'

She turns away.

'Did your mum know?'

No answer. It's like she doesn't even hear.

'Kat!'

Now she rounds on me. 'Oh, for God's sake! No. Of course she didn't!'

'Are you sure?' It's hard to imagine Chloe Clarke, even thirty-five years ago, pushing a man like Arty Robbins into a pit, but it's not hard to imagine her trying – not if she knew he was abusing her underage daughter . . .

'I think I would have heard about it, don't you?'

Maybe not if Chloe Clarke knew that Arty Robbins was dead.

'I'd really like to go somewhere warm and dry now,' says Kat.

'I'm sorry.'

She just looks at me.

'It's . . . I think Mum found out. About you and Arty. That's the thing. I think that's what she and Dad were arguing about. And whatever happened in the Shelley that night, between him and Mum, I think that's what it was.'

Kat nods like this is old news. I suppose, for her, it is. It's what she was afraid of, back then when it happened.

'Did you know he attacked my mum after we left? Actually *attacked* her. I remember the bruises. That's why there was a policeman when I got home.'

Kat still holds her umbrella over us both. It's not quite big enough, and I feel the drops of water sliding off and hitting my shoulder. I'm cold. She sighs and I hear the defeat in her. 'He was nice at first. He knew what he was doing – not like the boys at school. He gave me presents. I was . . . I was pretty fucked up back then. I went to him. I was hoping to find out something about my dad. My real dad. You know? His little brother. He said he could help.' She stops. 'Does any of this really matter now? It was thirty-five years ago.'

'Thirty-five years ago, someone killed him.'

'What, and you think it was *Mum*?' Kat howls with

laughter. It's a beautiful sound; and for a moment I have her back, my indomitable Kat.

'No, she was at the Shelley all night. Actually, I was wondering if it was you.'

Kat stops. '*Me?*'

'Or Gary.'

'Fucking hell, Nicola!'

'Kat! Just . . . I need to know. Whatever you did – whatever you know – I won't tell a soul, I promise. I just need to find a way to save Declan.'

'Nicky, Dec's my cousin. He can be a jerk and we don't talk much these days, but he's still family! If I knew something, don't you think I'd tell the police? Christ! No, I had nothing to do with it. I have no idea who did it, OK?' She picks up the pace again, almost marching me down Church Lane. 'I'm not proud of who I was back then. Actually I'm pretty fucking mortified you found out; and yes, I was happy when Uncle Arty vanished out of my life. But he's gone now, and I certainly didn't . . . Jesus, I *told* you, I was with Gary the whole time you were with Dec. No one else knew about me and Arty, and I'd really rather—'

'Did Gary know?'

'No!'

'Are you sure? Are you *absolutely* sure there's no way he—'

'Jesus, Nicky! Now you think *Gary* did it? I *told* you! He was with me.'

'I—'

'Anything to save Dec, is that it?'

'No! I—'

She pulls away from me, leaving me standing in the rain. 'I was going to go to fucking Ikea. We were going to have stupid Swedish meatballs, and then I was going to buy some ridiculous flat-pack furniture and laugh at Gary as he tried to put it together, and maybe get a pointless picture of some kittens and maybe a rug, and a lampshade I don't need called NurdleFlurdle or something. And then you called and said it was really urgent, so I dropped everything and came and . . . And instead of Ikea, I'm standing in a fucking graveyard in the pissing rain talking about . . .' She sniffs, and oh God, is she crying? She *is*. My best friend for nearly thirty-six years and I've done this to her.

'I'm sorry,' I say, and I'm crying, too.

Kat stares at me, and I know she's looking for something to make everything better and undo this. And I want it too, and I know I've pushed too far, too fast, too hard, and all I can think is to talk about Arty's murder instead, which shouldn't be any better and yet somehow is. How absurd is that?

'I think it might have been my dad,' I say.

'*What?*'

I tell her about the mud on Dad's jacket. How I thought she was right – how she *did* see Dad in the park that night.

About what Dave told me as I left Mum's house on Thursday and how I don't believe him. By the time I finish, I'm done. Spent and sobbing. I turn away from her and start back for the church.

'Nicky?'

I don't want to look. I don't want another memory of Kat's face that way, stricken with grief and betrayal.

'Nicky!' I feel her hand on my arm, grabbing me, spinning me round. I flash back to that Monday morning after my night with Dec – Mum smacking the bowl of Shredded Wheat out of my hands . . .

But the slap doesn't come, and then Kat has her arms around me. After what I've put her through, she still wants to comfort me.

'Daft bloody cow,' she says. 'Your dad? *Your* dad?' I can tell that she's fighting back the tears but she squeezes me a little and then lets go. 'Come on, before you catch pneumonia.'

We walk quickly through the rain, heading for the shelter of the High Street. Kat says she's going to call a taxi and take me home, because she's right, I *am* soaked to the skin. She tells me I'm an idiot, and how can I possibly think that my dad had anything to do with Arty Robbins' death. I watch her as she talks, remembering the party and the way she looked at him, so intense. I didn't understand but now I do. She was afraid. And earlier, outside, just after we arrived and I told her

I'd seen Arty slipping into her house . . . I thought it was the scandal of her mum having an affair with a married man that frightened her but it wasn't. She was terrified, and I was too busy thinking about Declan to see the truth.

We reach the High Street and scurry into the shelter of the shopping mall. I'm shivering and cold and I want to sit in a corner with a hot chocolate, but Kat says I have to keep moving to stay warm. I tell her about her mum's photographs, and so we go into Boots. The young man behind the counter takes the negatives and tells me the prints will take two or three days, then asks whether I want to collect them or have them posted to my home. I give my address and then ask for a second set of prints to be delivered to Kat's mum. I don't want to come out here again, not unless I have to.

'What are you looking for?' asks Kat.

'I thought Declan might be in one of them, so he could prove where he was. Even if he isn't, I'll see who was still there. I'll probably know who they were. They might remember something.'

Kat makes a face. 'It was more than three decades ago. They'll probably be dead.' She drags me to a waiting taxi, tells the driver to take us to her flat, then pokes me.

'What?'

'I don't mean to pry but . . . is there something going on between you and Declan again?'

The question shocks me back to the present. 'What? No!'

'I'm just trying to understand why you're getting so involved in all of this. You guys split up more than two decades ago. I know, for you, it's still like it was yesterday, but in a way that makes even *less* sense.'

'I don't—'

'Why are you putting yourself through all this? Why not let it go? Let the police do their thing. If he's innocent – I mean, it's been thirty-five years . . . It would be hard enough to prove he did it even if he *did*, unless they had a witness. So why?'

'I . . .' Truth is, I've been asking myself the same question. I don't know why I'm playing amateur detective. I could say it's because I know Declan didn't do it, but it's more than that. Maybe Kat thinks it's because I want him back, but it's not that, either. I'm not sure it's even about Declan at all. I can't seem to let it go. I remember what I saw but I still don't understand what happened.

'I don't know. It feels like . . . it feels like if I could help him, it would make things right.'

Kat snorts. '*He* was the one having an affair!'

I don't want to talk about me and Declan. 'I keep thinking about the man you saw in the park. Whether it really was my dad or whether it was someone else. And if so, who.'

Kat shakes her head. 'I was so sure. But if it wasn't your dad . . .'

I'm sinking into myself, the cold and now the warmth

getting the better of me. I feel odd. Numb and sleepy. 'What is it?'

'The police are still charging Dec, even after you told them he was with you. I mean, you were with Dec, and I was with Gary, and if Dec *did* do it . . .' She gives me a pointed look. 'Or Gary or me – or *you*, for that matter – well, we were all with other people until after midnight. So the police must think it happened later; but if it *was* after midnight when he died, then where the hell did Arty *go* for all that time? It was *his* party, for God's sake! His moment, his chance to show off all the money he had and everything he'd done and how everyone loved him.' She wraps an arm round my shoulders. 'No. Trust me. Arty Robbins had too much of an ego. He wouldn't have missed all that. Whatever happened, it happened while you were with Dec.'

'He was looking for you,' I say.

Kat makes a helpless gesture. 'Are we saying he wandered around the park for hours in the dark, hoping he'd find me hiding under a bush or something?'

Maybe we are. 'I don't know. What if it *was* Dad you saw? What if Mum isn't telling me the truth?'

'Why wouldn't she?'

I shake my head. I don't know how to explain that summer. There *was* something between her and Dave, whatever she says, whatever Chloe Clarke thinks.

'Anyway, you said it yourself. Whoever killed Arty

Robbins went down into that hole to cover him up. And it rained that morning, so they would have been covered in mud. Not just a few streaks on a jacket.' Kat flashes me a smile like she's done something clever. 'Now, we need to get you in a nice hot bath. But,' and she squeezes my hand, 'please don't let anyone else find out about me and Arty, OK?'

She takes me back to her flat and puts me in the bath, and puts my clothes in the washing machine, lends me some of her own and feeds me hot chocolate until I feel better. Then she takes me out to lunch and we talk about her mum and her photographs, and the holidays they had before her dad left. I ask her who she thinks killed Arty Robbins and Kat says we'll probably never know, but certainly not Declan, and I should tell him she said so. It's like magic, the way Kat can make everything OK again.

When I get home, there's a message from Declan waiting on my answerphone, asking me to call. He sounds scared. When I ring, he picks up almost at once.

'Nix, thank God!' His voice drops low. 'I know why they're charging me. They notified my solicitor this morning. I know what they've got.'

'What are you talking about?'

'That test they cocked up first time around? They found blood under Dad's fingernails. It's mine. They've got my DNA.'

15

Saturday 8th to Tuesday 11th February 2020

I never told anyone what happened that night when Arty Robbins burst into Declan's room and didn't know I was there too, hiding under the bed. After a couple of days, when it turned out that Arty had gone missing, it didn't seem to matter – I was simply glad he'd gone. For a long time, I used to imagine that Declan and I were the only ones who knew the truth, that no one else knew what his dad was really like; but, of course, we weren't. Anne Robbins certainly knew, even if she pretended that she didn't. I think Mum and Dad knew, too – Dad with his *good riddance to bad rubbish*. Maybe *everyone* knew, and it was just that no one ever said anything. Maybe that's what you got for buying the school a new minibus.

Declan asked me, years later, if I could imagine what it was like having that as the last memory of his dad. The last memory I have of my own dad, hollowed out by cancer, isn't much better, but at the time it made me think of Kat, who has no memories of her real dad at all.

And for a moment I'm back with Detective Scott asking, *Was Daniel Robbins there that night?*

'Nix? Nix! Are you still there?'

'Yes, I—'

'I don't know who else to talk to. My solicitor called. I have to go back to court next week. Wednesday. They're going to revoke my bail. They're going to lock me up, Nix. Nix, I didn't do it. I don't really remember what happened that night after you left, but I swear I didn't kill him. I'd remember *that*! I know I would.'

All those years living together and not a whisper of suspicion? No. And I don't care how long ago it was – you don't forget a murder. 'Declan, it's just a mistake, OK? It's all going to be—'

'Don't! Don't tell me it's going to be OK. Because it's *not* going to be OK.'

'Declan, you didn't—'

'Nix, you're not *listening*!' I can almost hear him tearing at his hair – what's left of it. 'This is what they've been waiting for. I'm done! They found blood under Dad's fingernails.

My blood. They're not going to drop the charges; they're going to put me on trial!'

On the phone, as Declan tells me how he's going to spend the rest of his life in prison, I try to talk him down. I go through it all again – everything I remember from that evening. I tell him he needs to inform the police about the fight with his dad and that he should call me as soon as he hears anything. And then I let him go, and I call the police station myself and ask to speak to Detective Scott. I'm going to tell him how the blood under Arty Robbins' fingernails was from Declan's smashed nose, and about the bloody hand-print on Declan's shirt. He probably won't believe me – not after I've already given a statement and told them how perfectly I remember things and yet somehow never mentioned this – but I'll stand up and say it all again in court, if I have to. I'm not going to let this happen. I'm not going to let Declan go to jail when I know he didn't do it.

It's already dark outside but Detective Scott is still at work. I tell him about the fight, about the blood. He asks me to come in next Tuesday after lunch to make another formal statement. He asks why I didn't mention all of this before. I tell him the truth: that I thought I was doing the right thing; that he didn't ask and I didn't see the point when I knew that Arty Robbins was already missing by the time I left Declan's house; that I thought it would only make things more complicated. He isn't happy but I don't care. When I'm done, I feel almost . . .

elated. It's silly, perhaps, but I finally know what it is they've got on Declan, and I know how to fight it.

I call Declan again.

'They're going to think we made it up,' he says when I tell him about giving a second statement. 'Now we know what they've got, they're going to say it's all lies.' I can hear it in him – how he's all but given up.

'Not if we can *show* them.' I tell him about Chloe Clarke's photographs. 'They'll be here in a couple of days. I can bring them over. We can go through them together.'

'Sure.' He sounds beaten.

'You might be in one of them. If they can see that you had a black eye, or swollen nose, or bruised cheek, or busted lip, it'll prove we're telling the truth.'

'And what if I'm not in *any* of them?'

'You said you went back to the Shelley after midnight.'

'Doesn't mean I'm in any of Chloe's photographs.'

'We'll know who was still there. I'll remember their names, and your solicitor can call them; and we'll find a witness who remembers you looking like you'd been punched in the face. It's going to be fine.'

'What if there *isn't* anyone who remembers?'

'Meet me in Wordsworth Park on Tuesday, after I've talked to the police,' I say. 'Mid-afternoon, by the entrance from the station. There's a bench there. You know the one.' Of course he does.

'You know I'm back in court on Wednesday?'

'I'll tell you how it went, what questions they asked. We'll go and have coffee in that café next to the playground. It's really good.' I have no idea if it's any good or not, but right now it's the only positive thing I can think of to say. 'We can go and talk to your solicitor, if you want; tell them about the photographs and everything. Their office is in Wordsworth Park, isn't it? I should have the photographs by Wednesday morning. We can go through them and find out who the people are, and then we can start calling them. I'll . . . I'll take Wednesday off work.'

'OK.' It's a dull, mechanical assent, like he can't think of a good enough reason to say no.

'Declan, when you said you saw Gary in the Shelley later that night . . . what time was that? You said he looked rough.' Kat says that Gary was with her, but he can't have been, not for the whole night.

'Christ, I don't know. Look, sorry. I've . . . There's something I'm looking into about Uncle Dan.'

'Kat's dad? The police asked about him, too. What's he—'

'Mum says she saw him there that night. I don't see how, but . . . Sorry. I've got to go.' He hangs up.

Dried blood from thirty-five years ago. Hard to believe, but when I can't sleep at half-past three in the morning and google it, I find they've used DNA to solve cases going back further still: fifty years and more.

After a lazy, disjointed Sunday spent dozing, watching telly and fretting, I get nothing done at work on Monday. Ed flutters around my desk more often than usual, until I lose my temper and snap at him to stop harassing me, saying that I can't concentrate. I storm out, memories looping through my head, over and over. Wednesday night with Declan. Gary, thirty-five years ago, skulking in the corner shadows of the Shelley, not watching Mum losing her temper with Arty Robbins but watching Kat . . . And then outside: *Tell me and I'll fucking kill him!* Kat says she never told Gary about her and Arty Robbins, but I remember the way he looked at her a week ago when she told him that Arty was dead. He was looking at her to see how he should react. He knew. He *knew*.

I head home from the library and wander aimlessly into a café. Anywhere to sit down. The memories are coming like waves, over and over, the same scenes. Kat and Gary in the car park of the Shelley. Kat watching Mum laying into Arty Robbins. The way Gary looked at Kat last weekend. The more I relive those moments, the surer I am.

Gary.

Gary and Kat left the Shelley right after me and Dec. If I had to guess, I'd say Gary took her to his stupid van in the Secret Car Park. They must have been there for quite a while. Detective Scott would laugh at me if I told him, but what if Gary *did* know? Maybe Kat never told him, but what if he figured it out?

I Know What I Saw

If I could find out who it was they saw heading into the park – if they're still alive, if they can remember something . . .

If, if, if. And yet something still doesn't add up.

I take a taxi home. Safer than taking a bus and having to pay attention to where I am. When I get back, there's a message on my answerphone. Someone I've never met or heard of before called Emily, calling from the HR department at the library. Apparently, there was some incident at work this morning. It takes an age before I realise that she's calling about me storming out. I don't call back because I don't know what to say.

Tuesday rolls round after an agony of waiting. I wake up to find an email: my photographs have been dispatched. Delivery expected this afternoon. I call work and leave a message to say I'm taking the day off because I'm not feeling well, and almost at once I get a call back. The same Emily who left yesterday's message. She asks if I'll be back in tomorrow and, if I am, could I drop in at nine-thirty to discuss the issues I'm having. I tell her yes, of course, and that I'm sorry about what happened. I'm not, but that's what she wants to hear, and it'll make her go away.

On the stroke of midday, I head to Wordsworth Park. I grab a sandwich and get to the police station and ask for Detective Scott, but Detective Scott has been called out and no one seems quite sure what to do with me. I wait and wait, tight as a drum, until eventually a policewoman I've never seen before comes to take my statement. She doesn't know me, doesn't know the case. I tell her about the night with Dec and about Arty Robbins bursting in on us and what he did. I don't say anything about Kat or about Dad's jacket or Chloe's photographs. When it comes to all that, to be honest, I wouldn't know where to start. She records it all and doesn't ask any questions, and suddenly it's over and I'm free to go, and it all feels like a crushing anticlimax. Half an hour later, I'm sitting beside Declan on the bench by the entrance to Wordsworth Park, tugging on my vaporiser. Declan is silent and far away, like he really doesn't want to be here. I've told him everything. Telling him about his dad abusing Kat was horrible, like I've betrayed a friend; which I suppose I have, but I had to tell him, because how else will he understand why I think that maybe it was his friend, Gary Barclay, who killed his dad?

'We could still go for coffee,' I say, 'if you like.' I'm wandering through memories of the evening after the Shelley: the two of us sitting against the tyre-swing tree, no one else around, knowing I'll be grounded for the rest of my life as soon as I get home, knowing that Dec is going to go away and that it might all be over . . .

He taps the police tracker on his ankle. 'My solicitor says it's a bad idea for us to talk.' He looks at me, waiting for some sort of reply. Huffs, when he doesn't get one. 'Mum's back in the flat now. I don't like to leave her on her own for too long, if I don't have to.'

'If you want any help with your mum,' I start, but he shakes his head.

'Can't lay that on you,' he says. 'Besides, she can mostly look after herself. It's just . . .'

It's just that if they put Declan on trial for murder and he's found guilty, they'll lock him up for twenty years, and his mum will be dead before he gets out.

'I'll bring her to see you,' I say. 'I promise.'

'Thanks, but . . .'

A different *but*. She hates me? She'd refuse to see her own son?

He knows about the photographs. He knows Gary and Kat saw someone in the park before midnight; and if Dad was alive then I'd simply ask him if it really *was* him, and why he was there and whether he saw anything. But he isn't, and that means asking Mum, and I already did that, and she said that she and Dad were together; and I know she was lying, and I thought she was lying because she was with Dave, but Dave said it was only for five minutes, but what if it wasn't, and how do I find a way to get Mum to tell me the truth, and oh God, I don't want any of this, I just want . . .

I don't think Mum will *ever* tell me what really happened that night between her and Dad and Dave, no matter how softly I tread. Then again, if it's not going to help me save Declan, does it even matter?

'The thing is,' Declan starts, and then crumples into himself and begins to shake, and it's a moment before I see that he's crying.

'There's still the photographs,' I say. 'They should show up this afternoon.'

He shakes his head. 'I'm not going to be in them. I *did* go out into the park. I don't really remember it but . . . But I know that I *did* go out, and it feels like I was gone for a long time. I'm not going to be in any photographs; and the police reckon Dad was still alive near midnight because some witness back then told that policeman of yours they saw him.' He shrugs, seeing the question in my face. 'I don't know. It's what my solicitor says.' Another shrug. 'They're going to say I did it after you left. And they've got a motive now, if they didn't have one already. Telling them what really happened . . . I think it's made things worse.' He looks so desperate.

'It's reasonable doubt, Declan.'

'Is it? After I left you, Mum's the only alibi I've got. She's been telling them I was at the Shelley the whole night, and they know that's not right. She's been telling them Uncle Daniel was there, too, which is just . . . I'd remember *that*, surely! Christ, Nix, I don't think she remembers it at all.'

'If there's a trial, I'm going to go up there and tell the world what happened – what your dad did to you.'

He makes a sort of high-pitched hoot of anguish. 'You and your magic memory against the whole London Metropolitan Police?' He shakes his head. 'I don't even remember half of it, not the way you tell it. You'd think I would, really, wouldn't you? You're not – you know – making it up, right?'

'Jesus! No.'

He takes my hand and squeezes it. 'It's what they'll say, though. You know that, right?'

'I think it might have been Gary Barclay.'

'Got any evidence?' He shrugs. 'Because if you do, now would be the time.'

'I need to find whoever it was Kat saw on her way back to the Shelley.'

'Someone in a dark jacket from thirty-five years ago? Good luck.'

Declan had a black leather jacket once. I remember him showing up in his Capri at the park on my sixteenth birthday. It was a glorious spring day, full of the promise of summer heat without actually being hot. I'd told Mum I was going to the cinema with Kat and I was sitting on a bench, juggling whether I should officially announce that Dec was my boyfriend, when there he was in that stupid lime-green car, black leather jacket and a white silk scarf wrapped around his neck. I remember the look in his eye. Being sixteen meant I was free.

God, I could laugh at myself sometimes. We were so naïve.

'You should have told them what really happened, the first time you spoke to the police,' he says. '*I* should have told them.'

It's 1985 and we're sitting on this same bench after school, me with my head in my hands. I'm grounded. I'm forbidden from seeing Declan, who's about to go to Clapham and might never come back. He tells me it's OK, we'll still see each other, even if it has to be a secret, even if he has to come up to Wordsworth Park every evening; that it's only a month until the summer holidays, that he'll wait . . .

Nine years later and I'm sitting at home. *Our* home. It's late and Dec's called to say he's going out with a few mates to the pub and he'll be back late, and is that OK? And I say yes, of course it is; and he says not to wait up, and then he's gone. He doesn't ask about my day. He doesn't tell me he loves me. Just: *See you later.* I remember wondering who he was with, and why I wasn't enough.

Is that normal?

I remember sitting there alone, and how empty I felt. I remember Dad, back in that summer after Arty Robbins disappeared, sitting on the sofa and staring at nothing. How he looked the way I felt – alone and hollowed out. Only a glimpse, before he realised I was watching.

But he never gave up.

Did I get it all wrong? Everything I saw vanishing from my relationship with Declan, everything I remembered that we seemed to have lost: is that simply . . . *normal*?

I Know What I Saw

The Declan of here and now gets up. I follow him along the path between the building site and the car park, watching him. There's not much left of the boy I fell in love with. He's filled out, etched himself with lines and wrinkles, sketched bags under his eyes. His shoulders sag and seem to droop with sadness. But when I hear his voice, the years fall away and there he is.

'I'm sorry, Dec.' Sorry for so many things.

'So am I,' he says. He keeps walking. Doesn't look back.

'I don't mean sorry for this. I mean for everything. For America. For leaving.'

'Maybe it was for the best.'

'Is that what you really think?'

He stops and stares at the hoarding around the building site as if he can see straight through it. I wonder: does he know where they found his dad? Was it right here?

'I think maybe this was a mistake,' he says. 'I think I should go.'

'How long would it take to walk here from your old house, do you think?' I ask. I'm thinking ten minutes. Ten minutes for Arty Robbins to get to the building site after he left us, although God knows why he went *there*, of all places. Someone else is there, too. They get into a fight. Somehow it ends with Arty Robbins falling into the pit. He breaks his neck. How long did it take to climb down after him and dig a hole and cover him? Thirty minutes? An hour?

Declan turns away. He starts back towards the station, and what can I do but let him go? Only I can't. I never could.

It's 1985. He sits beside me on the grass, and I love him so much it terrifies me.

Ten years later. I'm alone in the woods and sobbing because Dad's dead and Declan and I were going to be together forever, and he promised me and . . .

'Declan!' I run after him. 'Dec!' I sound on the edge of hysteria. Maybe I am; maybe I'm crazy because half of me is somewhere else, watching Declan in a pub with a woman I don't even know, and my heart has just broken in half. But what if I was wrong, like I was wrong about Kat and Gary, and about Arty Robbins and Kat's mum, and maybe even about Mum and Dave and Dad? What if I was wrong about everything? 'Dec! Please!'

He lets me catch up. Up close, all I see is how tired he is, how exhausted he looks. There's something in his eyes that isn't simple weariness at a past that won't leave him alone. A touch of regret?

'What do you want from me, Nix?'

'I don't know!' Absolution? No. Explanation? No, not that, either. What I *really* want is to go back in time and change it all. 'Just . . . stay a bit, will you? *Talk* to me!'

He sighs. 'I'll stay for a coffee, but not long, OK?'

We turn and walk together back into the park, the playing fields, the playground and the coffee shop and the car park.

I Know What I Saw

I want to go back in my head to that summer. I want Declan to take me in his arms and drive me to that place by the river . . .

'How long were we at your house before your dad showed up? Fifteen minutes? Maybe twenty?'

He puffs and shrugs and I feel his impatience. 'About that. Can't have been much longer.'

In my memory it feels as though we barely sat down before Declan's dad came crashing through the door, but I know that can't be right because that would mean he left the Shelley at the same time as we did, and I know that Dec and I talked for a bit before we started kissing. It's what Detective Scott says about memories being subjective – like how hiding under the bed felt like half an hour but can't really have been more than a few minutes.

'Maybe we can make Gary think we know something. Trick him into giving himself away.' In my head, the words sound hopeful. Out in the open, they sound desperate.

'Jesus!' Declan shakes his head. 'Gary's a mate! Nix, I have to go to court tomorrow. The police have my DNA. They reckon I was out looking for Dad after you left. They know we had a fight. They're going to say I'm a flight risk and that I should be in custody. My solicitor says there's a good chance they'll win this time. She puts a brave face on it but sometimes you can tell when someone thinks they're fighting a lost cause. They're going to lock me up, and there's going to be a trial and fuck knows how that ends. So unless you can show up tomorrow with a signed confession or something, just . . . drop it, OK?'

We're walking the same way Gary and Kat would have come that night on their way back from the Secret Car Park. I picture it in my head. The path from Shelley Street to the High Street, cutting the park in half, exactly as it does now. Wordsworth Lane cuts it in half the other way. Kat and Gary were in his van in the Secret Car Park, a hundred yards down Wordsworth Lane and tucked among the trees. The fences around the playing fields mean you have to walk up Wordsworth Lane until you reach the path. From the path, you'd see anyone heading for the building site . . .

No. There are fences *now*, but there weren't any *then*, not in 1985. I know that because I used to walk across the fields all the time, and so did the rest of us – and why wouldn't Gary and Kat do the same? Why go the long way and not across the field? And if they walked across the field, then whoever they saw was nowhere near the building site. They couldn't have been.

Declan picks at a fingernail. 'Mum said Dad was having an affair. When we thought he'd run away . . . But Kat? Jesus. He was her fucking uncle!'

I walk faster now, cutting sideways towards the playing fields. 'Everyone was at the Shelley. No one saw Arty. It doesn't make sense that he was out here for an hour on his own, so either he was with someone or . . .'

Or what?

I stand at the edge of the playing field, tracing a line to where the Secret Car Park used to be. It was dark. Gary and Kat couldn't possibly have seen anyone near the building site.

I tried to hide behind a see-saw. They were in the playground, then, already close to the gates. Kat said she thought it was Dad. The lights near the gates meant they would have seen him clearly, which makes it weird that she got it wrong. So maybe she didn't.

'I never stopped loving you, you know,' says Declan. 'Right from the first moment I saw you, I never stopped. But *you* did. We had it, and then somewhere along the way you lost it.'

'What? *Me?*'

I see the old pain in his face. And there's the rub, because it's not true – at least not the way he thinks. I *didn't* stop loving him. Ever. I couldn't.

I shake my head. 'No, I . . .'

'You went off to America. You knew I couldn't come with you. You knew exactly what you were doing.'

'You were seeing someone else.'

'I bloody well was not!'

I know what I saw but I don't know how to explain it,

even to myself, in a way that makes sense; and we went over this so many times before we finally called it quits, and we never really got to the bottom of it. No use dragging it all back up now.

'I was scared,' I say.

'Scared of *what*?' He turns away and then stops and turns back, his arms flailing in exasperation. 'I don't need this, Nix. Not now. Not with everything else. Jesus Christ, this could be my last day of freedom! They're going to send me down tomorrow. I could *die* in prison for something I didn't even *do*.'

I'd seen Kat's dad walk out of her life. I'd seen Declan's dad abandon his family. I'd seen my own parents: how easy with each other they were when I was small, and how all that gradually changed until so little was about feelings, about passion – not like me and Declan . . . And then, after we were married, I saw how we slowly and steadily took each other for granted and I couldn't stop remembering how it didn't used to be that way. How our love had faded.

And then I saw Declan and that woman in the pub together. The way his eyes ate her up. The way she kissed him. The freshness of it. The way he seemed to spark. It was obvious.

I look at him. Really look at him: old and sad and beaten. Maybe I'm wrong. I've been wrong about a lot of things. Maybe there's some other explanation; and I want to ask him, I want to tell him what I saw and ask if it wasn't what I thought. I want him to tell me I'm wrong and make it into something I can believe, because I *want* to believe.

'I saw you kiss her, Dec.'

Silence. I can't look him in the eye. What if he tells me I'm right? And does it even matter? It was twenty-five years ago. I can't change the past and, whoever she was, she's long gone; but I *can* change the present, so isn't that what I should do? Forget this? Forget it all, as best I can? Except that I *can't*. I can't forget *anything*.

He's looking at me, bewildered, like I'm some sort of alien. 'You saw *what*?'

I turn and walk straight up to him and wrap my arms round him and hug him tightly. He freezes, startled. It's like hugging a postbox.

'I saw you,' I whisper. 'I saw you together, and it was the last straw. I knew you didn't love me any more and so I left. I left because we'd lost what we had and it was the only way I could save myself. I left because I knew that if you found someone else then *you'd* leave *me*; and if you did that, I wouldn't survive. I saw you when she kissed you and . . . we'd been ghost-walking through our lives for years, and I . . .' I run out of words as I cling to him.

'You really thought I was seeing someone else?' he asks.

'You *were* seeing someone else. I *saw* you!'

'Jesus, Nix! No! No, I *wasn't*.'

'Wednesday 19th April. Dad was in hospital. He was getting worse. I needed you. I called you but you didn't answer, so I went to find you. I waited outside your office and I saw you come out with some woman I didn't know. Long, dark hair, almost to her waist. Glasses. Big lips. I knew something wasn't right and so I followed you. You went to a pub. The Fox and Hound. You bought two glasses of white wine. You sat next to her, too close. You looked at her with the look of a lover, and then she kissed you. You did nothing to stop her and everything to encourage it.'

I stare at him and he stares back, open-mouthed and bewildered. I almost want him to tell me it never happened, that I'm imagining it, because if he does then I'm going to slap him and walk out, and it would make everything so much easier.

'Jenny,' he says after a long silence, and I can tell he remembers. His face turns grey. 'Christ! That was Jenny, but we weren't *seeing* each other. OK, there was some weird spark, but . . . Shit, Nix! OK, no, it was more than that; we were really attracted to each other and we both knew it, but we kissed, once, and that was all that ever happened. And I'm sorry you had to see it, I really am, but we didn't have an *affair*. Fuck! She had a fiancé. She was happy with him, and I had you and *I* was happy too, believe it or not. We saw each other outside work what . . . twice, three times maybe. Just a stop for a drink on the way home, and that was that. All it ever was. If we'd both been single, sure, but . . .' He rounds on me. '*You're* the one with the perfect memory. You tell me when we saw each other. Go on. When do I need to account for? When did you not know exactly where I was?'

'I . . .' I can't.

'That day you saw us? She was moving to York. It was her last day and we were probably never going to see each other again, so we decided to go out for a last drink together, only the two of us, because we knew nothing could happen and it would be safe. Up until now I'd forgotten she kissed me, but yes – it was our ten seconds of *what if*? That was all it ever was. The sum total. Ten fucking seconds. Was that wrong? Maybe. But there was never any *affair.*'

This is where Declan tells me to leave. Sends me home, back where I belong, me and Chairman living alone together. Or is this where I slap him and call him a liar, because the clarity of his memory tells me how much that one shared moment meant to him?

There's a long silence.

'It wasn't only that,' I say quietly.

More silence, then Dec exhales, a long sigh that I know is his way of letting something go.

'I know.' He turns away and seems to shrink a little, fiddles with something in his pocket – a nervous tic, something for his hands to do. 'I know, and I felt it, too. It wasn't . . .' He gives a bitter chuckle. 'I don't even know how to describe it. We were . . .'

'Adrift.'

'Yeah.'

'It wasn't that you were having an affair,' I say. 'I believe you when you say that you weren't. It was that you were *thinking* about it.'

He shakes his head. 'I'm not sure I understand that. But . . . maybe that doesn't matter any more. I forgive you.'

I let that sink in. It's an odd feeling. Not the huge pathetic relief I'd expected. Some of that, yes, but with a spike of anger and a big dollop of fear. The fear is that forgiveness means he's stopped caring. The anger – do I *need* forgiving?

'I haven't,' I say. 'I haven't forgiven either of us. I don't think I ever will. I'm not sure I can.'

He looks at me, long and deep. 'Why?'

'Because we were special!' God, how stupid I must sound. 'We were so perfect, like we were the whole world. And then it stopped being like that. It changed. It became,' and I'm floundering for words that don't even exist, '*ordinary.* I hadn't had anyone else. You were the first, the only . . . Oh God.' I look away. 'Because I could remember what it was like when we were together at the start. I could remember every kiss, every special moment. I could remember all the little things that we didn't do any more, everything we'd lost.'

I choke up. Dec smiles, gently shaking his head. I feel his arms slowly wrap themselves around me, hugging me tighter.

'I never stopped being in love with you,' he says. 'Not even after you were gone. I know what you mean. About the distance between us. I thought that was you. I thought you'd decided I was boring.'

I believe him. For the first time in a very long time, I believe him. I think about all the years we lost – the decades I wasted because I was afraid – and I start to cry.

'Hush,' he whispers. 'It's OK.'

'No,' I sob. 'It really isn't. We were the best, and we threw it away. *Both* of us.'

He stares right through me, as though he's looking all the way to the stars.

'I don't want to go home.' I suddenly don't care about Mum and Dave and Dad, and who killed Arty Robbins; I care about this man in front of me who might only have one day of freedom left. 'I want to be with you.' I want us to stay like this, the way we used to be all those years ago.

I let him hold me and it's perfect. It's all I ever wanted.

16

Tuesday 11th February 2020

This time, I don't resist. This time, I let myself have what I want. Declan. My Dec. We go back to his flat and he leaves me alone to make tea. I watch him laugh and smile and feel like I could do this forever, reliving our life together. He opens a bottle of wine and we order food, and then his mum shuffles out of her room, and for an instant I'm speechless at how haggard she looks. Anne Robbins was never a strong woman, not even twenty years ago when I last saw her, but now she looks like a ghost, as pale and thin as a stick.

'Mum, you remember Nicola?'

Anne Robbins looks at me for what feels like an age, then shuffles into the kitchen for a biscuit, turns round and shuffles out. If she recognises me, she gives no sign.

'Is she . . . ?'

'She's had a long day,' says Dec, with just a hint of apology.

I pour myself another glass of wine. I'm a little tipsy now, which makes it easier.

'I don't think your mum ever forgave me for who my dad was,' says Dec without bitterness; and he's right, I don't think she did.

'Come here.' I open my arms to him, and I don't know whether it's the wine or whether any of this will still mean anything in the morning, but right now I don't care. He comes to me and wraps me in his arms and pulls me into him, and I tilt my head and kiss him, and he kisses me back, and for a moment I'm sixteen again.

My phone rings. I silence it.

'I want to stay with you tonight,' I say.

My phone beeps. Someone leaving a message. I don't care. Everything I want is right here. We stagger into the bedroom, locked together, and fall onto the bed and cling to each other, holding each other as though we're afraid to let go.

An hour later, the phone in the lounge rings. We wait for it to stop but a minute later it rings again. This time, Dec puts on a robe and goes out to answer it. The conversation is short and muffled. I hear him, exasperated: 'What? So no one's even talked to them? But what if he *was* there?'

I can't make out the rest. I don't care. I'm wrapped in my

own glow. When he comes back, he has our abandoned glasses and the half-empty bottle of wine.

'My solicitor,' he says. 'About tomorrow.'

I sit up. He's trying hard but he can't quite hide how shaken he is. 'Has something happened? Should I . . . ?'

He kisses me. 'She wants to meet before we go to court, that's all. Maybe we can take those photographs of yours. See if you're right.' He sighs. 'Remember I told you how Mum says that Uncle Dan was at the party that night? I don't see how that can possibly be right. I mean, he'd been gone for fifteen years, so it would have been a big deal, and I don't remember anything at all. But still . . . You'd think someone would follow it up, right?'

I think of the photographs. 'Would you recognise him?'

He shakes his head. None of us would. Except maybe Kat's mum.

We drink a little more. Dec asks about America. I tell him about the tests I did, and the people I met who were like me. When I see he's only half listening, I kiss him again, and he kisses me back, and it turns out to be one of those evenings where kissing is better than talking. We make love for a second time and afterwards Dec falls asleep, like he always did, while I lie awake in the gloom, looking at his sleeping face. He's changed so much, but all it takes is a flicker of thought and I can see him as he was when he was twenty, or twenty-five, or eighteen, lying beside me.

I don't know how long I've been watching him – I'm not tired and I'm in no hurry to stop – when I hear a noise outside in the hall. I almost wake him up, thinking *burglar*, then remember that his mum is staying here, too. I'd almost forgotten; or rather, I'd put her presence out of my mind, too focused on Dec – but now it seems an opportunity. I put on his robe and creep to the door to look, and there she is, shuffling down the corridor.

She stops when she sees me. This time there's no doubt: she knows who I am. She watches me, and I watch her back.

'Can I get you something?' I ask.

'Some water,' she says. Her voice crackles with hostility.

I go to the kitchen and pour a glass of water. Anne Robbins settles in the lounge. I give her the glass and turn away, but she catches my wrist, her bony fingers trembling.

'Why are *you* here?' she asks. Her grip tightens and then she lets go in disgust.

'I was with him on the night his father disappeared.' Her knuckles clench white. 'I'm trying to help him. I'm his alibi. At least . . . until he went back to the Shelley.'

She looks away, then looks back. 'Declan says his father hit him and that you were there. Is that true?'

'Yes.'

'You Walkers. Arthur loved that boy. What on earth did your mother say for him to be like that?'

'I don't know,' I say, which is true, but the way she looks

at me – all full of suspicion and disgust – makes me go on. 'She knew what he was doing. I think she threatened to call the police if he didn't stop.'

Anne Robbins almost spits at me, 'And what business was it of any of the rest of you, what happened in our house?'

Why is she defending him when she was the biggest victim of all? I don't understand. 'He was having sex with a schoolgirl,' I say. 'Someone I knew. She was underage. Mum found out.'

'Liar!' The look Anne Robbins gives me has such venom that I take a step back.

'Do you want me to help you back to your room?'

She shakes her head. 'Get me my blanket.'

I fetch the blanket from her bed and bring it back. I give it to her and she waves me away.

'A proper nerve, your mother, spreading filth about my Arthur while she was carrying on with David Crane.'

I flinch.

'Oh yes. Those evenings working in the Shelley? Everyone knew.'

I bite my lip. I want to say something mean and spiteful, like how at least Dave wasn't fifteen. 'I'm sorry Arty used to hit you,' I say instead. 'I'm sorry we didn't see it sooner.'

'People talk such nonsense.' She doesn't look at me. 'Marjory simply made up what she wanted to hear. Spiteful little liar, just like your mother.'

'I remember the bruises, Mrs Robbins.'

She ignores me.

'Mrs Robbins . . . was Declan with you that night?'

Now, at last, her eyes fix on mine. She leans forward and catches my arm again. 'Yes, and that's what I told them. And don't think for one moment that he's going to take you back, after what you did to him.'

The way she looks at me is like she *wants* me to know she's lying, like she's daring me to call her out on it. I think of the curtains in Declan's bedroom, closed at midnight when I saw him leave, open the next morning.

'Did you go back home that night?' I ask.

'All of them so worried about your precious mother – as if she hadn't brought it on herself. It was Arty's birthday!'

'Was Declan's uncle there that night?'

Anne Robbins turns away as though I'm not there, pulls the blanket around herself and settles into the armchair, and doesn't answer when I ask again. I don't know what to think. How much does she *really* remember?

I slide back into bed and find Dec only pretending to be asleep. I kiss him and then I close my eyes and drift, exhausted and content. My alarm will go off in a few hours and I'll have to get up. I'll take the day off work. I'll have breakfast with Declan and then we'll go to see his solicitor, and I'll wait outside; and then I'll talk to this Angela Watson myself and tell her about my memory and everything I know. I'll ask her what she needs me to do. I'll go with Dec to court, bleary and rumpled in yesterday's clothes, hair a mess, bags under my eyes . . .

But happy.

It's light when I open my eyes. I look round, dazed for a moment by waking in an unfamiliar room. There's no clock beside the bed. I reach for Dec but he's already up. I feel for my phone under the pillow. It's not there.

Sod it!

I lie still, luxuriating in feelings of warmth and happiness. The flat is quiet. Dec's robe hangs on the back of the bedroom door so he must already be dressed. Maybe he's gone out to bring warm croissants and pastries fresh from some nearby bakery. I bask in the idea, until the need to pee drives me to the bathroom. The light streaming through the curtains there reminds me that I should call the library to say I'm not going to be in. I go to the kitchen for a glass of water, and I suppose I should really get dressed so that when Dec comes back, we can go home and find out whether there's anything in Chloe Clarke's photographs . . .

Shit! I *can't* take the day off. I've got that stupid appointment with bloody Emily from HR.

Shit! What time is it?

I go back to the bedroom. My phone isn't in the pocket of my jeans, which is odd, because I know it was there last night and I swear I never took it out. I feel stupid, poking at my scattered clothes in case it fell out while we were undressing each other, but I think I would have noticed. When I search the bedroom and still can't find it, I go back to the lounge and use Dec's house-phone to call myself. My phone rings from the lounge table, which makes no sense because I *know* I had it in my pocket when we went to the bedroom; and yes, it might have fallen out, but not into a different room.

I'm late. I need to get home and get changed in order to go back out. I need to go right now.

A string of notifications lights up. The latest is a missed call, the one I just made. Behind that is a text from Kat, a couple of missed calls from Mum, a waiting voicemail and some more missed calls. I flick them away and dial Dec but the call doesn't connect, so I pick up the voicemail.

Nicky, it's Kat. I've been calling all night! Where are you? I'm with Mum and those photos you got done are here. No Dec, but they reminded me of something: I think I saw him that night. Late, outside the Shelley. If you talk to him, tell him good luck for tomorrow. Tell him we've got all our fingers crossed.

I go to the text that I flicked away. Kat again.

Mum's photos arrived. No Dec :-(

Dec went to the Shelley less than ten minutes after I got home. I *saw* him leave. It's what he told me the next day. It's what he always told me . . .

I scramble into my clothes and try his phone a second time. Still straight to voicemail. Has he got it turned off? I leave a message: *Dec, it's me. Answer your phone. I need to go. I have to get to work. See you later?*

I pause at the door on my way out. A part of me wants to go back to Anne Robbins and shake her awake and not let her go until she tells me what she really remembers, but what if it's nothing? Do I really want to know?

On the hallway floor, I see a shape half covered by a fallen scarf. It looks like an old mobile phone, but then I see it has a strap . . .

Dec's police tracker. He's cut it off.

Oh God. *Why?*

I run back to Dec's bedroom, poking his number into my phone yet again. Still no answer. I rush out of the flat, determined to find him before he makes this worse than it already is . . . but as soon as I get outside, I realise I don't have the first idea where to go. I run along the High Street, looking into coffee shops and cafés, but he's not there. I call again and again but his phone doesn't even ring. He's turned it off.

I check my in-box. Nothing from Declan, only an email telling me my photographs have been delivered.

I don't know what else to do. I need to get home so that I can get changed so I can go to work. I'll be late, but I should squeak in for half-nine. And what else *can* I do, except wait to see who calls first: Dec or Detective Scott, wanting to know what I was doing at Dec's flat last night, and do I know where he is, and not believing a word I say when I tell him I have no idea, and it's all so stupid. It doesn't *matter* if Dec's not in the photographs! He was probably upstairs with his mum, or asleep. What matters is that *someone* must remember him coming back to the Shelley with a bloody lip and a black eye . . .

I wave down a taxi and jump inside almost before it stops. In the back seat, I call Kat.

'Nicky? Jesus, what time . . . Oh, right.' I hear her yawn.

'What do you mean you saw Dec outside the Shelley?'

'What?'

'Your message. Last night.'

'*You* didn't pick up your phone. Hot date?'

'Kat!'

'Right. Dec. Yes. It's no biggy, but . . .' I hear a languid stretch to her voice, a tone I know, and then the rustle of sheets.

'Why aren't you at work?' It's already twenty to nine. I know why *I'm* not at work, but why . . . ?

'Sweetheart! Self-care day.' I almost hear the shrug. 'So yesterday I had the afternoon off and went to see Mum. I thought, maybe . . . Oh God, *promise* you won't say anything about – you know.'

If she's taking a day off work, could Gary be there too, lying next to her? I have to be careful not to say anything about her and Arty. It's hard. Even thinking about it makes me angry.

'I don't see why—'

'Promise me!'

'OK, I promise.'

'Anyway, I went to see Mum, and your mum and dick-face Dave were there, too; and just after I showed up, this delivery guy comes to the door with a package that turned out to be your photos. Mum opened them up and we all looked through them. I tried to call you in case you wanted to come over, too. Anyway, you've probably looked at them already by now, so—'

'I haven't.'

'Oh.' Kat sounds surprised. 'Well, there *are* some pictures from after midnight. They're not very good, and I have *no* idea who anyone is. Dec isn't in any of them but it was late, right? Anyway, we got talking about that night and I remembered that I *did* see him. I remember thinking it was really important that Mum didn't see me and Gary together, so I made him stay outside when we got back while I checked to see if the coast was clear, which it bloody well wasn't because *everyone* was looking for us, and Mum had a complete meltdown at me and then put me to work collecting empties and washing glasses. I don't know for how long, but I think I saw Dec come in – I remember *that* because I wanted him to find Gary . . . Anyway, I didn't get to talk to him, but then Mum said I could go home, so I got my stuff and went. And that was when I saw Dec again. Outside the Shelley – can't have been more than ten, fifteen minutes later. He didn't see me, and I wanted to go to bed, so I didn't say anything, but—'

'You saw him there? Outside the Shelley?'

Kat sighs, long and loud. 'Maybe he went out for five minutes to clear his head, I don't know. Anyway, I'm sure it was him, so that's good, right? He was there, like you said. Gary reckons the two of them hung around outside for a while, too, but I'm not sure he really remembers it.' Her tone turns curious. 'You sound different. Are you at home?'

'I'm in the back of a taxi and I'm in a bit of a rush. I was with him, OK? Last night. At his place. I stayed over. Now he's gone missing. He's supposed to be in court this afternoon.'

Silence stretches out between us. I check my watch. A quarter to nine, but I'm almost home.

'Jesus!' says Kat at last.

My head is spinning. The curtains. The curtains in Declan's room. I closed them before we started kissing, before his dad came back. They were closed when I saw Dec leave the house later, when he turned and looked up and saw me and waved. I never thought much of it, but when I looked the next morning, they were open . . . Which means *someone* was back in his room during the night. And I asked Dec so many times about that night, and he always said that he went to the Shelley and stayed there with his mum, and why would he lie about something like that?

I have his mum's words in my head: *Yes, and that's what I told them.*

What does she really remember?

On the other end of the line, Kat takes a deep breath. 'Nicky . . .'

'What?'

'I was thinking—'

'Kat, I'm in a real rush. I'm late. I'm going to have to hang up in a minute.'

'Nicky, hear me out. Arty Robbins was a violent, abusive, manipulative piece of shit who hurt everyone around him. Me, Dec, his wife, your mum. Whoever pushed him in that hole, they did the world a favour. I know you want to help Dec, but . . .'

'But?'

'I remember seeing him outside the Shelley. That's it. I don't think he was heading anywhere. I think he was just sort of standing there. I really don't know, but I was thinking I could say something else. You know – if that would help – I could say I saw him go upstairs. I don't know, maybe I really did? Maybe that's what really happened. I could say I was there until two or three in the morning, with him. No one would know.'

Straight-up lie to the police? 'Do you . . . do you think he did it?' The taxi slows to a stop, waiting to turn right across the traffic and into my street.

'No, I don't, although we both know I'm a shit judge of character, right? But I've been thinking: maybe whoever did this to Arty Robbins doesn't deserve to go to prison. And if you and Dec are back together, and he makes you happy—'

'You *do* think he did it!' The words crack between us like a whip, out fast and harsh and too quick to take back.

'No! I don't know what I—'

'I have to go.' We're moving again.

'Nicky—'

'I'm sorry.' I hang up. I can't take this.

The curtains. The curtains in Dec's room were open the next morning, which means someone went back. I always thought it was his mum or maybe his dad. It didn't seem to matter. But if his dad was dead and his mum stayed all night in the Shelley . . .

'Miss?'

We've stopped. The taxi driver has turned to look at me.

'Can you wait here? I need to get changed and then I need to get to the British Library.' I look at my watch. Ten to nine. Five minutes to get changed, fifteen minutes to get to the library, another ten minutes to get to HR and I've still got ten minutes to spare. 'I'll only be a few minutes.'

I dash out, not waiting for an answer. Christ! Dec always

said he never went back home that night. Why would he lie about something like that? Because he had to change his clothes? Because they were covered in mud?

No. No, no, no . . .

I try his number again, and again it goes to voicemail. I don't understand where he's gone.

My phone. He must have taken it. I mean, it doesn't have legs or wheels of its own, so *someone* carried it from the bedroom into the lounge, and I know that someone wasn't me . . .

He saw the message from Kat: *Mum's photos arrived. No Dec :-(*

He must have woken in the night and seen it. Maybe the phone fell out of my pocket and it was lying on the floor; maybe he trod on it or something. He must have picked it up and taken it into the lounge. He saw the message from Kat. And there was that call last night from his solicitor . . .

Oh, Dec, what have you done?

I stand at the door, feeling stupid as I search my jacket for my keys, and suddenly I'm in 1994, just before Christmas, sitting at home on my own, crying because Mum's been on the phone and told me that Dad's got cancer and it's not looking good, and maybe he has three months or six, if he's lucky; and all she can think of to say after she tells me is what a shame he won't ever get to be a grandfather, because he would have loved that; and she's right, and he would have been great, but I can't shake away the accusation that lies in her words – that I've left it too late, that I should have got on with it, that somehow it's *my* fault. Declan isn't home and Kat isn't answering her phone, and so I have a drink or two to steady my nerves, and maybe I have one too many, because the first thing Declan says when he rolls in at nearly ten at night is: *Christ, are you drunk?* We argue and I can't bring myself to tell him about Dad because it's all too horrible, so I run to the guest room and lock the door and climb into bed and I don't come out until morning; and Dec only knocks on the door once and asks to come in and then tells me, when I don't answer, that I'm not being very grown-up.

It wasn't the last time I slept alone—

Focus! *Shit!* Almost nine and I'm standing outside my front door like a lemon. My keys aren't in my jacket, they're in my bag. I let myself in and . . .

Straight away, I know something is wrong. The air feels odd. There's no miaow from Chairman, no pad of paws as he comes to rub against my legs to demand his breakfast. I go to the kitchen and his food bowl is empty. Of course it is, because I didn't come home last night and so he didn't have his supper, so he should be all over me, telling me he's hungry, and please get on with things . . .

I don't have time for this. I've got a taxi waiting outside and I need to—

I hear a chirrup from the lounge. I run in and there Chairman is, curled up on the sofa, stretching. And I can't put my finger on it but the air still feels wrong. I scan the room. Everything is where it should be. Just a light blinking on the landline phone that I almost never use – a message waiting on the answering machine. I press play but it's a few seconds of static and then the line goes dead. The call isn't from a number I recognise, but it was made twenty minutes ago.

Dec?

More likely one of those auto-dial marketing calls.

I don't have time. I need to get changed and *go*.

I hear a noise from the bedroom. The slight creak of a board. I freeze. Did I imagine it? Or is there someone else here? I reach for my phone, finger hovering over the emergency call button as I move back to the lounge doorway and look into the hall. 'Hello?'

No. *Focus!* I'm imagining things and I don't have time.

The bedroom door is ajar. It should be open. It's always open so Chairman can get in and out.

'Is there anyone here?' The front door was locked when I got back. The windows are closed. There's nothing out of place. Just a . . . *wrongness* in the air. Or maybe I'm bringing things back from my memories. Too many different times and places, all crashing together at once.

Chairman rubs against my legs and then trots into the kitchen and miaows at me. *Breakfast, please!*

I push the bedroom door open. The room beyond is . . .

Exactly as it should be.

Five past nine. I'm jumpy, that's all. This thing with Dec going missing has me on edge. My work clothes are laid out neatly on the bed, as I left them. I pull off my jeans and climb into a skirt. No time for make-up or anything like that – a dab of lippy in the taxi, that's all. I yank my T-shirt over my head and tug on my blouse. I'm starting on the buttons when I feel the skin prickle on the back of my neck and feel a whisper of movement behind me and . . .

I turn and . . .

And there's a man in my room. Right in front of me, and I can't see who it is because he's holding up my dressing gown, coming at me with it. I cry out and lift my arms to cover my face and then he's on me, the cloth wrapped around my head, smothering me. I stumble back, blind, struggling to breathe, my arms flailing to push him away. I trip on the edge of the bed and then I'm falling. One hand smacks against the bedside table as I try to catch myself. I feel the lamp go flying and hear it shatter on the floor, and then my head bangs against the wall as I crumple, ripping at the cotton wrapped around my face, yelling and screaming. I tear it off, terrified, eyes wide, but there's no one, and all I hear are fading footsteps.

I sit for a long, long moment, too stunned to move. When I haul myself up, I'm shaking so much that I almost fall again. It takes a few seconds before I steady myself. I pick up the ruin of the bedside light and clutch it like a club, then shuffle into the hall.

The front door is wide open.

I go back to the lounge and look out through the window to the street below, in case I see someone running away.

Nothing. Just a waiting taxi.

Back in the hall, I close the front door and lean against it, waiting for my heart to stop racing. In the nook by the door is my little table with its notepad and pen, and its collection of junk-mail waiting for recycling.

Mail . . .

The photographs.

They should be here: a packet of them lying on the floor by the letterbox.

But they're not.

17

Wednesday 12th February 2020, 9.10 a.m.

Do I call the police? What do I say? That someone slipped into my flat and attacked me but I have no idea who it was? That they took something that wasn't even here before I left? As far as I can see, they didn't touch anything else. My laptop is on the table beside the bed, where I left it. Everything is exactly where it should be. Everything except the one thing I need.

I fumble my phone out of my bag and call Kat. It rings and rings and finally goes to voicemail. I hang up and try again and the same thing happens. On the third try, she picks up.

'Nicky! What the hell—'

'Someone broke into my flat,' I say, which stops her cold. '*What?*'

Words pour out of me as I tell her what happened: how someone was here in the flat and they attacked me and I didn't see who it was, and now they've gone and they took the photographs and I don't know what to do and it's all too much, because I've been thinking about the curtains in Dec's room that were open when they should have been closed, and how I don't think his mum remembers whether he was there, and now he's gone missing and I just spent the night with him, and of course he didn't do it but oh God, no one really jumps bail unless they're guilty, do they?

I have to stop to breathe.

'Wait . . . someone *attacked* you? Jesus Christ, Nicky, are you OK?'

'I'm fine.' I'm not fine. 'They just pushed me over and ran away. I fell, that's all, and—' I'm not fine at all. I'm shaking like a leaf.

'Nicky, what you do is call the bloody police. Right now! And get out! Whoever it was, are you sure they're gone?'

'As sure as I can be.' What if they *are* still here, lurking, hiding under the bed or something? What if the open front door was a trick? I hadn't thought of that – and it's stupid, I know it is, but what if they're just waiting for me to hang up before they spring out again and . . .

'*Are* you sure?' Kat sounds as scared as I feel. 'Because if you're not, then you should get out and call the police straight away.'

Chairman walks in a circle around me. He looks at me, curious, and butts his head against my hand. Somehow that makes me feel a little better.

'Nicky! Just get out and call the police. You can come here, if you want to. Or . . . no, find a café that's close. Somewhere that's public. I'll meet you there. You shouldn't be on your own.'

'No. No, I . . . I think I'd better stay here.' She's right, I *should* call the police. But it feels so stupid.

I don't want to be scared like this.

'Do you want me to come over?'

I *won't* be scared like this.

'Just . . . Kat, stay on the phone while I look round, OK?'

I check the front door. It was locked when I got home from Dec's place and there's no sign of damage. I check the windows and find them locked, too, like they always are. I go back into the bedroom and open the wardrobe and leap back in case there's someone lurking inside. There isn't, of course, and I feel a fool.

A soft thump makes me jump almost out of my skin, but it's only Chairman, leaping off a windowsill. He watches me as I look under the bed, and I feel even more stupid than I did when I checked the wardrobe. I peer into the bathroom. It's all empty.

'OK,' I say into the phone, 'I've been scared witless by my own cat but there's no one here.'

Chairman follows me around, rubbing himself against my legs. He wants to know what I'm doing. He still wants his breakfast.

'Good,' says Kat. 'Now call the police!'

I stand in the middle of the bedroom, looking around. 'I don't understand. How did they get in?'

'Nicky, are you sure you don't want me to come over? It's not a problem at all – I've got the day off.'

'You want to stay with the break-in victim while she waits for the police?' I try to make it sound like it's nothing. 'It's not much of a self-care day, is it?'

'You're my friend and I'll stay with you for as long as you need me. I could call Gary, too, see if he could come over.'

'He's not with you?'

'No, he's working. When *isn't* he? He was supposed to take the day off too, but . . .' I hear her sigh.

Gary. I keep coming back to that night; to the venom in him while he was talking to Kat when he thought they were alone. *You tell me who he is! Tell me and I'll fucking kill him!*

But Gary was with Kat that night. She said so.

'You were with your mum yesterday evening? Looking at the photographs from the Shelley?' Unless it all happened after they went back . . .

'Yes, but—'

'Was Gary with you?' But then where did Arty Robbins go for those missing two hours? Besides, Kat never told Gary about her and Arty Robbins . . .

'No. Just your mum and—'

'But you told Gary about them when you got home, right?' Unless . . .

Kat may never have told him about her and Arty Robbins, but perhaps he knew all the same. Gary definitely had something against Arty. I saw it in the way he looked at Kat that Sunday when she told him Arty was dead.

'Nicky, where are you going with this?'

'That night: were you with Gary the whole time, after Dec and I left?' I keep looking for who was missing for long enough to hide a body, but what if someone pushed Arty Robbins into that pit and then left him there, and only later went back to hide what they'd done?

'I . . .' Kat pauses. I can almost hear the realisation hitting her down the line. 'Until past midnight. After that, I went home. Nicky, you're not suggesting—'

'Kat!' I snap. 'My front door was locked. The windows are locked. You and Mum are the only ones with a spare key.'

There's a long pause from the other end of the line as I hear Kat move through her flat and rummage through a drawer. 'It's still here.' I hear the edge to her voice. 'Are you *sure* you don't want me to come over?'

'No, no, it's—' I stop, trying to control the thoughts racing through me. 'Sorry. Thanks for . . . You're right. I'm being stupid. I'm going to call the police now.' The idea that it was Gary is still prowling around my mind. He's been here before. He knows where I live. He knows where Kat keeps my spare key. He could have made a copy. And he's the only one, apart from Kat, who had a reason to kill Arty Robbins.

My hands are shaking. I need to collect myself before I call the police. I hang up and sit on the bed and stroke Chairman and go back to 1985, to the night of the party, to watching Mum have it out with Arty Robbins. I see her as she was, furious as a tiger. Her anger is outrage and a primal disgust. I see her stab at his chest with her finger . . .

Dave Crane at the bar, watching like a hawk . . .

Was Kat close enough to hear what Mum was saying? She must have been terrified, but she couldn't let it show.

And Gary, watching Kat with that same intensity . . . *I'll fucking kill him!*

I check the door and the windows one more time. There's no sign anyone forced their way in, and lock-picks and snap-gun gadgets are for *CSI* shows, not for real life. Nobody broke into this flat. Someone let themselves in.

It's gone nine. It's a weekday. I should be at work. I should be there right now, at that stupid meeting with HR. The flat should have been empty. It should have been easy for him, whoever it was: slip in, find the photographs, slip away again. If I hadn't come home when I did, I might never have known. Lost in the post. Just one of those things.

But the photographs, if they were here, should have been on the floor by the front door. The man who attacked me was in my bedroom. Why didn't he just *take* them? Was he after something else? But if so, *what*?

I pick up the phone to call the police and then stop. I'm going to sound stupid. No one broke in. They came in with a key. They didn't take anything – not that I can prove.

I wasn't supposed to be here. I only came back because I needed to change.

A nasty thought creeps into the edges of my mind. I don't want to look at it but it won't go away. What if Kat's lying? What if they were in it together?

No. Not my best friend.

I try calling Dec, for the umpteenth time. Dear God, why did he have to run away? Why today? Because he was afraid they'd lock him up until he went to trial? They certainly will now!

His number goes straight to voicemail, as it has all morning. I leave another message: *Dec, it's me. We need to talk. You need to come back. I think I know who killed your dad.*

Gary. Maybe Kat was telling the truth; maybe she never *did* tell him about Arty Robbins, but that doesn't mean Gary didn't work it out. Maybe he overheard Mum telling Dave after Arty attacked her. Maybe it was just the way Kat looked when Mum accused Arty in the Shelley. Maybe she said something later, when they were alone together. Kat says they were together until after midnight, but her mum said she was back before then; and Kat also says she went back into the Shelley on her own, checking that the coast was clear, only to discover that everyone was looking for us. Did Gary wait outside, like she says, or did he go back across the park to his van? Did he see Arty Robbins and follow him? Did he lure him to the building site with threats and blackmail? Or did he do it earlier, while he was waiting out in the park for Kat? Did he go back again later and bury the body in the middle of the night? Did he kill Arty Robbins on purpose, or was it an accident?

Chairman climbs onto my lap, purring like an engine as I stroke his head and scratch his chin. Gary was in the park. He had a reason. He had a temper. I remember him sitting in his van, Adam Ant singing 'Stand and Deliver' while four policemen forced their way into some stranger's house. A search warrant, so the rumours went. Drugs. And Gary was into his weed back then . . .

And now he's on the brink of some big property deal in Docklands.

I go back to the lounge and play the message on the answering machine a second time. Still nothing. Was that Gary, calling ahead to see whether the flat was empty? I check the number against the number I have in my phone for

Gary Barclay, but he's too clever for that. I google it, on the off-chance, but nothing comes up. I play the message again, and then again, listening hard, but all I hear is a subdued roar of traffic in the background.

I call the number from my landline. It rings twice and then goes dead. I get my coat. Outside, the taxi is still waiting, impatient, meter still running. I ask the driver if he saw anyone come out of my building and he says no, but I see he has one of those dashboard cameras. I tell him I've just been attacked and that the police might want to look at the recordings. I pay him what I owe and add a fat tip. I don't ask for his number and I don't write it down. I've already got all that in my head.

I settle into a café that has a couple of spare seats. It's gone half-past nine. I call work and ask for Emily in HR. She doesn't pick up, so I leave a message on her answering service and tell her I was attacked on my way to work this morning and that I won't be in because I have to deal with the police. Then I buy myself a sandwich and call Detective Scott. I start to tell him that Dec is missing, but he already knows.

'I was just attacked in my flat,' I say. I tell him what happened. He takes a few details and checks to make sure I'm somewhere safe, then tells me to stay where I am.

'I'll have a uniformed officer come to take a full statement.'

'It was about Arty Robbins' murder,' I say. 'The only

thing they stole was a copy of the photographs Chloe Clarke took that night. You've got copies, too. I need to see them.'

'I'll think about that. I do have some questions about the statement you gave yesterday.' He asks if I could come to the station.

'There's something else.' None of this makes any sense unless you know about Kat and Arty. I have to tell him.

I can hear him waiting. Deep breaths, Nicola.

'Arty Robbins was sexually abusing my best friend. Katherine Clarke. She was fifteen at the time.' I'm sorry, Kat. 'She was fifteen.'

'You're telling me Robbins was sleeping with a schoolgirl?' I can hear him trying to put the pieces together in his head; and that he knows a can of worms opening when he hears it. 'Anyone going to back that up?'

'Kat, obviously.' I can't decide whether he's taking me seriously.

'She'll talk, if I ask her to come in and give a statement?'

'Do you have to?'

'This is a murder investigation, Ms Walker.'

'My mum knew about it. That was what the fight was about, between her and Arty. I think my dad knew, too. And Kat's boyfriend – husband, now. Gary Barclay.'

I tell him I'm happy to talk to him in person but I won't go on the record about Kat unless Kat says it's OK. As soon as he hangs up, I call Mum.

I Know What I Saw

'Hi, Mum.'

'Nicola!'

'You called last night. What's up?'

'Called? No, I don't think so.'

'I got two messages saying you tried to call. Last night.'

'Oh. Did I?' Mum sounds confused. 'I was next door with Chloe—'

'And Kat. Yes, I know. The photographs.'

'Yes.'

I wait for her to say more, but she doesn't.

'Mum, can you do something for me?'

'Of course, love.'

'Can you do it right now?'

'Nicola, what's going on?'

'The photographs. They're really important. Can you pop next door and ask Mrs Clarke if I could borrow them? I made a second set but they . . . they've gone missing.'

Mum sounds less than impressed but agrees that yes, she can. I ask her to call me and then gnaw on my sandwich, too distracted to taste what I'm eating. The fear is sloughing off, transforming to anger.

Gary. It *has* to be Gary! Who else? Gary, and he's made me scared of my own home.

No. Think, Nicky Walker! *He's* the one who's scared. He's scared of those photographs.

I scan faces as people pass the café window, feeling paranoid in case he's there, in case he's following me. Maybe this is a mistake, but this is about *me*, about something *I'll* remember.

My phone rings, Mum's name flashing up. 'Nicola?'

'Mum,' I breathe, 'did you find the—'

'I'm sitting with Chloe. She wants me to say thank—'

'The photographs,' I snap. 'Have you got the photographs?'

'Yes, love. They're right in front of me.'

'Mum, I need you to do me another favour. I need you to meet me in town, and I need you to bring them.'

'But, love, they're not mine. I—'

'Mum! Someone broke into my flat this morning. They were after those pictures. They took them. There's something in them about who killed Arty Robbins.'

'But I—'

'Tell Mrs Clarke that it might be dangerous to keep them.' It's only as I say it that I realise it might even be true.

'Oh, love . . . does it have to be today?'

That's all Mum has to say? No *How are you* or *Oh my God, how terrible* or even *What did they take*? I don't think she's even absorbed what I said. She sounds bewildered.

'Would it be OK if I stay over tonight?' I ask.

'Tonight?' She makes it sound like I'm asking her to sacrifice her firstborn. 'Dave and I are going out.'

'I don't want to be on my own, OK?'

Mum grudgingly agrees to leave right away. I choose a pub I know, with a quiet basement. We'll go through the photos together. I'll find what Gary Barclay is trying to hide and then I'll take it to Detective Scott and it'll all be over.

Back on the High Street, I can't shake the idea that Gary is somewhere near, following me. It's ridiculous, because he'd have to have been following me all morning, ever since I got home, and why on earth would he bother when he already has what he came for? And yet the feeling haunts me, and then another thought comes: what if he's on his way up to Wordsworth Park right now to get the other set of photographs from Mrs Clarke? What if she really *is* in danger?

I dive into another coffee shop. I know where he works, so I do an Internet search for his office and get a number. I call the switchboard and ask for Gary Barclay. They put me through to some secretary, who tells me that Mr Barclay is with clients at the moment.

'But he's in the office, yes?'

'He's this moment gone into a meeting. He should be free in fifteen minutes or so. Can I take a name and a number so he can call you back?'

I should hang up. I've got what I want. Gary's gone back to the office, probably so that he can pretend he never left. He must have just got there, but that's OK because it means he's not following me and he's not on his way to Wordsworth

Park, so I know I'm safe, and so are Mum and Mrs Clarke . . . but I'm scared, and I'm boiling with anger.

'Yes,' I say. 'Tell him Nicola Walker called. He's got my number.'

Stupid. *Stupid!* I know I've made a mistake as soon as it's out.

As I reach the station, I see three waiting taxis and slip inside the first. A taxi feels safer. Enclosed. I tell the driver to take me to Princess Street. As we pull away, my phone rings and I almost jump out of my skin.

'Ms Walker?'

My heart skips a beat. The voice is Dec's solicitor. 'Do you know where Declan is?'

'Ah. I was rather hoping to ask you the same. He's due in court.'

'He told me.'

'If he doesn't show up, there's really not much I can do. Do you have any means of contacting him?'

'Only his mobile number.' Which she already has and which is still going straight to voicemail.

'I see. Well, thank you. Ms Walker, if Mr Robbins does happen to get in touch, please ask him to call me. It would really be *very* helpful if he could make himself known. I can stall, but not for long.'

I promise to call her back if Dec gets in touch, not that I think he will. Where *is* he?

I Know What I Saw

Almost as soon as I hang up, the phone rings again. *This* number I recognise. Work. I shunt it to voicemail. I don't want to hear bloody Emily from HR tell me how they're very sorry but they've had to start a disciplinary process. I don't need that – not today.

The taxi isn't making much progress through the traffic. From the window, all I see are red lights and cars and milling people.

'Has there been some sort of accident?'

The driver laughs. 'This is normal.' He flashes a grin into the mirror. 'You in a hurry?'

'A little.'

He shakes his head. My phone rings for a third time.

'Nicky?'

I freeze.

'Hello?'

It's Gary. I almost hang up. Calling him seems so stupid now. But if I hang up . . .

'Look, Kat told me you had a break-in. And about Dec. I'm sorry, Nicky. If there's anything we can do.' He pauses. 'Are you OK?'

'I know it was you, Gary. I've already talked to the police.' Christ, what am I doing?

'What are you talking about?' Tension cracks the edge of his voice. Good! Now he knows how it feels.

'You killed him, Gary.'

'*What?*'

'You killed Arty Robbins.'

'What the fuck? Why the hell would I kill Declan's dad? I didn't even know the guy!' I hear the ugliness in his voice, the brutal edge I remember from thirty-five years ago, before he started trying to hide what he really was behind that veneer of refinement.

'Because you knew Arty Robbins was the boyfriend Kat was trying to keep a secret, that's why! Because you knew he was shagging her.'

There's a long silence, then, 'Jesus, Nicola. You're sick, you know that?'

The line goes dead. The taxi driver is watching through the rear-view mirror. I catch his eye and he looks away. I'm gasping, panting like I've run halfway across London. What have I done?

18

Wednesday 12th February
2020, 11.30 p.m.

Two months after Kat came to see me in America, she called me. She was distraught in a way I'd never heard before. Between the sobs, she told me she was in hospital. She'd had a late miscarriage. What should have been her second son had been born twenty-two weeks early, a stillbirth. I was the first person she told, even before Gary. I was still wrestling with how I felt about being divorced – I suppose I'm still wrestling with it now. I listened to her without really listening, without truly hearing the pain she was in, and then asked what I could do. Nothing, she said. I was in America, after all. It would be silly for me to come all the way back simply for her. She had her mum and Gary, and

Gary's family. She just needed to tell me, that was all. I said the right things, held her hand as best I could down a phone from five thousand miles away. At least, I *think* I did. I tried to, wrapped up as I was in my own misery. I can't help thinking, though, that if it had been the other way round, Kat would have been on the next plane. She would have dropped everything to come to me, and she would have stayed until she knew I was going to be OK.

She was always there for me. I wish I could say the same. And now I've told her secret, probably to the one person she most wanted not to know. I told it to save a man who, until recently, I hadn't even spoken to in ten years.

I reach the pub on Princess Street in time to see Mum go inside. I expect to navigate through the lunchtime rush, but the place is almost empty. I order two coffees and go down to the basement, hoping we'll have the place to ourselves, but two men are there ahead of us, poring over a script and reading aloud. The language sounds like Shakespeare but I don't recognise the play.

Mum goes very still when she sees me. The colour drains out of her like she's seen a ghost. She gets to her feet. 'Oh . . . oh, Nicola, I'm so sorry.' One hand moves to her half-open mouth as she comes out from behind her table and hugs me for a very long time. 'I'm so sorry,' she says again. 'It's just . . . When you told me on the phone, it didn't register. Have you been to the police?'

'It's OK, Mum.' It's not. It's very far from OK. He came into my flat. He has a key, which means he could come back, and I've told Gary I think he's a murderer.

I'll carry the memory with me for the rest of my life. Now and then, when I least expect it, I'll find myself sprawled on the floor with a dressing gown wrapped around my face, helpless and struggling to breathe, not knowing whether there's someone standing right over me, about to do something much, much worse.

'I'm not hurt. Just . . . shaken up,' I say.

We sit down and stare at each other. 'And you didn't see—'

'No. I didn't see his face.'

Mum reaches across the table to take my hand in hers. 'Did you call the police?'

'Yes, and I'm going to see them later. I wanted to see the photographs first, though. It's why he was there – to get them.'

'Love, half the people here are dead!' Mum puts three envelopes on the table. 'You should really let this go. Let the police do their job.'

Three envelopes? But there were *four* sets of negatives.

She pushes them across the table.

'Is that all of them?'

'Yes, love.'

I open the picture wallets. Three sets, each wallet in the order they were taken. The first pictures I look at are obviously from before any guests arrived. There's the Shelley, almost empty, with bunting hanging inside and the tables pushed together in the saloon bar, loaded with plates and cutlery for the evening. There's a picture of Vincent standing beside the *Fifty Years* banner, holding up a pint and grinning for all he's worth; then one of him and Madge, then one of Kat's mum, then one of Dave, then one of Mum and Mrs Clarke together, all of them in their Mary Shelley aprons. They look happy. Excited, even.

Except Mum. All I see there is tension.

I skim forward. The pictures are of the party guests as they arrive, posing by the Mary Shelley sign, the pub steadily filling up. I recognise faces even if I can't put names to them. People I used to see in Byron Road or Tennyson Way, or in the park now and then. By the time I reach the end of the first wallet, the guests are still arriving. I haven't seen any of me or Dad or Arty Robbins.

Mum watches with a curious interest as I start on the next wallet. It's the second film, because the pictures are still of people beside the Shelley sign. I find Gary in his long, dark coat and his quiff, trying to look sultry, and feel a stab of fear and guilt.

'Nicky?'

I'm shaking.

'Nicky? What is it?'

'I'm OK.' *Breathe!*

I Know What I Saw

I used to think he was a bit of a joke but now I wonder: a spate of burglaries a few months after the party; cars that went missing every month or so. There was a mugging one night, not long after Dec moved to Nottingham. It made the news because the victim ended up in hospital and nearly died; Gary was with Kat when it happened, but he knew the men who did it. That was the first time Kat broke up with him. I remember how upset she was, shocked and shaken. *He's not like that*, she used to say.

Isn't he?

My phone rings. An unknown number. I send it to voice-mail and move on. I find Dad in his leather jacket outside the Shelley. The next picture is of Mum and Dad together. Dad's smiling, happy, Mum's stiff and wooden . . .

The one after is of Dad and Dave, arms round each other's shoulders, both of them grinning like they could take on the world. I stop and stare at it, looking at Dad, but if he had any idea that something was going on between Mum and Dave, there's no sign of it here. The photo after that is of Dad and Dave again, this time with Mum in the middle. It reminds me of the picture of me and Dec and Kat, which must be in here, too. The Three Musketeers. Mum looks brittle enough to shatter.

I put the picture carefully down, side by side with the first. Mum sits on the chair beside me and squeezes my knee.

'Thanks for doing this,' I say, still looking at the picture of Mum and Dad. 'Mum, I think it was Gary Barclay who broke into my flat.'

'Kat's *husband*?'

'They have a spare key. He's been to my flat before.'

'Nicky . . .'

'I think he knew about Kat and Arty Robbins. I know *you* did. And Dad. I overheard you on the night before the party. You said that some things couldn't go on. Some things you couldn't brush under the carpet. You were really angry . . .' My eyes are watery as I look at her. 'I spent the whole of that summer thinking you and Dad were about to get divorced, did you know that? I thought that was what you were arguing about, but it wasn't. You were arguing over what to do because you'd found out Arty Robbins was abusing my best friend.'

Mum looks at me for a long time without saying anything. 'I didn't know you knew,' she says at last.

'I found out a few days ago.'

'She was his niece.' Mum hisses the words, then wraps an awkward arm around me and gives me a little squeeze. 'Oh, love. It's so long ago. What does it matter now?'

'I need to know the truth, Mum. If someone doesn't do something, Dec's going to go to prison for something he didn't do, and I don't think I can live with myself if that happens.' Not to mention that the real killer just broke into my bloody flat.

'You don't owe that man anything!'

'Maybe not, but I was married to him for several years and I know he's not a murderer. And it's not about what I owe *him*, Mum. It's about what I owe myself. And I know you couldn't stand Dec, and I know that started on the night Arty Robbins attacked you; and I don't think I can really blame you for that – not after what Arty did, not after everything you knew. But Dec was *never* like his dad. He was never anything but kind to me. So will you *please* tell me?'

Mum takes back her arm and draws in a deep breath. It hisses out between her teeth and then she slowly nods. 'I saw Arty a couple of months before the party. I was upstairs and I saw him come out the back door of Chloe's house. It was a bit odd, him coming out the back, but he was Kat's uncle, and Chloe was working for his dad at the Shelley, so I didn't think much of it until I saw him again a few weeks later.' She sighs and shakes her head. 'I knew there was something not right that time – the way he slipped out the back and down the alley. I thought Chloe was at the Shelley, but I wasn't sure. Then I saw Arty again on the evening before the party. I *knew* Chloe was at the Shelley this time, and you were supposed to be next door with Katherine, too. I saw Arthur come out and take a few steps down the garden, and then he turned and . . . He was fiddling with his belt, still doing up the buckle, and I just had these . . . these horrible thoughts. So I ran out, and I was going to bang on the front

317

door, but the curtains were open a crack and the lights were on. So I had a peek.' Mum looks away. Whatever she saw, it's still there. 'I still see Katherine as though it was yesterday. She was obviously upset and . . . it was clear what had been going on. And she was fifteen. *Fifteen!*'

Mum sighs. 'I thought . . . I don't know what I thought. I didn't know what to do. I went back inside, and then you came sneaking in through the back door, claiming you'd been in the bloody park, and it was such a relief I almost burst into tears. I suppose you were with Declan?'

I nod.

'I wanted to march over to the Shelley right there and then and tell Chloe but instead I waited for your dad to come home, and he talked me out of it. *Not our business*, he said. I told him that having a child-molester living across the road from my teenage daughter very much *was* our business, thank you kindly. I told him I was planning to go to the police. He blathered something about you and O-levels, and being sure about things before making wild accusations, and then he said something that actually made sense: *Whatever you do, make sure the blame lands where it belongs, because if you're right then it's not her that's in the wrong, it's him; and don't you dare make her suffer for it more than she already has.* And that made me stop, because there wasn't anything the police would be able to do without dragging Katherine into it; and her mum, too. And then everyone would know – and I couldn't do that to them, not without talking to them first. Then your dad said that maybe he should have a quiet word with Arty, to tell him it had to stop, and that made me angry again, I'm afraid. A *quiet word*? Brush it under the carpet? No. So at the party, I told Arty Robbins exactly what I knew and what I thought of him. I kept Katherine's name out of it but I told him in front of Anne and anyone else who happened to be listening, and I made sure they all knew enough to work out for themselves what he was doing.' She puffs out her cheeks. 'Maybe I should have waited for your dad to have his *quiet word*, but I'm not sure we wouldn't all still be waiting even now, if I'd done that.'

'Did anyone else know it was Kat?'

'I don't think so. Not before . . . Dave did, after – well, you know.'

'After Arty Robbins attacked you?'

Mum nods and looks away. She looks older than her years right now, frail and ancient. I feel how the burden of that night is crushing her, but I have to do this. 'Mum, what else happened that night? Were you and Dad really together for the rest of the evening?'

She doesn't answer. It's hard not to shout and scream. I *need* her to tell me, and I can feel how close it is to coming out.

I rest a hand on her arm. 'Mum . . . Dad's gone. I know

that. And I love you; and I'm sorry I don't like Dave, but I understand that he makes you happy, and you have every right to that. It's *my* problem, not yours; and I know Dave was Dad's best friend, and so *he'd* probably be happy, too. But I need to know . . .' I struggle for the words. I need to know because this was a part of why I ran away from Dec. 'I still think about it, Mum. I can't stop remembering. I need to know the truth.' Because if I'm wrong – if it wasn't Gary Barclay – then not only did Mum have an affair with Dad's best friend, but maybe that mud I remember on his jacket means that my dad was a murderer.

Mum takes my hand and squeezes it hard enough to hurt. She reaches into her bag and pulls out her purse and opens it, then takes out a picture. It's at least ten years older than the ones on the table in front of us, maybe as much as twenty; faded, the colours all washed-out. Her and Dad and Dave.

'I met Dave before I ever knew your dad. I was nineteen. Dad was Dave's best friend. I didn't think much of him at first. He sort of ignored me, and I knew it was because he liked me and I was with Dave, and Dave was his friend. I started to tease him. I don't know why. I flirted because it made him uncomfortable. And then – and I really don't know when or how it happened – eventually the feelings became real. I think *he'd* been in love with *me* right from the start, and I think Dave knew that, too. Poor Dave saw it all play out right in front of him: your dad and me oblivious to what was really going on until it was far too late. And you might think that would be the end of any friendship, but it wasn't. Dave let me go, like a perfect gentleman. He was your dad's best man at our wedding, and he was always there when I needed a shoulder and your dad wasn't around, or when I needed . . . someone else. It was perfect.'

She looks at me long and hard and squeezes my hand again. I smile, because I remember.

'Money was tight that summer when Arty Robbins disappeared. I started doing shifts at the Shelley now and then. Dave got me the work, and of course it meant we were together more than usual and . . . I know what you're probably thinking.' She shakes her head. 'Your dad got to thinking it too, that summer, but nothing *happened* – not like that. But I did have a moment . . . And, of course, your dad picked up on it.' Her voice cracks as tears roll down her cheeks. 'He used to call us the Three Musketeers.'

I wince like I've been slapped. Me and Kat and Dec. *We* were the Three Musketeers. 'What happened that night at the Shelley? After you told Arty Robbins what you thought of him?'

It takes a while for Mum to gather herself. 'I told you, love. I went out to calm my nerves and Arty followed—'

'After that. After you went back.'

'I went home with your dad.'

I look her square in the eye. 'Mum, I know it was a long

time ago. I know it doesn't really matter now, but it matters to *me*! I remember that summer. *All* of it. I remember the three days when Dad walked out as though they were this morning. I remember you both pretended everything was OK after he came back, and maybe it *was*, but something happened that night when Arty Robbins disappeared. Mum . . .'

I'm on the brink of tears. Mum's fingers curl like claws. I think she's wrestling with how to tell me something she should have told me thirty-five years ago. 'Love, your dad didn't have anything to do with what happened to Arty Robbins, if that's what you're asking.'

'Then what *did* happen?'

She lets out a long sigh. 'Your dad went looking for him. He was furious. Dave and I went outside. We went into the park. I thought I ought to tell Dave what it was all about – Arty and your friend Katherine – and I didn't want anyone else to hear. It was only supposed to be for a few minutes, but then . . . Dave had an idea that something else was going on, you see. That Arty was abusing Anne, too, but Anne wouldn't say anything and so Dave didn't know what to do; and Arty was hurting so many people, and we both felt so helpless, because there was nothing we could do that wouldn't hurt them even more. We were both so angry and stuck and . . .'

I wait for more but it doesn't come. 'Dave said you were only gone five minutes.'

Mum pauses to blink away the tears, then shakes her head. 'It was a bit more than that, love.'

'Dave said he and Dad had a fight.'

'Your dad came looking for us, that's all. He took me home and that was the end of it, but he knew something had happened. He knew both of us too well not to see it straight away. One stupid mistake and it nearly cost us everything. But we told him the truth in the end and he let it go.' She takes my hand and squeezes again. 'I chose your dad, Nicola. I chose him when I married him and I would have chosen him again every single day he was alive. Dave knew that, even when . . .' She looks away. 'I know I'm not like you, but I haven't forgotten your father. First and last and always in my thoughts, your dad.' She stumbles to her feet. 'I'm sorry, love. I think I need the bathroom.'

I watch as she weaves between the chairs and climbs the steps from the basement. The actors have gone, too. Alone, I think about Dad as I flip through the photographs on the table. I remember a family picnic from when I was six, not in Wordsworth Park but somewhere else. I remember sausage rolls, and Dad trying to make me laugh by stuffing three into his mouth at once. I remember the seaside on the south coast when I was eight: some beach made of stones as big as my fists, piled up by the sea so they were almost like giant steps. I remember paddling in the water and how cold it was, and getting in so deep that it was up to my waist and the waves were breaking around my chest, and then losing my footing and feeling the stones disappear from under me, and then Dad's hands around me, hauling me back into the light. He always used to laugh when I told him about that. *You weren't going to* drown*, love! The water was only shallow.* But that's how I remember it. Dad's hands pulling me from the cold and the black. In my head, I was going to die and he saved me.

The last pictures in the second wallet are of me and Kat and Dec outside the back of the Shelley, the same place where Arthur Robbins attacked Mum ten minutes later. I start to cry. I can't help it. We were so young, so full of what the world had to offer, so certain of everything: of who we were and what we wanted, and of what we'd become. And look at us now. Maybe Kat can say yes, it all turned out OK, but me? My lonely life with only Chairman for company, too afraid to get close to anyone because I can never forget how it hurts when I lose them. And Dec? He had so many dreams and now God knows where he is – on the run, with the police after him, facing the prospect of spending the rest of his life in jail because they think he's a killer . . .

Where are you, Dec? Why did you run?

Deep breaths. In, out. In, out. I pack away the second wallet of photographs and open the third. The first pictures are of Arty Robbins giving his speech, which I know came right after the pictures of me, Dec and Kat. Then Vincent and 'For He's a Jolly Good Fellow', which I remember, and I know all hell is about to break loose. I flip through the rest. There are a dozen pictures of the crowd in the Shelley, a handful more of people I've already seen and then . . .

Nothing. The pictures just stop. Nothing from later in the party at all; nothing from that fourth reel of film, and I *know* there are more, because Kat told me only this morning.

I go back to the picture of Vincent and Arty Robbins, the one Mum mentioned to me a week ago. It's exactly how I remember Arty, in his denim jacket, blue jeans and – yes, I guessed right to Detective Scott – a white polo shirt. He stands with Vincent, a pint in his hand, the two of them looking like they're having the time of their lives. Mum said it was minutes after he'd attacked her, but however hard I stare, I see nothing of the abused wife in tears in another room; of a schoolgirl seduced and threatened and on the edge of a nervous breakdown; of the bruises on Mum's neck. The more I look, the more I wonder if Kat was right and I should let it all go, if maybe I should call Gary Barclay and tell him it doesn't matter what I know, because actually he did the world a favour.

Good riddance to bad rubbish . . .

WHAM! A memory of this morning crashes in out of nowhere, like a train rushing through a station. Suddenly

I'm lying on the floor, thrashing at the cloth wrapped around my face, listening to feet running away, heart racing fit to burst.

I don't know how I'm going to go back home now, even if it's only to pick up a few things before I go and stay with Mum.

And then there's Dec. Maybe *I* could let it go, but the police won't.

Mum comes back down the stairs, each step taken with deliberate care. She looks grim, her eyes red and puffy. I get up to help her but she shoos me away, picking her bag up from under her chair. She's shaking, and I don't want to be alone tonight, but I've done this to her. It's my fault. I should have seen how this would upset her.

'Mum, this isn't all the pictures. There were more. Some from later.'

'I don't think so, love.'

'But there were four films and—'

Mum rounds on me. 'It's hard on all of us, you know! I barely remember what Arty Robbins even looked like. I can barely even remember what your father . . .' She wobbles and loses her balance for a moment. Her hand shoots for the table, looking for support but only catching the edge. It tips over. Photographs rain across the floor.

'Mum!' I rush to her but she bats me away as I try to steady her.

'Leave me alone, Nicola. Just leave us alone!'

I back away, powerless, as Mum rights the table and picks up the scattered photographs. There's nothing I can do. It's my fault. I've done this to her. And maybe a little part of me is glad, which only makes me feel even worse, but *this* is how it feels to be ambushed by a memory.

'Mum, there were more pictures! From later on. You must have seen them last night.' But she's ignoring me, and I can see that's the way it's going to be; that nothing I can say will make a bit of difference, and it makes me so *angry*, the way she does this – just shuts down and shuts me out, the moment life gets difficult.

She stuffs the photographs back in their wallets, all out of order, stuffs the wallets into her bag and heads for the stairs.

'Mum, for Christ's sake! Just for once will you stop and try to listen to me? Why do you always have to be like this? At least Dad *tried* to understand!'

She stops for a moment. 'I hope you find what you're looking for, Nicola,' she says, 'but you won't find it here. I was only ever trying to keep you safe.'

'Mum . . .'

There's another film. There were four sets of negatives. Someone's taken it. Mrs Clarke? Kat?

Out on Princess Street, she can't stop me standing in the rain beside her as she hails a taxi.

'Mum, I'm sorry.'

'So am I.' A taxi pulls up. She gets inside and it pulls away, and I'm left standing in the drizzle, slowly getting wet.

I head for the nearest station. I don't know where to go now or what to do. Go home, I suppose. Pack a bag, if I'm going to stay in a hotel tonight. I need to feed Chairman. But first I have to see Detective Scott.

19

Wednesday 12th February 2020, 2.30 p.m.

Detective Scott comes into the coffee shop in Wordsworth Park five minutes after I arrive and finds me lost in a memory. It's 2009 and I'm at Heathrow Airport, trying to manage three suitcases through Arrivals. The great experiment of America is over. I'm coming home. I've told Mum and Kat but I'm not expecting either of them to be waiting for me at the airport; and yet here she is, Kat, beaming, arms open to wrap me in a giant hug as she takes two of my cases, and I'm so happy to see her that I almost—

'Where's Declan Robbins?' Detective Scott sits across from me at the table. He doesn't bother ordering a coffee or anything; just gets straight to it.

I tell him I have no idea.

'Ms Walker, if you have any means of reaching him, I implore you to urge him to turn himself in. He's making it far worse for himself by doing this.'

I tell him I'll do what I can. Then he asks about this morning, so I tell him about how I got home and there was someone there, and that they attacked me; and no, I didn't see who it was but I'm pretty sure I know, because all the windows were locked and the door was locked, too, which I think means it has to be Gary Barclay, because the only other person with a key is Mum.

'I did make some enquiries,' says Detective Scott. 'It seems Mr Barclay was at his place of work when the incident occurred. I've had it confirmed by at least one witness. I've got someone over there interviewing, to make sure.'

He asks who Gary Barclay is and why he has a key, and so I tell him about Kat and Chairman and how she comes over to feed him from time to time.

'It's once in a blue moon,' I say. 'The last time was six months ago.'

'Was anything taken?'

I tell him about the photographs. I show him the delivery confirmation email and tell him about the second set that went to Kat's mum; and that Chloe Clarke, Kat and Mum all looked at them together last night.

'You think I'm making it up?' I show him the bruise on the side of my head where I hit the wall.

'About your intruder?' He shakes his head. 'Of course not. Do you have somewhere else you can stay for a few days?'

I shake my head. 'I could find a hotel, I suppose.' After this afternoon, staying with my mother is not an option.

'If I had to hazard a guess, I'd say that whoever broke into your flat came at a time when they expected you to be out. You caught them by surprise. The most likely motivation behind the assault was simply escape.' He raises a hand before I can protest. 'I don't mean to belittle your experience, Ms Walker. What you've described *is* a serious criminal offence, and I can assure you it will be investigated as such. If you feel yourself in personal danger then I can recommend—'

'I'll just find a hotel,' I snap. I wonder if he realises how patronising he sounds, and I still half expect him to tell me I'm crazy or making it up, but then he surprises me. 'Ms Walker, I'll be the first to admit I was sceptical when you gave your initial statement. And as for your second . . . this fight between Arthur and Declan Robbins? Frankly, a lot of us think you made that up to make our lives difficult.'

'I—'

Again he holds up a hand. 'I believe you.' He smiles and, for once, I think he actually means it. 'It was the bit about the boots. It *was* a rattlesnake, Ms Walker. It would have been helpful to Mr Robbins' case, though, if you'd told us everything right at the start, so I do need you to be straight with me. It can be off the record for now, but you need to tell me what you know – *all* of it. Then we can talk about whether you need to give another statement. Let's start with what's in these photographs. What is it that you think we're missing?'

'I won't know until I see them.'

'All right,' he says. 'I might see what I can do.' Then he cocks his head and peers at me. 'You didn't mention the sexual abuse of Katherine Clarke in your previous statements. Why was that?'

'I didn't know.' It's tempting to point out he didn't ask.

'But you do now? How?'

I tell him how I saw Arty Robbins sneaking into the back of Kat's house, how I thought he was seeing Kat's mum, then about Mrs Clarke's diary. I tell him about the conversations with Kat that I remember from the party and then last Saturday by Dad's grave. 'She says she never told anyone, and that no one ever knew. I'm not so sure. Mum did. Look—'

'Gary Barclay.' He snaps his fingers as he stares into space, reaching for a memory. 'I *knew* that name rang a bell. Gave a statement to your Constable Simmons at the Mary Shelley in 1985. Claimed to have seen Arthur Robbins shortly beforehand, heading off into the park.'

'Wait – he said that back in 1985?'

'Yes.'

'But . . . No!' Kat said it was Dad. 'You've not spoken to him since?' Oh my God, *that's* why they think Arty was still alive when Declan left to go back to the Shelley . . .

Detective Scott shakes his head. 'He's hardly going to remember it better thirty-five years later. And, I have to say, the case against Declan Robbins remains pretty strong.' He makes a sour face. 'Despite your best efforts.'

'Even if Gary has an alibi for this morning, that doesn't mean he didn't push Arty Robbins into that pit. He knew Kat was seeing someone else. He threatened to kill whoever it was. I heard him.' But if it wasn't Gary in my flat, then who was it? Kat?

Kat could easily have taken her mum's photographs, too. The missing envelope . . .

No. No, no, no.

Detective Scott sighs. 'We'll take a statement, Ms Walker. Let's wind this back. You returned home shortly before nine this morning. Your front door was locked. Moments after you entered, you were assaulted by an intruder. You didn't see who it was and they made good their escape. On recovering from this incident, you discovered that a set of photographs you believe to have been delivered the previous afternoon was missing, and there was no sign of forced entry. Is that correct?'

I nod.

'You didn't see the intruder at all? Not even a glimpse?'

'I *saw* them, but I didn't see their face. I didn't see who it was.'

'Can you be sure the intruder was a man and not a woman, Ms Walker?'

I stop and think about this for a few moments. I heard a noise. I turned and saw a shape, obscured by the dressing gown. Then a hard shove and running footsteps. 'Are you suggesting it was Kat? I called her only—'

'I'm not suggesting anything, Ms Walker. I'm trying not to make assumptions; but as far as I can tell, your contention that the intruder was Mr Gary Barclay is based purely on the assumption that the intruder had access to a spare key, and we're fairly confident it couldn't have been him. So? Man or woman? Can you say for sure?'

'No. Although whoever it was, they were a bit taller than me. Not huge or anything, but definitely taller.'

'OK. Right. These photographs. I don't doubt they were there, Ms Walker, or that they're now missing. It's just, you don't have any proof, and I'm wondering: why would someone put themselves at risk when we already have a set of those pictures in evidence?'

The scepticism in his voice should be a warning but I plunge on regardless. 'You don't have *all* the pictures – only the ones Kat's mum didn't throw away. She still had the negatives. I took them to be developed.'

'Negatives?' I see a flash of annoyance. 'Right. So there are more pictures than the ones we collected – ones that you claim may be critical to this case – and now they're gone. Have I got that right?'

I bow my head.

'How many keys do you have?'

'Four. I have one.' I pat my bag. 'There's a spare in the flat. It's still there. Kat has one and Mum has one as well. You know, just in case . . .'

'All accounted for?'

I nod.

'Any visitors in the last couple of weeks who might have had access to the spare you keep at home?'

I shake my head.

'Really? No one?'

I feel stupid, but it's been months since I had anyone in my flat.

Detective Scott flicks a glance towards my bag. 'Would it have been possible for anyone else to gain access to your key recently, without your knowledge?'

'I . . .'

'You were with Declan Robbins last night, correct?'

'I . . . yes.'

'And you stayed overnight?'

'Yes.'

'And this morning, he was already gone when you woke up?'

I nod.

'What time was that?'

'About . . .' I see where this is going. 'What: Dec got up early, took my key, copied it, brought it back, left again and then, instead of going straight to my flat to take the photographs while he knew for sure I wouldn't be there, he hung around so that he was still there when I got home?'

'Unlikely, granted. Has he had access to your keys previously?'

'No!' But he *has*. He could have taken them last week, when I went to see him. Except that he never went out, so how could he have made a copy? And why?

My head is spinning – memories of last night and of all the nights Dec and I had together, and of this morning, and of my phone on the table instead of in my pocket, and of the way Anne Robbins looked at me when I asked about that night.

Detective Scott gives me a look with a lot of sharp edges. 'Let's move on to the part where you decided you were going to do our job for us. These photographs. Who knew you had them?'

'Kat,' I say. I can't look at him. 'And . . . and Dec.'

'Anyone else?'

'I don't think so. Well, obviously Mrs Clarke knew I had them.'

'Right.' He makes some notes. 'You said you had two sets developed. Where's the other one?'

'My mum has them, unless she's given them back to Mrs Clarke.' I almost tell him I've already looked through them and that the ones from the end of the party are missing, but I think I've already stretched as far as it will go his willingness to indulge me.

'I take it the negatives are gone?'

I nod.

'Right. What I want you to do, Ms Walker, is go home and wait for uniformed officers to take a formal statement – as I already asked you to do earlier. From your account, we're talking about robbery and assault. Print out the delivery statement and any other documentation you have for those photographs. We'll take it from here. And, Ms Walker, please leave the police-work to the real policemen in future. We'll be taking statements from Mr Barclay and Mrs Clarke as soon as possible.'

'Don't you need to send some specialists or something, to take fingerprints?'

Detective Scott takes a deep breath and lets it out very slowly. 'Don't touch anything until the officers arrive, OK? Now, Ms Walker, I'm going to ask again: where is Declan Robbins?'

'I don't know.'

The memory of the curtains in Dec's room burns me. Someone opened them in the night, between the time when I saw Dec leave and when I woke up the next morning . . .

'Ms Walker?'

I snap back into the present. 'Sorry!'

'Do you have any idea – any idea at all – where Declan Robbins might have gone? It's vital that he turns himself in.'

I'm about to tell him the honest truth: that I don't have a clue, that I'm as bewildered as anyone, that I can't imagine him leaving his mum in the state she's in . . . and then I realise it's not true. I *do* have an idea where he might have gone. Scotland. Harris Lodge. The card I saw on the table when he invited me to dinner. It wasn't there last night.

'No,' I say. 'None.' And then, 'Have you investigated Arty Robbins' brother?'

'Daniel Robbins? We made some enquiries. Unfortunately he passed—'

'Thirty-odd years ago, in a bike accident. I know, but that was long after Arty Robbins was killed. Did you know he was Katherine Clarke's biological father?'

Silence hangs between us. Detective Scott is trying to lure more words out of me, but I'm wise to that trick.

'No,' he says at last.

'Declan's mum seems to think Daniel Robbins was at that party back in 1985.'

'I'm aware of Mrs Robbins' statement.' The way he says it, with a sardonic curl to his lips, it's like he doesn't believe a word of it.

'No one else seems to know a thing about it. *I* certainly don't remember anyone mentioning him, and given that Daniel Robbins had been estranged from his family for fifteen years, it seems that him coming back would have been a big deal.'

Detective Scott shrugs. 'So Daniel Robbins wasn't there.'

'But why would she make up something like that? What if he *was* there, but hiding?' What if *he's* the face hiding in Chloe Clarke's photographs?

Detective Scott sighs. 'I'd like to go back for a moment to an earlier statement that you gave, if that's OK?' he says at last. 'Can you describe again what Declan Robbins was wearing that night?'

I tell him. He checks his notes.

'That's exactly what you said before.'

'I know,' I say. 'I remember saying it.'

He makes a note. I wonder whether it says: *That Walker woman is a liar.* 'Did Declan Robbins change his clothes at any point, that you're aware of?'

'I . . . don't know. His shirt, probably.'

'His shirt?'

'There was blood on it. I remember his dad's hand-print.' I shudder. 'I assume he put on a different one when he left.'

'But you didn't see?'

'He had a sweater on.' Why is he asking about Dec changing his clothes?

'What sort of sweater?'

'Some white thing.' I close my eyes and go back to that night, standing at the window looking down onto Byron Road. 'No, not a sweater. It was a tracksuit top.' I need Detective Scott to go and talk to Kat and Gary. I need him to start believing me. 'Detective, I don't know if it means anything, but I saw something the next day. It didn't mean much before, but . . . When I came down for breakfast, Dad's jacket had streaks of mud on it. That orangey clay mud.' I don't need to explain – he knows I mean mud from the building site. 'I had other things on my mind at the time, but . . .' Sorry, Dad, but I need the detective to start looking at someone who isn't Dec. 'It was a black leather jacket. That's all I can remember.'

Detective Scott gives me a long, hard look. 'I see.'

He's not writing any of this down so I go for the kill. 'There's one more thing. Katherine. She was with Gary Barclay in the park that night. Last week she told me it was my dad they saw on their way back to the Shelley, not Arty Robbins. She told me earlier today that she remembers seeing Dec when she left the Shelley again late that night, too. He was outside. It was past midnight.'

Detective Scott narrows his eyes. He knows I'm playing

him but he can't quite see how. Well, fine. I'm hardly going to
spell it out for him, but Kat will tell him she thinks it was Dad
she saw in the park, and he'll put that together with the mud
on Dad's jacket . . .

Anything to save Dec – is that it?

I suppose it is.

Detective Scott takes another note and gets up to leave.
He doesn't offer to shake my hand. 'Go home, Ms Walker.
We'll have some officers with you later this evening. And,
Ms Walker . . .' He pauses, waiting until he knows he has
my full attention.

'Yes?'

'I have to warn you that the obstruction of justice is a serious charge, as is withholding information from the police.
I'm going to ask you one more time—'

'I really don't know where he is.' I look him in the eye
until he gives a little nod. Then I watch him go. I haven't
made him happy.

When I reach my flat, an hour later, Kat is squatting
against the front door and I'm so pleased to see her. She's
exactly what I need. The one person I can always depend on.

'Kat—'

'You fucking bitch,' she says.

I stare, dumbfounded, hearing the tremor in her voice.
She looks awful. Her eyes are red from crying. 'What? Kat,
what's happened? What—'

'You told the police about me and Arty. You promised you wouldn't tell *anyone* and you did!'

'I had to! I—'

'I was fifteen. It was thirty-five *fucking* years ago! You think I'm proud of it? The police have been on the phone to Gary as well. They're poking about where he works, asking where he was this morning. He's a fucking wreck. What the *hell* is wrong with you?'

'Kat, I'm—'

'What? You're sorry? Here's a thought for you: stop being sorry and start being fucking different. Why are the police going after Gary? What did you say?'

'You told me you didn't tell anyone about you and Arty, but I saw the way Gary looked at you the weekend before last. He knew! He *knew*, Kat.'

'Yes. He did! Of course he did. I told you that no one knew *then* – not *ever*! Gary knows about what Arty did to me because I *told* him. I told him after I told him I was pregnant with Max and he asked if I'd marry him, and I thought he should know what he was getting. Ten years after it happened, Nicky. Ten fucking years later, and I remember it like it was yesterday – the way I suppose you remember everything – because it was the scariest thing I ever did. So no, Gary didn't kill Arty in some mad crime of passion or revenge or whatever, because I promise you, he did *not* already know *any* of it until I told him.'

'I—'

'I called Gary's office. He was there all morning. He's got a pile of witnesses. It wasn't him in your flat, OK? But you know that, because you already know who *did* do it; you just don't want to admit it.'

'Kat—!'

'*Don't!* You're not the only one who has nightmares because of things that happened years ago. You're not the only one to have memories you wish you could forget. You don't need to have some special condition for that, you know?'

We stare at each other. There are tear-streaks on her cheeks. We've been friends for nearly forty years.

'I don't understand you,' she says. 'I've been there for you through thick and thin, since we were teenagers. Dec's my cousin, but I took your side when you left him because you were my friend. It didn't even make any sense – you leaving the way you did. What did he do wrong? He was nothing but good to you and you fucked him over and I still stood by you. I've always been there for you. I really don't understand you. I really don't.' She wipes away a tear. 'Is it jealousy? You screwed up your own life, so now you want to fuck up mine, too?'

Three-quarters of my life. Kat's all I've got left and I can't let this happen, but I don't know what to do.

'Kat, when you were with your mum yesterday, looking

at those photographs, were there only three films or were there four?' I can't stop myself. 'Did you take one?'

The look she gives me is one of utter contempt.

'There were four films, Nicola. And no, I didn't take one.'

She walks away.

'Kat! *Kat!*'

I stand in the doorway after she's gone, numb, the hurt in her voice echoing inside my head; and Mum's hurt, too, as she got into that taxi. I'll have these moments with me forever, undiminished. And for what? Dec's still out there, on the run. I'm no closer to knowing who really killed Arty Robbins.

I go inside. Chairman is curled on the bed. I sink beside him and start to cry.

20

Wednesday 12th February 2020, 8.00 p.m.

Hi, this is the answering service for Kat and Gary. We're sorry we can't take your call right now, but we're either out stuffing our faces or too busy getting naughty to be answering questions about double glazing we don't need or the accident in which we were innocent – in which, frankly, we probably weren't even involved. If you're a real person, then call my mobile. The message ends with a giggle.

I'm lying on my bed with Chairman curled beside me, fast asleep. I envy him. I've tried Kat's mobile half a dozen times and left three messages telling her how sorry I am, but she doesn't want to talk to me. I have three missed calls on my mobile from work. The police haven't come to talk to me about the break-in and I won't sleep a wink here tonight, but Mum doesn't want me and I doubt Kat's invitation still stands.

I suppose Gary could have lied to Kat about being in the office all morning, but I don't see how he could fool the police. I suppose Kat could be lying about that night at the Shelley, but it doesn't matter. She can't have spent the *whole* night with him. Mrs Clarke obviously didn't believe our story about being out in the park, but it would have been all-out nuclear war if Kat hadn't come home until the morning. Gary could have gone back later, found Arty Robbins and . . .

But then I could say the same for Dec, or for Dad, or for anyone; and it's Dec's DNA under Arty Robbins' fingernails, and I'm right back to Kat's question: where did Arty Robbins go for all that time?

What can be in those photos that someone doesn't want me to see? Yet there must be *something*, otherwise why steal them? It doesn't make sense.

I need to see that fourth film of photographs. I need to know what happened to them – why Mum only came with three. Someone had to have taken them last night, and that means it was Mum or Kat or Chloe Clarke. It must be Kat protecting Gary, or Mum protecting Dad, or Chloe Clarke protecting . . . I don't know.

I get up, put on a coat and jumper, take my keys and head

out. The street outside is dark. I walk quickly, looking back over my shoulder every few seconds in case there's someone following me. There isn't, of course, but I only relax when I reach the lights of the High Street and the bus station. I should have called a taxi.

There's a minicab office by the station. Ten minutes later, I'm in the back of an old Ford that smells of stale cigarette smoke. A week ago I wouldn't have touched a taxi like this with a bargepole – not with all the stories you hear – but now . . . now this feels safer than going by bus.

I call Mum.

'Nicola?' I hear the sigh in her voice. She sounds drained.

'I'm sorry about earlier.'

'Yes, well.' Which is Mum's way of saying she'll pretend it's all forgiven and forgotten, because that's what's expected of mothers; but actually it isn't either of those things.

Half an hour later, my taxi stops at the end of Byron Road. I pay the driver, then get out my phone and pretend to make a call until he pulls away. Once he's gone, I knock on Chloe Clarke's door; but there are no lights on inside the house, and no one answers.

Now what?

I can remember the number for the house-phone, but I've never known the number for her mobile. Kat would know it, but Kat won't talk to me. Mum probably knows it too, but I don't want to bother her again. Besides, I know Mum. She writes all her phone numbers on the old Rolodex she's had since before Dad died, which she keeps on the desk in the conservatory . . .

I walk to the alley that runs behind our house and duck inside. It's pitch-black and I have to use the light from my phone to see where I'm going. I half expect an impassable mess of brambles and rubbish – a few more decades of accumulated neglect – but it's no worse than it ever was. There's still a shopping trolley and an old bicycle, just not the ones I remember.

I pick my way to the gate into our back garden, reach over and fumble for the latch. The bolt slides back, creaking a little but not rusted solid. One good shove and I slip through. It's been a long time since I was out here: the lawn is smaller, half devoured by Mum's conservatory, and Dad's vegetable patch has been replaced by flower beds and a rockery. The garage is where it always was, with its collection of ancient plant pots tucked behind it. Most of them are empty. A couple are filled with earth and the dead stems of some shrub or other.

The flowerpot I remember is long gone, replaced and renewed, but I'm guessing Mum's habits haven't changed. And I'm right: under the third pot, I find a key.

I check the time. Five past nine, which means I probably have a good hour or so before Mum and Dave come back from wherever they've gone. I could wait, I suppose, but I don't want to.

I open the back door and tiptoe inside, creeping like a mouse even though I know there's no one at home. I force myself to relax and turn on the kitchen light, which makes me feel a lot less like a burglar. I head to the dining room and through into the conservatory, and there it is: Mum's Rolodex, right there on the desk in the same place it's always been.

I flip through until I find Chloe Clarke, but Mum only has the number for her house-phone.

Shit!

And now I don't know what to do, so I go into the lounge to sit down and think, and probably to wait for Mum and Dave to come home; and there they are, on the coffee table, the wallets of Chloe Clarke's photographs. One, two, three, *four*!

As easy as that.

I crash onto the sofa and grab them, flipping through them, one by one. I find the pictures from the beginning of the party and put them aside, then the wallet with the picture of me, Kat and Dec, and the one of Arty Robbins and Vincent.

Why did Mum only bring three when we met? Did she just find the fourth wallet later, when I told her that one was missing, or was she lying to me earlier?

The last wallet has the pictures I want. The first few are still from when Dec and I left the party. Then they change. There are suddenly fewer people in the background. The faces are red, the eyes more blurred. People are tipsy, if not outright drunk. I find a picture of Kat taken from the side as she's cleaning glasses behind the bar, which has to be from after she and Gary came back from the park. She looks so young. Then another where she's turned towards the camera, looking annoyed, maybe startled by the flash.

There's a clock in the background. Two minutes to midnight . . .

I flick through the rest. Stolen portraits of couples whose faces I recognise but whom I never really knew, grinning at me, glasses raised; people who lived near the park, but who were never a part of my life. I see Jason Clay's parents, which is as close as I can get to a name for anyone . . .

And then the photos stop, and the next two pictures are of the morning after: the pub empty except for the litter of the night before. Then a couple of a sunset; one of some crocuses; and a series of Kat in her school uniform, holding up her O-level results, looking like she'd rather curl up and die than pose for a picture.

No Mum or Dad. No pictures of Gary, of Dec or Dec's dad, or even of Vincent or Dave or Dec's mum.

No pictures of anyone I know, except Kat.

I go back to the start and look again, more carefully this time. A couple of shots after the photos of Kat, I see a figure in the background that's probably Gary. I can't make out his face, but I don't know anyone else who wore a long coat like that. I start checking the background faces in the other pictures in case I can spot Dec, but the only person I find is Dave, right at the end, working the bar again.

Dec was probably upstairs. Even if he wasn't with his mum, it was past midnight and it wasn't like he knew anyone at the party, so of *course* he was upstairs. I'm stupid to think I'd find him. None of this proves anything.

I don't understand. Someone doesn't want me to see something – something that's right here in front of me. But what?

I go through the pictures one more time, peering at each of the faces. Would I recognise Daniel Robbins if I saw him? Only if he looks like Dec or Arty, because I never met him in the flesh. But there's nothing. Just the two pictures of Kat, the figure in the background that's probably Gary, and the pair of photos that catch Dave working behind the bar.

Dave . . .

My eyes fix on him. He's wearing different clothes. I remember perfectly well, but I ferret out the first wallet of photographs to be sure, and there he is. Dave, Chloe and Vincent, all in their green aprons. Vincent and Dave are wearing white shirts underneath and pale-blue jeans.

The light is bad in the two photographs from the end of the party and I can't be sure of the colours. Dave is in the background and a little out of focus. But his trousers are dark, maybe even black, and the shirt he's wearing is striped.

Detective Scott's constant questions about what people were wearing . . . *Did Declan Robbins change his clothes at any point, that you're aware of?*

I sit there, staring, trying to work out whether it matters. And then it hits me, and I feel so stupid. Kat even figured it out last Saturday in the graveyard . . .

Whoever killed Arty Robbins went down into that hole to cover him up. And it rained that morning, so they would have been covered in mud. Not just a few streaks on a jacket.

Whoever it was, they had to change their clothes before they went back to the Shelley.

Dave.

Mum was with Dave . . .

But only until Dad found them . . .

Mum has a spare key . . .

Oh Christ, it was *Dave* in my flat, not Gary.

My memory flashes back to 1985. Not to the night of the party but to the night a few weeks later when Mum and Dad said they were going out to the pictures, and then Mum came back on her own and Dad didn't come back until three days later.

Susan, if you think you made the wrong choice—

Oh, for fuck's *sake, Craig . . . You want me to be honest? You just remember you said that.*

The only time I ever heard Mum swear. I thought they were talking about Dave.

I Know What I Saw

I know what you're probably thinking. Your dad got to thinking it too.

What *I* thought was that she and Dave were having an affair. I'm pretty sure Dad thought so, too.

He knew something had happened. He knew both of us too well not to see it straight away.

Jesus! Mum knew, even back *then*?

Craig . . . it's not what you think.

It finally makes sense. The tension in our house that summer – it *was* about Dave, only Dad and I both got it wrong. Mum and Dave weren't having an affair; Dave was the one who killed Arty Robbins. And Mum was keeping his secret.

One stupid mistake and it nearly cost us everything. But we told him the truth in the end, and he let it go.

She told Dad? And he went along with it? Why? Why would he do that?

I'm scared. Horrified. Angry. I scoop the photographs up and then hesitate. I never liked 'Uncle' Dave after that summer, but now I realise I don't know him at all. I don't know what he's capable of, but I *do* know he's a murderer, and that *he* was the one who broke into my flat and attacked me.

All the years thinking Mum and Dad had been on the brink of divorce. All the years thinking that was what it looked like: the tension of a kept secret. All the years, and Mum never said a word, even when the police arrested Dec. She *knows* he's innocent . . .

I fumble the photographs and spill them, as memory after memory of Dec crashes into me: our last year together – the last few months – everything I thought was going wrong because I believed I was seeing a repeat of what I'd seen between Mum and Dad, and I knew where that led. All the years of thinking Mum and Dad's marriage was a sham when it wasn't *that* at all. The secret eating away at them was a murder.

I take the two pictures with Dave in the background. No one will notice. All I have to do now is find Dec and bring him back, then talk to Detective Scott and show him what I've found, and then somehow make Mum tell me the truth—

Lights outside. The headlights of a car slowing down. Turning. Pulling into the driveway.

Mum and Dave.

I leap across the room for the light switch and then stop at the last second. I'm already too late. If they see the lights go out, they'll know there's someone inside. I have to get out, right now . . .

The car door opens.

The photographs! They're scattered across the table. I stuff them back into their wallets and put them back where I found them as I hear footsteps and then a key in the front door. But now I've left it too late to dash through the kitchen and out the back without being seen. I dive into the darkness of the dining room instead. There's another way out. The conservatory.

The front door opens and then I hear Dave's voice. 'Susan?'

Not Mum.

Just Dave.

21

Wednesday 12th February 2020, 9.30 p.m.

'Susan? Hello?'

I'm hiding behind the dining-room table. It's ridiculous. If Dave comes in and turns on the light, he'll see me. If he does that, then I'm trapped. But there's nowhere else.

I hear the slight rustle of his clothes in the hallway as he shifts from foot to foot.

'Hello? Is somebody here?'

Why is he calling for Mum? Isn't she with him? They were going out together, so why isn't she . . . ?

I hardly dare breathe. I hear him move, and I can't tell if he's coming this way. He'll see me if I make a break for the kitchen. But the conservatory has its own door into the garden.

I start to creep out from behind the table.

The scrape of something metallic rings from the lounge.

I freeze. Dave calls out again:

'Whoever's here, I'm calling the police!'

He moves back into the hallway. I scurry behind the conservatory desk, almost tripping over a waste-paper bin. I barely catch myself.

Dave is talking like he's on his phone. 'Number seventeen Byron Road. Yes . . . yes, I think so. I don't know . . . The lights were turned on and . . . Yes, disturbed . . .'

Where's Mum? Why isn't she here? Oh my God, has he *done* something – has he done something to *Mum*?

I remember her face in the pub in Princess Street. The shock of it all. The horror. Did she realise, right there, that it was Dave who broke into my flat? That it was Dave who attacked me? What if she confronted him, like she confronted Arty Robbins?

Dim moonlight spills through the conservatory windows. My heart races. I look round for something I can use as a weapon. I look down and see inside the waste-paper bin . . . wallets of photographs.

I draw one out, slow and delicate. I open it. Even in the gloom I can see it's one of the pictures from the Shelley. Inside the wallet, as well as the photographs, is an envelope full of negatives. The photographs from my flat.

'Yes, thank you. You'll be here in a minute? Thank you.'

I Know What I Saw

You'll be here in a minute? I was almost ready to believe he *did* call the police, but not any more. They never say that. There's no one on the other end of that phone.

He's at the doorway. I curl up beside the desk. The light comes on and I'm dazzled. I blink furiously, trying to clear my eyes. He's just inside now; I can see him through the gap between the desk and the wall, brandishing a poker. There's nowhere for me to go. All Dave has to do is take another two steps into the room and turn and he'll see me and . . .

He takes a step.

Another.

He starts to turn.

I burst out of hiding and launch myself at the conservatory door, wrench the handle and shove. It's locked and it doesn't move. I whirl back, clutching the rubbish bin like it's a shield, and grab a potted plant from the windowsill.

Dave stares at me. 'Nicola? What—'

I throw the pot, plant and all. He's too surprised even to flinch, but I miss and the pot smashes on the wall behind him. He lurches a step backwards into the hallway. I shove at the conservatory door again, frantically working the handle even though I know it's futile. It's locked and there's no key, and the only way out is past Dave.

I whirl and throw another potted plant. This time he ducks out of the way. The pot smashes against the door frame.

'Nicola!'

'You killed Arty Robbins!'

He's still holding that poker.

'It was *you* in my flat!'

'Nicola, wait . . .'

I run at him, wielding the bin like it's a shield. I shout something – I don't really know what. Dave raises the poker and yells back, but my head is too full of how he's a murderer, how he killed Arty Robbins, how he took Dad's place, how he was in my flat, how he *attacked* me, how I need to get away and how it's all his fault Dec's about to go to prison. I swing the bin and crash into him, because straight past Dave is the only way out. I career off him and cannon into the wall behind, then lunge for the kitchen as he staggers. He grabs my arm, spinning me round.

'Nicola!'

I rip free and stumble for the back door, flailing to keep my feet, grabbing at anything to stay upright, trying to reach the door, my balance all over the place. One swinging hand grabs the kettle, desperate for any purchase. I fling it as Dave comes at me. It hits him in the chest. He grunts.

'Jesus Christ!'

I collide with the sink, stumble another step, crash into the windowsill beside the door and I'm at the door – almost there – but Dave's still coming at me, so I grab the first thing to hand, Mum's knife block, and throw it, knives and all. He cringes back, hands raised to protect his face. I go for the door and get it open, then an arm grabs me from behind, wrapping around me, pulling me back into the house. I hear someone roar 'Fucking hell!' and know it must be Dave, but it's not the Dave I know, not a voice I recognise. He holds me and keeps pulling and pulling, and I'm screaming at him and I have both hands on the door frame, holding on for dear life . . .

'Nicola, will you just—'

I let go with one hand, grab his arm and bring it to my teeth and bite. Dave howls and tries to pull away, and I tear myself free and run like I've never run before, helter-skelter down the back garden for the gate and the alley beyond. I look back and see him still coming after me.

'Nicola! Wait! *Nicola!*'

Brambles rip at my legs but I don't care. I crash into the abandoned shopping trolley and bounce off it and then I'm out of the alley and in the street – Shelley Street, with its lights and its Neighbourhood Watch, and its bus stop with its CCTV camera.

I'm free. Scratched and cut and bruised and battered, but free.

I know who killed Arty Robbins.

22

Wednesday 12th February 2020, 9.40 p.m.

I run past the Mary Shelley. I should probably go inside and call the police and stay where there are people, but I'm too afraid that Dave will follow me, so I keep on going through the park. When I can't run any more, I speed-walk as fast as I can along the dark path beside the building site. It's only when I reach the High Street and the station that I stop and call Mum, terrified she won't pick up, that it'll ring and ring and ring because she's lying dead in a ditch or something . . .

She answers. 'Nicola—'

'Mum!' I'm gasping between every word. 'You're all right! Where are you?'

'Love, what on earth is the matter?'

'*Dave!*'

'Dave? What about him?'

'Arty,' I shout. 'Arty fucking Robbins! Dave killed him. And you knew! You've always known.'

There's a long silence at the other end of the phone. Then, very quietly: 'Nicky, I don't know what you think you—'

'I went home, Mum. I was looking for . . . I let myself in with the key you keep in the flowerpot behind the garage. I found the photographs Dave stole. I saw what you were trying to hide. He changed his clothes. At the end of the party he's wearing different trousers and a different shirt.'

'Oh, Nicola, he probably just—'

'Mum! I found Mrs Clarke's negatives in the conservatory bin. He took them! He came to my flat and he *took* them, and he *attacked* me! And you knew it was him, didn't you? This afternoon you knew it was Dave, and you saw how scared I was and you could have told me the truth, but you didn't say a fucking word and I—'

'Nicola!'

'And then he came back and found me, and he tried to hit me with a bloody poker and I was terrified he'd done something to *you*.'

Another long silence.

'Mum?'

Nothing.

'Mum, where are you? I . . . I need to see you're OK.'

Another silence, and then 'Nicola,' she whispers, 'what happens now?'

'What do you mean, *what happens now*? The police need to—'

'Nicola, I'll . . . tell you everything, but . . . please – please don't call the police until we've had a chance to talk. It's not what you think.'

'How can it not be what I think? He killed Arty Robbins! Mum, where *are* you?'

'I'm at the cemetery, love.'

'The *cemetery*?'

'I'm with your dad.'

I stand in the middle of the pavement, stunned. Mum went to see Dad's grave? Tonight?

'Your dad had a part in this too, love.'

There's a line of taxis outside the station, waiting for the next wave of tired late-night commuters coming out of central London. I jump into the nearest and tell the driver to take me to Saint Joseph's. We get to the church and I walk round to the graveyard and there's Mum, sitting on a bench beside the door into the nave, under a pool of light. I stand over her and throw the two photographs of Dave down beside her: the one from the beginning of the party and the one from the end. One of him in a white shirt and pale-blue jeans, the other in a striped top and dark trousers.

'Nicky—'

'Don't!' I recoil as she reaches for me. 'I know what happened that night. You mouthed off to Arty Robbins about Kat. He followed you outside. He attacked you. Dave stopped it. You took Dave out into the park . . . Maybe you really were only trying to explain, but Dad was looking for you an hour later, and it can't have taken a whole hour to tell Dave about Kat and—'

Mum starts shaking her head, but I'm not going to stop, not now.

'Arty went looking for Kat. He went to her house but he couldn't find her. He went home. I was there, with Dec. I hid under the bed while he punched Dec in the face. Then he left and went out into the park, still looking for Kat. You were out there, weren't you? You and Dave. And Dave was in love with you, and so he lured Arty to the building site where it was dark and no one would see, and pushed him over the edge. Then he went down into the pit to hide the body, and by the time he was done he was covered in mud, so he went home and changed his clothes.' I stab a finger at the photographs. 'And that was why no one saw him until past one o'clock. And you knew! You knew all along. When did he tell—'

'Stop!' Mum gets up. 'Just stop!'

'Mum!' I'm shaking. She reaches for me again, and again I flinch away. 'I can't—'

'I wasn't going to let Declan go to prison,' says a voice. I spin round. There, on the edge of the darkness, stands Dave. I back away.

'It's not what you think,' says Mum, but she doesn't look at me.

Dave holds up his hands, a false gesture of peace. 'Nicola—'

'No,' I shout. 'No, don't you come near me!'

The darkness of the cemetery is all around. Dave takes a hesitant step towards me. I see a fresh cut on his face. I retreat, fumbling for my phone. My hands are trembling and I almost drop it. I want to turn and run but somehow I can't. I can't look away, either. The moment I do, he's going to come after me . . .

'I'm calling the police!' I stab a finger at my phone.

'I didn't kill him,' says Dave.

'You broke into my home. You attacked me!' He keeps walking towards me and I keep backing away, and Mum's not doing anything. And now I know – I know they were in it together, all along, all of it.

Dave touches a finger to his face. 'I could say the same about you.'

A voice on the other end of the line. 'Emergency—'

'Police! I'm in the cemetery of Saint Joseph's church! Wordsworth Park . . .'

Dave lunges for me. I hear Mum call something but it's

lost in my own scream. I dive away and bolt into the darkness, yelling at my phone, 'There's a man – he's trying to kill me! David—'

My foot catches the edge of a grave. I sprawl into the sodden grass, and Dave is on me before I can even start back to my feet. He snatches the phone out of my hand and throws it into the night.

'Stop!' he snarls. 'I didn't kill him. Will you just . . . *listen*!'

'David! Get off her.'

Dave lets me go. He hauls himself to his feet and takes a step away. I stay where I am, lying on the ground, staring at them both. I haven't got the strength to move.

'I didn't kill him,' says Dave again, quietly now. 'But I *did* bury him.'

I quiver, forcing myself back to my feet on wobbly legs. 'You were in my flat.'

He nods. 'Chloe's pictures. I knew she'd thrown out all the ones from the end of the party. But then she gave you the negatives . . . And last night we went over, and there they were. We went through them, all of us together. No one else noticed, but I knew if you saw them, you'd work it out.' He shakes his head. 'I should have taken them all, but then you'd have known they were gone. I thought I'd be clever. Just slip out the ones that mattered and maybe you'd never know. And then you came back.' He shrugs. 'I'm sorry if I hurt you.'

'You're *sorry*?' I can hardly hold my voice together. 'So you and Mum—'

'Your mother had nothing to do with this.' Dave stares me down.

But she did. I see that. That was the secret she was keeping from Dad until . . . until they told him. 'Dad?'

'Do you really want to know?' asks Dave.

I have to grab hold of a gravestone to stay on my feet. I stare at Mum. She sighs and bows her head.

'Oh, love . . . You said I never liked Declan. I suppose that's true. You said you thought it was because of Arty Robbins – because I thought Declan might turn out the same. It wasn't that, love. It wasn't that at all. I couldn't stand having him around because I couldn't bear the guilt of what I did to the poor boy. It wasn't David who killed Arty Robbins. It was me.'

Sirens in the distance . . .

Dave stands a few feet away, hands clenched into fists. I don't know whether it's fear or fury I see in his face. Mum, though – Mum looks calm.

'I tried calling you last night,' she says. 'I was . . . I was going to tell you everything. After the photographs – I thought you'd have seen them. I was going to . . .' She sighs. 'But then you were out, and I had your key, and Dave said *Why don't I just go and get them? She'll never know.* And I thought . . . I thought: what's the harm? I thought you'd be at work.'

I turn and scream in Dave's face, 'He came at me from behind. He threw a robe over my face and pushed me to the fucking bed!'

Mum looks away. 'I'm sorry. It wasn't meant – I mean . . . Oh, love, I don't know what I mean. No one was supposed to get hurt, but . . . After you told me someone had broken in . . . We had a lovely meal tonight, Dave and I. And then, well, I didn't know what to do, so I came here to sit with your dad for a bit because . . . I thought this might be the last time I'd get to see him.'

The sirens are close now.

'I couldn't keep a secret like that, you see. Not from your dad. And when I told him, he understood. I mean . . .' Another long sigh and then a tiny bitter laugh. 'It took a few days, didn't it? But that was my fault. By then, he'd got it into his head that it was something else. I should have told him the day after it happened but . . . I honestly didn't know how he'd take it.'

'Mum, please,' I beg, 'just tell me what happened.'

The sirens stop.

'There's nothing much to say. Your dad went looking for Arthur. Dave and I went outside, and I told Dave about Kat. We walked around the park for a bit. We were up near the building site when Arthur found us. He was like an animal. He came right at me. He had blood on his hands. Dave tried to stop him and I ran away, shouting for help, but Arty kept coming and then suddenly . . . Oh, I didn't know where I was and it was dark, and all of a sudden there was this pit in front of me, and Arthur – I thought he was going to kill me. Dave tackled him and they started fighting. I should have gone for help or called the police but instead I stood there like an idiot. And then Arthur had Dave on the ground and he was kicking him and kicking him, and there was a shovel lying there, propped up against a pile of wood, so I took it and I ran up behind him and . . .'

Tyres crunch on the gravel track up to the church. Mum's voice cracks.

'I didn't think about it. I hit Arthur on the head with it. He fell into the pit. And then he didn't move.'

I hear the bang of a car door from the far side of the church and then the crackle of a radio, a quiet voice and footsteps, full of purpose. Mum pulls out a hanky from her sleeve and blows her nose.

'I thought that was it. Twenty years in Wormwood Scrubs, or whatever. I thought you'd be a mum yourself by the time I saw you again. And then Dave took the shovel out of my hands and made it all go away. Your dad found me while Dave was still at it. He was worried sick. I told him I'd slipped and fallen. That was how he got mud on his jacket – from me. Your dad took me home while Dave was still in the hole, hiding what I'd done.'

The police come round the corner of the church, dazzling their torches in our eyes.

'I had to tell him in the end. I had to.' Mum smiles. 'Do you know what he said? "Good riddance to—"'

'"—bad rubbish",' I say and nod, because yes, I do. I remember perfectly.

She holds out her hands, waiting for the cuffs.

23

Friday 14th February 2020

The taxi stops at the top of the driveway into Harris Lodge. I pay the driver and watch him pull away, then walk down the drive. I wonder for a moment if I'm ready for this, then decide that I am and knock on the door. When no one answers, I knock again. This time I see a twinge of movement at the corner of a lace curtain upstairs. I hear footsteps inside and then the door opens.

'Nix?' Dec looks terrible, like he hasn't slept for days. He certainly hasn't shaved. 'How did you—'

I step up, take his face in my hands and kiss him. It's a long kiss, the way I used to kiss him thirty-five years ago. I don't let him go until I feel the tension shimmer out of him and turn into something else.

'If you bothered to turn on your phone,' I tell him, 'you'd know that your solicitor has been trying to reach you. So have I. So have the police.'

He closes his eyes and nods. 'I know, I know. It was stupid. I should . . . They were going to lock me up. I saw the message on your phone and . . . and I heard you talking to Mum. I knew you must think I'd been lying all this time, that maybe I *had* done it. I couldn't stand it, the thought of losing you again, so soon after . . . But Mum kept saying that she'd seen Uncle Daniel, and I didn't remember; and it was like no one else saw him, so I thought she was wrong until you told me about Kat. And then I thought: what if he *was* there? What if he knew? Kat was his daughter. What if he came back for her and discovered that his own brother . . . ?' He shivers. 'Well, you know. And Mum told the police, and they weren't even bothering to look and . . .' He trails off. 'Daniel lived up here. Near here, anyway. He's still got family in these parts. I thought I might find something.'

'And did you?'

He shakes his head. 'He was never there. Mum made it up.'

I touch a hand to his cheek to silence him. 'I have a message for you from your solicitor. She's asking the CPS to drop the charges. She's confident they'll agree.'

The look on Dec's face is delicious. His mouth hangs open. Eventually he'll find his words and start asking who and what, and how and why, so I kiss him again before he has the chance. I can't be doing with all those questions right now.

I don't know what the police were expecting when they reached the cemetery that night, but probably not what they found. Right there and then, I have to say, I was a bit disappointed they didn't Taser Dave. When they didn't, I was about to tell them everything – starting with how he'd attacked me – but the look on Mum's face brought me up short. I saw despair and resignation and love. I saw the way she glanced past me at Dad's grave. And I saw how Dave looked, too. He wasn't angry or threatening; just an old man who'd once done something wrong to protect some-one he loved.

I told the police that some youth had tried to snatch my bag, but that he was disturbed when Mum and Dave showed up, then I gave them a perfect description of Gary Barclay, back when he was eighteen. Mum and Dave backed me up. I still don't like Gary, even if he didn't kill anyone. I still don't like Dave, either, but maybe I need to rethink that.

The police searched the graveyard. They found my phone for me, which was nice, but of course they didn't find my phantom mugger because my phantom mugger never existed. They weren't happy about that – there isn't really a way out of the graveyard except past the church and the way they came in. Eventually they took a statement and went away. *Typical hysterical woman – probably imagined it.* I could almost hear them thinking it.

'What happens now?' asked Mum when they were gone.

We went back to Byron Road. Mum and Dave told me how Dad knew that something was up and how, in the end, it was Mum who put her foot down and insisted they told him the truth. She took him to see Dave and told Dad what she'd done, and how Dave had buried the body because they were both angry and afraid; and when she was done, she told Dad she'd go to the police and admit the truth, if that was what he wanted, and so would Dave. They would have done it, too. It took Dad three days to think about it – those three days he walked out on us in early August that year, but in the end he decided he was OK with Arty Robbins being dead, thank you very much.

Good riddance to bad rubbish.

By the time Mum and Dave finished talking, I just wanted to go to sleep. We turned in: Dave in the guest bedroom, Mum in her own bed, and me on an air-mattress on the floor beside her. And of course neither of us could sleep a wink, even if we were exhausted, because everything was horrible; and tomorrow Mum would be going to the police and I might never see her again outside of a prison. She promised to tell them everything, to make sure they dropped the charges against Dec. Dave told her she should say it was an accident: that Arty fell. For once, I agreed with him. The police wouldn't be able to prove Mum was lying and it would be enough to get Dec off the hook. Not Mum and Dave off the hook, because she never reported it and someone was dead and they'd covered it up; and the police wouldn't let that slide, not even after so many years, but at least it wasn't murder.

It was three o'clock in the morning when I saw the way to save them both.

Dad.

Mum was still awake, so I told her about Gary and Kat seeing Dad in the park, looking for her; the mud I'd seen on Dad's jacket, and how I'd already told Detective Scott; how it was all there for the police to put together, because Dad was the only one who didn't have an alibi, even if he had nothing to do with it.

'You could say it was Dad,' I said.

Of course, Mum looked properly horrified, because how could I suggest such a thing? And I know, it *is* horrible; but I was thinking, you see, that Dad made a choice that summer. He'd heard the truth and chose not to say anything because he loved us – all three of us – Mum and Dave and me. He protected us with his silence; and, as I remember him and how he was in the days afterwards, I know he made his peace with that choice.

Keep the family together, love. Don't mind me. I'm dead. Doesn't matter to me what they say.

His last gift to his family. Something like that.

I don't want to lie to Dec. If I'm honest, I just want to go back to being sixteen . . . well, maybe not quite *that* far. Say, twenty. I want to be that version of myself again. I want *us* to be that *us*; but I suppose there's no getting away from all the years that have passed, so I'll settle for a fresh start. I pull out the bottle of wine I brought, pour us each a glass and tell Dec how Dave and Mum went out into the park, and how Dad went looking for them. I tell him how Arty went looking for Kat. I tell him about Kat seeing Dad, and about the mud on Dad's jacket the next morning. I tell him how everyone's best guess now is that Dec's father and mine got into a scuffle, which somehow ended with Arty at the bottom of that pit with a broken neck. I don't tell him how Dad became the judge of his father's life; or how Mum told me later that, actually, it wasn't so bad a secret to live with – how it made her love Dad even more, knowing that he knew.

Dec looks at me, unconvinced. 'So . . . after all this, they're saying it was an accident?'

I raise my glass and take a sip, then look at him over the top of it, long and hard, and shrug. He doesn't believe it. I can't say I blame him. What I want to ask is *Do you really want to know?* but there's only one answer to a question like that, and usually it's the wrong way to go, and some things it's best *not* to know; because *knowing* something is one thing, but *understanding* it is something else entirely; and when it comes to that understanding, I'm in the same murky water as everyone else. Do I want to know more about Dec and the woman he was with, on the day Dad was dying? I remember what I saw with perfect clarity, like I remember everything, but I don't know what it *meant*, not really; just like Dad saw Mum and Dave and thought it meant one thing when actually it meant another. Dec says it was nothing. I'm not sure I believe him. But I *do* know it was half a lifetime ago, so maybe it shouldn't matter any more.

'Dad knew he was down in that pit,' I say. 'I don't think there's much doubt about that. As for the rest? You should call your solicitor.'

I build a fire in the fireplace. Dec turns on his phone. I don't know what Angela Watson of Lainton Legal Associates says, but Dec looks happier when he's done. He calls Detective Scott and his happiness turns to sheepish embarrassment. Running away was stupid, and I can't imagine Detective Scott pulling his punches about that. Dec's embarrassed, but not scared.

'Is it over?' I ask.

Dec closes his eyes. He takes a deep breath and lets it out, long and slow. 'They haven't dropped the charges yet but . . . yes. I think so.'

Not the end – not yet – but maybe it's the beginning of it.

'You always told me you stayed the night in the Shelley,' I say. 'Did you really?'

Dec smiles and shakes his head. 'I honestly don't know. I did go out into the park and wander around. I don't know how long for. I was supposed to be looking for Dad, but I was thinking about you. *That's* what I remember. You, and how I didn't want to leave for bloody Clapham.' He chuckles, as if amazed at himself. 'I remember I couldn't sleep. I remember going home early, and looking up at your window and wondering if you were awake. Then going inside, scared in case Dad was there. But he wasn't. So I got changed for school, and left.'

And that, I suppose, is when he opened the curtains? But when I ask, he only shrugs. He doesn't remember. 'Probably,' he says.

We order in some food, and drink the rest of the bottle of wine. We talk about old times, happy times. It gets dark and the fire burns low, and Dec suggests we should turn in; and I say yes, but that he should go first, because I need a few minutes to be alone. He doesn't ask why. He was always good that way.

I sit in front of the fire in Harris Lodge and let myself go back there. To hiding under Dec's bed, listening as Dec took a beating from his dad; to the bruises on Anne Robbins' face;

to the fear in Kat's eyes as she talked about her 'boyfriend' who wouldn't let go; to the marks on Mum's neck after the party. I bring the memories back, one by one, and then carefully put them away. And when I'm done, I take the pictures of Dave from the party – the ones that prove he was the one who buried Arty Robbins – and I throw them into the flames.

I watch them burn.

As long as they drop the charges against Dec, Mum can tell whatever story she likes. As I sit here, I don't know what she'll do. When I left, I don't think *she* knew, either, but I'm happy that she gets to choose. I'll call her tomorrow and find out. Then I guess I'll call Gary and tell him I'm sorry for accusing him of murder and assault. I still don't like him, but I owe him that.

That's for tomorrow. For tonight, I have one more thing to do.

Kat doesn't answer when I call, so I leave a message telling her how much she means to me. I talk about our friendship: the times she covered for me when I started seeing Dec, the times she picked me up when I was down. The words of kindness when Dec and I were falling apart, and that insane trip out to America, which just might have saved my life. Waiting for me at the airport when I came back; and how there are a hundred other things, and another hundred behind those, and that I remember every single one. I tell her that I love her and hope she'll forgive me, but that even if she doesn't, I'll still be grateful, because she's the best person in the world and it's been a privilege to be her friend.

I hope it's enough.

I sit for a while, watching the flames, then head up the stairs for bed, and Dec. I don't know where this is going to take us, but it doesn't matter. Somewhere new. Somewhere that isn't the past.

Acknowledgements

Thanks are due to a lot of people, some of whom I can name, some of whom remain anonymous. Mostly I'd like to thank my agent, Robert Dinsdale, who put a huge amount of effort into trying to make this project work, even if I was a little hard to work with at times, and Sonny, whose editorial notes unerringly found ways to make the story stronger. Thanks also to Mandy Greenfield, who did the copy-edit, to Dan Balado for proof-reading and to the Arrow production and publicity teams. And a special thank you to my wife Michaela, whose endless curiosity first brought hyperthymesia to my attention, along with the throw-away you should use this in a book, and whose patience was sorely tested by the consequences . . .

About the author

S. K. Sharp is the pseudonym for Stephen Deas. Stephen is the author of over twenty works of sci-fi and fantasy. He lives in the South East of England with his wife and two children.